To Me,

Y0-BOE-427

1981

From
Mom and Dad

Rated PG

Rated PG

Virginia Euwer Wolff

ST. MARTIN'S PRESS • NEW YORK

Library of Congress Cataloging in Publication Data

Wolff, Virginia Ewer.
  Rated PG.

  I. Title.
PZ4.W8577Rat   [PS3573.05613]   813'.54   80-14382
ISBN 0-312-66400-1

Design by Manuela Paul

For Anthony,
Juliet,
Craig,
and Art

Folks, I'm telling you
birthing is hard
and dying is mean—
so get yourself
a little loving
in between.

Langston Hughes
"Advice" from
Montage of a
Dream Deferred

Rated PG

one

I'm not the average bungler. I go for the ninety-ninth percentile, the nearest miss, the almost-smithereens stroke. Much like a mole on one breast (I've got one of those too), it's something you live with and notice from time to time, but you don't get hysterical.

This large-scale bungling, the smithereens stroke, has direct bearing on what I'm about to tell you. It's a highly subjective account of one of the things I did on my summer vacation. Parts of it are so immature I could puke, and parts of it are mature as hell.

Every time I get on an airplane I wonder what the world is coming to. It's clearly coming to a dead end, and just slowly enough, seductively enough, to keep us interested.

Armed with appropriate philosophical doubts about the nature of existence and the dependability of flotation cushions, and studiously disguised as a non-bungler, I made my way into the throat of TWA's latest pride and joy. Having taken my usual ballpoint pen-jabbing approach to Seat Selection, and having won in a soft but determined voice my customary argument about keeping my violin at my seat, I bumped down the aisle, hugging the violin case to my belly grocery-bag style.

I was going to a Suzuki conference in San Francisco.

People don't look up when you squinch past them into a seat on a plane. They stick a finger in the book to keep the place and duck out so you can get by, taking the opportunity to count the house. The face behind *Point Counter Point* finished a sentence, turned its attention to the aisle, and accompanied by an unbending of long legs lifted itself several inches above my head, adroitly missing slamming into my violin case on the way up. I thanked the legs and scooted in, propping the violin between my right knee and the window. Long blue legs fell into place, *Point Counter Point* opened again. I buckled my seat belt and read the nausea instructions, tucked winsomely just in front of my knees.

A page turned to my left. Some people only talk to you after you're in the air, some don't say a word the whole flight. I sneaked a sideways glance, squinting in the afternoon sun. Nudging forty—from which side I couldn't be sure—eyes that probably knew a good idea when it came along, mouth that if you saw it in a snapshot you'd wonder what it'd just finished saying. Okay, Seat Selection, I'm ready to hold my end of a conversation ever so politely up when you are. I turned to the oxygen-mask information.

Something very like Mickey Spillane's little mind-nagging detail scratched away at the back of my skull. I looked again. The mouth. A laugh going on a few inches behind it, maybe. I couldn't see the left hand. With my fingers shaking in authentic fear I got out a pen, tore the front flap off my ticket envelope and wrote on my right knee, trying not to ballpoint my yellow wool lap:

> I thought you'd already read everything he ever wrote.

I stuck the ticket-flap in the upper-right-hand corner of *Point Counter Point*. The book took a few seconds to drop.

"Bitsy, for christ's sake!" As if he'd just fitted "xenogamous" into the *Times* crossword puzzle.

He still had the intractable lock of hair. I counted three gray ones in it.

"Hayes, these things don't happen. I don't know if I—maybe I—" Moving with ambivalent terror, I was going to change seats.

He was laughing. "Bits, you've got that inimitable lack of composure; I'd know you anywhere. I really would. How the hell did you recognize me?"

How indeed? "You get yourself in the papers now and then. Not that I read them. But I noticed you narrowly missed that—that ambassadorship or whatever it was—"

"Yeah, I missed three of them." He pointed to my violin. "You really still play that thing?"

"I really still do." I was trying to calm down.

"Are you good?"

"I'm fair. Are you good at what you do?"

"I'm okay. Could you jump up and give us a little Sibelius right now?"

"No! I mean no. How's your family, Hayes? Shall I change seats?" Maybe he wanted me to.

"No. Mine? Fine. Very fat and happy, all of them, as a matter of fact. In Tokyo. I'm on my way there. Yours?"

"Fine. No cosmic mishaps so far—"

"You warm? Take off your jacket, Bits, it's—"

"No!" I wasn't anything resembling paranoid about my new yellow wool jacket, but I'd tended, in recent years, to be more or less sensitive about my arms.

"Sonofabitch, Bits, now I know what I wanted to tell you. I owe you a letter. Sorry."

"Forget it."

"I do. That was very considerate of you, the part about ten thousand fascists racing through my backyard and tearing out my fingernails. I owe you an answer."

He didn't. Not really. Like Mercutio, not so deep as a grave nor so wide as a church door, but it would do. He always said his *s*'s like José Ferrer. It used to knock me out.

What I'd meant to do was get to the Suzuki conference.

"Where do you live, Bits?"

"New York." I'd stopped shaking.

He laughed. "I can't imagine you living here."

"Oh, Hayes, you know everybody comes from someplace else."

He nodded his head. "Wow, Bits, you've still—"

"Will you please call me Beatrice? That's my name."

"No, I will not. You've still got all those freckles."

"How very Norman Rockwell of you to notice, Hayes."

"Now why do you have to go and spoil a perfectly good

conversation like that? Bits, it really feels funny running into you—every once in a while you come popping into my mind—''

''Asking you what everything means.''

''Right. Did I know?''

''No, you didn't know everything. Would you like me to tell you a thing or two?''

He closed his book. ''Yes, as a matter of cold fact. Did you ever figure out where the ducks go in the winter?''

Engines roared, we rolled forward, turned around, sped down the runway like some kind of furious attack, and sloped into the air. Nobody else would have bothered themselves asking me a question like that.

Since I didn't know whether I hated him or not, I wasn't going to tell him outright that I did or I didn't. That may sound terribly glib or terribly melodramatic. But after you've heard the rest of it you'll know whether I should or shouldn't have. I want to be honest with you, and the most honest thing I can say is that it's your choice. Feel free to make a guess right now.

I decided to stay seated exactly where I was. I snorted convivially at him and he bought me a drink.

''Not going to tell me, are you, Bits?''

Hard cold facts: he was six feet and one-half inch, a certified Capricorn with green eyes and a villainous penchant for—but I get ahead of myself.

''No, because it's a meaningless question. What've you been up to, Hayes?''

He clinked his plastic glass against mine. ''Well, a hell of a lot of mileage, a small amount of petty intrigue, a tennis elbow—''

''Where'd you get that?''

The laugh started in his throat. ''There's that inquiring mind again, Bits. You'll be happy to know it's still in the same old place. Right in the middle of my arm.''

Jets sighed into a lower key. We hit the clouds and an air pocket. Every time I said something he laughed. Damn his eyes. Westward ho.

*   *   *   *   *

Into the thirsty stretches of my Presbyterian girlhood two portentous figures strayed, within a month of each other. One was a book and one was a person. I'd hardly recognize either of them now. And a taste for the portentous was, like a pancreas, something I didn't even know I had.

I was fifteen and in the advanced stages of illiteracy when I wandered into a rummage sale on a June afternoon in Oregon. Out of the bright blue and green of the day I ambled into the church basement and was hit with the familiar stench of mildewed shirts and dirty cake tins that makes a rummage sale the unique thing it is. Leafing through Biblical atlases and torn editions of Longfellow, I inched my way along and was just about to move on when I came across the opening sentence:

> If you really want to hear about it, the first thing you'll probably want to know is where I was born, and what my lousy childhood was like, and how my parents were occupied and all before they had me, and all that David Copperfield kind of crap, but I don't feel like going into it, if you want to know the truth.

I picked up the book without reading any more, paid twenty-five cents for it and got out before I had to talk to any of the old ladies, who already smelled moldy, just from being in the same room with the shirts and things.

At the Chevron Station I hitched a ride home with Casey Parker in his doubled-up logging truck. Fire season cut the day and the dollar short for loggers, in the same way that too-late frost or too-early snow dashed our bumper apple crop into the juice bins every few years. Living off the land was never an easy business; Casey's weathered hands lay on the steering wheel in dusty acceptance.

"Can't argue with the weather, can you, Beatrice?" He reversed the hump-backed truck into the one street in town without a glance in the rear-view mirror.

"No, I guess you can't, Mr. Parker."

"The Lord provides and the Lord decides, that's all there is to it. How's your apples?" We crossed the creek and took the corner in low gear.

"Pretty good so far. Eighteen thinners, I think."

"Ain't nothin' gonna stop them little green things from growin', is there? Only coddling moth, or fire-blight . . . "

"Or an early drop . . . " We laughed in the sun.

"You ain't been over to see the heifer lately. She's big. Milkin' enough cream for every strawberry in the valley. Good cow, Matilda. Waltzin' Matilda. Just wait'll the berries are ripe, then you come on over and get some cream.''

He slowed down at our mailbox. "Look at that mountain. Bigger than life. Sure don't care about the loggin' business, does she?''

"No, I guess not. Thanks for the ride. I hope you get a longer day tomorrow.'' I climbed out of the truck.

"Keep playin' that fiddle of yours, now. You was real good in church—you sounded just fine, you and your mom—''

"Thanks—hey, thanks a lot.'' We'd played Brahms.

"So long, Beatrice.'' The truck rumbled up the road.

I started reading my book on the way up the driveway, but it got jiggly, so I walked the half-mile or so with my finger stuck in page eleven. I couldn't believe it: even the trees looked different. I'd never had a crush on a book before.

I read it through that night and cried.

My brother took a look at the book, decided it was dumb, and told me so. A few days later I gave it to my best friend Judy, who said she "enjoyed it,'' cleaving our friendship for about a week. So much for trying to share your love with a third party, I said, and we picked up where we'd left off.

We'd left off with Debbie Reynolds. Trying to be her. Judy had almost made it; she was a cheerleader and had got the bright-eyed bounce down to a science. It was harder for me. I was short enough to be "pert,'' but very bony and too freckled. One night when we were sitting in front of Judy's mirror stuffing wads of Kleenex in our bras, I'd contrived a ponytail, a dusty blond ponytail, and a new name.

"What do you mean, your name's Bitsy?'' Judy asked, trying to even herself out to a 38-D. "Somebody that plays the violin is gonna be called Bitsy? You're crazy.''

"Listen. The ponytail bounces when I walk, you saw that. People call Debbie Debbie, they're gonna call me Bitsy. And you can be the first.''

"Good God,'' she said, but she agreed to be the first.

Holding onto my new name was tricky. Nobody could remember to use it, and Mother wouldn't even try. Neither would my brother, who'd suffered a bleeding love for Debbie the year before.

I wondered what had got into him. By mid-June it was only the principle of the thing.

By the time the American Legion's Fourth of July parade came along, I'd read my book three or four times, and everything looked different. I marched along in the band, my snare drum bonking my knees, noticing for the first time that something I'd always thought was glamorous and patriotic was downright silly.

Everyone in the valley, plus lots of tourists, came to see the parade, swelling the population of four hundred to about a thousand for a few hours of Bingo, duck-shooting on conveyor belts, and money-making for the American Legion. White, icy Mount Hood sat just beyond the football field, not caring any more about the Fourth of July than she did about the logging business.

After the parade, Judy and I changed into Debbie shorts and launched plans to spend the afternoon eating all the free food we could get and avoiding mothers.

The high school lawn was cleverly disguised as a carnival, and we worked our crowding way into several booths, offering our services to anyone who wanted a break. We got apple pie, two Bingo games, and four hot dogs. We turned down dates for the dance that would follow the fireworks, agreeing by hand signal that the boys who asked us were slopheads.

I couldn't have predicted the next thing that happened.

It began just like anything else.

The sun was sliding down the sky when we traded inquisitive glances with two tall boys near the 7-Up booth who seemed college age. They didn't have the squinty look of the boys we knew; something about them didn't belong to tractors amd pear trees. Judy must have seen free 7-Up in their eyes (she had an exceptional sense of these things) and we sauntered past in an imitation of Jeanne Crain in *State Fair*.

"Would you two girls like a 7-Up?" She was right.

"I guess so, if you want to buy," she bounced, hands on hips. I wiggled minimally, just a little Debby.

The sun was in my eyes. I didn't even see the sweating green bottle that found its way into my left hand.

"Have you got names?" somebody said.

"I'm Judy and this is . . . "

"I'm Bitsy," I said too quickly.

"Okay, Bitsy, I'm Hayes. Do you live around here?" Some people like curly hair and dark eyes. Some like blonds with glasses. In a fraction of a second the sun went behind his head and I realized I was a pushover for an irreverent mouth.

Judy told him we did.

The four of us backed off a little, like a square-dance formation. We'd paired off in the reflexive way that is exclusive with the very young. A drunk in a ten-gallon hat lurched through the crowd, spilling part of his can of beer down my shorts.

"Little girl, this town of yours it up to its ass in Snopeses," Hayes laughed.

"You noticed?" his friend said.

"And that one in particular depresses the hell out of me," Hayes said high above my left ear.

I looked up. "That sounds like a book I read."

"You read books? Plus one for you." Judy ambled away with the other guy. "What book?"

"*Catcher in the Rye.*"

"Oh, him." He put his arm around me.

"You've read it?" I wondered if he'd cried over it. But I knew guys didn't cry. "I thought it was only me . . . "

"Well, it's not," he said rather finally. "You want some beer?"

"Hey wait—do you know anything about the ducks, then? Where they go in the winter? I know it's a dumb question—"

He eyed the question. "No, it's not dumb. I just never had anybody ask me, that's all." He thought a moment. "Tell you what I'll do though. I'll let you know the minute I find out. Now what about that beer?"

"Okay, but I don't like it much." What would Debbie have said?

"Maybe just a little. We've got some in the car. Just an eensy minuscule sip to fortify your id."

"What's an id?"

He took my hand and we changed direction, going toward the parking lot. "How old are you?" he asked.

"Fifteen. And what's minuscule? I've got a lousy vocabulary."

"It means little."

"Okay. How old are you?"

"Twenty."

"Wow!" I stopped again. Our hands sort of snapped, like a dog straining a leash. "I didn't think you were that old."

"Yes, and I'm going to chain you to the back seat of my Chevrolet and rape you."

I looked down at the bridge our hands made, the knot of hands like a picture in a Sunday school book. "You're not, are you?"

He shook his head. "No, I'm not."

So I went with him. The other one turned out to be Fred, and the four of us sat in their Chevy and drank Olympia beer, Judy and I listening to the tales of their travels. They'd driven all the way across the country, they'd been to racetracks, nudist camps, the Grand Canyon. They wanted to know about our mountain, and we told them the Indian legend about the two mountains that fell in love and couldn't reach each other so they finally erupted in one huge burst and then died.

When we all started having to go to the bathroom, Fred, who was one of the blondest people I'd ever seen, moved the car to the edge of somebody's early corn—a built-in bathroom with a view of the fireworks on the football field.

The conversation skipped around, and Judy and I didn't understand a lot of it. When they started talking about Trotskyites and reactionaries, we excused ourselves and squatted among the cornstalks, watching Roman candles break up in weeping willow designs above our heads. Between the big words, they told us Fred had an uncle in Seattle whom they were ostensibly going to visit.

"What does 'ostensibly' mean?" I asked.

"It's what you tell your parents you're gonna do," Hayes told me.

Then I found out about the willing suspension of disbelief.

"Hold it!" I said to Hayes in the middle of something he was saying to Fred. "What did you say?"

"What did I say when?" He put his right hand on my right knee.

I let it stay there. I didn't know it was a sexy gesture. "What's that about suspending?"

"Oh. Well, I was driving along with my friend Freak this morning through your monumental forests, and we decided we didn't believe it. It was damn near primordial; we didn't see a human soul for hours. We stopped the car, got out, and stood by the side of the road—no human voice came to our eager little ears. We couldn't imagine anybody actually living here. Like a land deserted, left to natural forces entirely. It's not like where we come from, not at all. It was like there wasn't another warm body left on earth.''

"And?"

"And here we are, here's a fortuitous moment of beer and fireworks and warm bodies, and I willingly suspend my disbelief.'' He said his *s*'s like José Ferrer.

"Oh." I didn't understand it completely.

"Let's put it another way. What were you thinking, at about eleven o'clock this morning?''

"You don't want to know that. It's dull, it's nothing.''

He took my free hand. "You don't really understand, do you,'' he said, lifting it up between us, "that I want to know who you are, what you are, how you cerebrate, what this hand does?''

I didn't know what to say. "You're kidding. You're—''

"Go on. Tell me I'm full of shit.''

No boy had ever invited me to do that before. That stuff had rules: girls could think it, boys could say it. This guy had a rule-breaking air to him, and I liked him for it.

"Okay, you're full of shit.''

"Sure I am. So's the whole world. Most of it, anyway. If we'd just admit it we'd be a whole lot better off. Do you know how many hypocritical shitheads I've bought good beer for, who won't even admit they don't know what a stupid word means?''

"No.''

"Too goddamn many. Let's get out and investigate this fascinating cornfield.'' He opened the door and pulled me out by the hand. We walked down the little slope to the mass of silvery stalks.

"You want to pick some?'' he said.

"No, but we can steal strawberries some night. They're not quite ripe yet. How long are you gonna be here?''

"Freak and I have to talk that one over. What's stealing strawberries about?''

"Oh, you drive into somebody's patch, you park right next to it. If there's no moon you use headlights. But not if the house is close to the patch. Some are, some aren't. The best way to do it is to start with somebody's cow—''

"With a cow?'' We both started laughing. It had never seemed funny before.

"Maybe we'd better whisper," I said.

"Okay," he whispered. "Hey, Bitsy, I'm gonna make a short, two-part speech."

"Go."

He reached for both my hands. "One, this whole thing is refreshing as hell. And two, I want very much to kiss you."

I stared straight ahead at the pocket of his shirt.

It wasn't exactly a movie kiss, but the beer or the fireworks or something was making me feel very strange. I decided it was like the big words, and I'd understand it after awhile.

We stood there looking at each other for awhile. Then he said, "What's the rest of this strawberry theft?"

"Well, you get a bucket, you wait 'til it's dark, and you go into somebody's barn and milk their cow—a Guernsey's best—"

"What's a Guernsey?"

"That's a cow. I guess you go to museums and operas and stuff all the time where you live, but here we learn about cows. Do you go to operas all the time?"

"Not all the time. Go on about this Guernsey."

"Then you take the milk and you steal the berries, and you have stolen strawberries and cream."

"Bitsy, if we decide to hang around, you've got yourself a strawberry-stealing buddy." He took my hand and we walked back to the car.

Judy and Fred were listening to the radio. We settled into the back seat and laughed for no reason that I could think of.

"You still didn't tell me what you were thinking this morning," he said after a few minutes.

"It's not important."

"You want to know about suspension, don't you?"

"Yes."

"Then get on with it and tell me."

"Okay. I was thinking—you sure you want to hear?"

"Tell!"

"I was thinking—" I started whispering. "—about Holden Caulfield. And being lonely as hell."

"Oh. Then, if somebody'd come along and said you'd meet your shining prince today, would you've believed them?"

"Of course not."

"Bitsy," he said in a very low voice, "princes come in all kinds of disguises. Sometimes they bear a strong resemblance to itinerant college boys who meet unusual girls who don't think anyone else knows about Holden Caulfield, and you give them a little time, and their princeliness just happens. Would you buy that for the moment?''

I took a deep breath. ''For the moment.''

''Then, theoretically, at least, what happens to this morning's disbelief?''

''It's gone, for the moment. It's suspended.''

''Did anything force you to suspend your disbelief?''

''Well, influenced me . . . ''

''Forced you?''

''No.''

''Was it suspended willingly?''

''I guess so. I didn't have anything to do with it.''

''Exactly. The willing suspension of disbelief.''

''Hey, that's good! Is that whole thing your idea? Did you make it up?''

''No, sweetheart, I did not. Some English snotnose did, a long time ago.''

''Don't call him a snotnose if you're gonna go around quoting him all over the place.''

''Jesus, you are refreshing. Let's have a beer.''

About halfway down the bottle, Debbie Reynolds disappeared in the middle of a genuine movie kiss, never to return. Hayes said he wanted to know about the girl he was kissing, but I couldn't think of much to say. I told him about Daddy building the log house with the stone fireplace and planting the orchard and then dying. And about the lady in the funeral home offering my brother and me some chocolate pudding before the funeral, and my brother saying no, so I thought I had to refuse, too, even though I loved it. I'd thought about it sitting in a dish upstairs while I was supposed to be listening to the minister talk about my father. I told Hayes I'd felt guilty about letting my mind wander that way, and he said you couldn't expect a five-year-old kid to know everything. And I told him how I'd started violin lessons the next year. And how my mother and brother didn't approve of me very much because I never read any books. It was the first time anybody'd ever asked me for my life history.

The boys got out of the car for a few minutes, leaving Judy and me to compare notes. She said they had possibilities, and I tried to sound like Debbie, for her sake. When they got back in, they said they'd decided to stay, and all we had to do was show them a place to pitch their tent. We thought it over for a while and decided we'd try the East Fork of the river. That way they could wash in the river and catch fish and live just like the Indians. They said that sounded fine.

We drove eastward on a nameless road whose pavement ran into gravel about a mile from the river. They said it looked like Vermont, and wanted to know if the river was cold. We told them it came right off the mountain.

We parked the car and got out where we could hear the river hurtling itself over the rocks below. Carrying sleeping bags, tent, poles, and a flashlight, we slid down the bank and found a flat spot. We took turns holding the flashlight and throwing stones out of the way, pitched the tent, threw the sleeping bags inside and got back in the car. It was Anxious Hour for mothers.

As we rounded the lone ponderosa pine at the bend in my driveway, Hayes leaned over and said, "Bitsy, we're going to be here for awhile. You and I are gonna get to know each other and figure it all out. What's your real name, anyway?"

"Beatrice."

"Well, listen, Beatrice girl. We're gonna take long walks in this woods of yours and explore the willing suspension and steal strawberries, okay?"

"Okay." I was surprised that anybody who'd listened to my dull life history was still speaking to me.

"And now I'm gonna kiss you good night, and then you run right inside that log house and put on your jammies and jump into bed like a good girl."

A kiss is a very funny thing, I decided. All you do is put your mouths together, and the warm breathing and the tiny little noises change the way you feel about feet, door handles, pine trees, all kinds of things.

I got out of the car and went inside. My mother made a habit of staying awake until I got home. She hunched up on one elbow as I walked through her room.

"Beatrice, do you know what time it is?" I headed for the bathroom. Judy's parents always asked her if she'd had fun.

"Yes, Mother, it's about twelve-thirty. We had something to

eat.'' I sat down on the toilet. I used to tell her the truth all the time.
All the time. But when *Mad* Magazine and extracurricular life
began to look attractive, she'd made it clear that she wasn't having
any of that useless and harmful stuff, so I stopped giving her any.
The change from truth to lies was easy; all I had to do was not think
about it very much.

"Whom were you with?"

I wanted to burst out the whole thing, how he knew about Holden
Caulfield, and the willing suspension of disbelief, but I couldn't
think of a way to say any of it.

"Some college students, Mother." I gave the toilet paper a
small spin and about nine feet of it rolled out on the floor. I'd had
more beer than I thought.

"Where did you meet them?"

"In front of the 7-Up booth."

"Where do they go to college?"

"Someplace back east. Probably Princeton or something."
Poor Mother, I made that up right on the spot.

"Was Judy with you?" She thought Judy was solely responsible
for my Debbie Reynolds phase. I wanted to tell her I was already
out of the phase, but I'd have to tell her how Debbie slipped away,
and the conversation would have gotten into one of the sticky areas
that Mother didn't want to have any of.

"Yes, Mother."

"I worry so, all the drunks on the Fourth of July . . . "

"Mother, I'm here safe and sound, practically in bed."

"Your father had some Princeton friends. Very stimulating
people, very cultured." Her hierarchy went: godly—cultured—
stimulating. "Your father was such a fine man. This house he built
with his own hands . . . "

"I know, Mother, I know he was." From my hazy memories of
my father, I had a feeling he'd have liked the willing suspension.

I rubbed two fingers of toothpaste around in my mouth. Walking
very slowly out of the bathroom and straight to her bed, I leaned
over, kissed her, and stood up with amazing good luck. I turned
around and got through the door, made all the correct turns, and got
upstairs without a light. We hadn't had electricity until I was eight
years old, and I'd memorized the whole house in the dark.

Could you fall in love if you were fifteen? People got married younger than that in the *National Geographic*. The only thing I was sure of was that I'd never in my life come across anybody like this Hayes person. I once had a great-uncle named Hayes, somewhere far back in the Pennsylvania part of the family—the part that thought Daddy was a lunatic to come and live in the forest and build a huge log house. Was that like falling in love? Doing something you'd never done before that would make your family think you were crazy?

Maybe Hayes and Fred would be gone by morning and that would be that, I decided, and got into bed.

They weren't.

two

Princes, when they swoop out from behind 7-Up booths, have a profound sense of camouflage, and manage to appear to parents looking just about like everybody else. And so, to my mother, Hayes looked like an itinerant college boy with a rakish flying forelock of nondescript brownish hair, who might have clever designs on her daughter.

For a musician, I've always had lousy timing. I should have taken chemistry the year before Hayes hit my life, instead of the year after. For one reason, I'd have known what a catalyst was. Hayes was a catalyst.

I began to hit the dictionary with an inflamed vigor that no one in my family, including me, would have suspected I had.

God worked in mysterious ways, according to my mother. On the morning after the Fourth of July she reminisced about seeing the northern lights around Mount Hood years before, when my father was alive, when the hay field wasn't even a hay field yet, when my brother was a round and cherubic two-year-old, and when I was swimming around *in utero*. "Like God's great magic fingers, aflame with color, Beatrice."

I'd never figured out why my father had to go and die when I was such a little kid; I'd promptly stopped eating and had contracted a troublesome and scary malnutrition disease. By the time I was seven the disease was cleared up, but it left me on the skinny side. It was just another of the mysterious ways in which God worked, I guessed.

At closer range were the mysterious ways in which Hayes worked.

On parents: "It's just that the older you get, the more chances you get, and the percentage isn't always on your side."

On National Forests, in one of which he and Fred were camped for the duration: "Quintessential, Bits? The five essentials: air, food, water, love, beauty. And here they are, right beside a river."

On the Universal Thump, when I told him I thought he liked people in the abstract only. (He'd taught me "abstract.") "The Thump, Bits? It's in Melville, which you've gotta read, this week if at all possible. It's like this: everybody gets thumped around by somebody else. When I'm President, I'm gonna set up a system where everybody sits around in a big circle and rubs everybody else's shoulderblades. You know, easing the Thump a little bit. And in order to facilitate this . . . " He took a deep breath and kicked Fiddle-Faddle, our chestnut mare, into a canter among the pine and cedar trees. I hung on tight behind him. " . . . I'm gonna make sure everybody in the country gets good and uncorked every two weeks. It'll be part of the national pension plan."

I'd ridden bareback behind lots of different guys, on lots of different horses. There was a good smell to it, pine pitch, horse sweat and T-shirt. This simply had more of all three.

"Hayes, do you really think you're gonna be President?"

He slowed Fiddle to a trot. "Well, to tell you the truth—now, I don't tell everybody this, most people being horses' asses and pricks to begin with—"

"Then how did you know I wasn't gonna be one? How come you just up and asked us about the 7-Up?" He'd already told me that most of the horses' asses and pricks—and the sonsofbitches and the mealy-mouthed, duplistic oafs—were located within the immediate environs of Washington D.C.

"I didn't, Bits. I didn't know. We were there, you were there wiggling, it seemed like a good idea at the time. I didn't know your

brain would be so full of that freckled trust. Hey, when I run for
President, are you gonna vote for me?''

"Holy shit, Hayes, what kind of dumb question is that?'' We
stopped to pick thimbleberries.

He made me get *Portrait of the Artist as a Young Man* from the
library thirty miles away. Mother had wondered for a long time
when I was going to stop going to seed.

I'd stopped. Abruptly.

But Mother had other questions. "Beatrice, just what do you do
with that college boy?'' She was churning butter on the back porch,
butter I was supposed to be churning. She really wanted me to go
around with the minister's son. What she didn't know about the
minister's son was that his hobbies were stealing hubcaps and
lifting people's blouses in the choirloft. And he only said about two
things. To girls he said, "Hey, Tits!'' And to boys he said, "Get
much?'' Mother would have been terrified of all that, so I didn't tell
her.

"What we do, Mother, is ride horses, we eat thimbleberries, we
cook fish, we talk . . . '' I left out the part about the pine pitch, the
horse sweat, and the T-shirt. "You know what he says? He says it's
wholesomely anachronistic around here; what with coyotes and
Chopin within shouting distance, it invites the willing suspension
of disbelief.''

"Churn for awhile, Beatrice.''

She went into the house to play Chopin.

She asked him the next day just what he thought of the poet
Coleridge. I never knew what he was going to say, and this time I
held my breath.

"Sam? Well, when you consider his marked fervor for the
improbable . . . '' I didn't even listen to the rest, supposing that
within twelve seconds the poet Coleridge would have become a
horse's ass.

Apparently not.

My mother told my brother at dinner that Hayes seemed like an
interesting young man. She quoted him.

"Marked fervor? Sounds like a comic strip to me. Right between Mary Worth and Judge Parker. Beatrice, you've gone from
lethargy to bombast in a few days.''

My brother had made something of a clean break with me a few years before. We had a collection of Mickey Spillane, and we kept it in the hayloft, at the end of a long tunnel. We used to take a flashlight and crawl through, hay in our mouths, and read *I, the Jury* and *Vengeance is Mine* and the rest of them. Just about the time I was figuring out that sex was basically a matter of zippers and light switches, my brother took his flashlight and the books and left the hayloft with them. He never explained why. Mother kept saying a thing from the Bible about putting away childish things. Every time I turned around he was putting away another one. By the time Hayes appeared on the scene we had very little to do with each other.

Hayes and Fred introduced us to the creeping jesus number nine, which had a lot to do with vodka. It was the purifying, original hangover cure. I'd never had hangovers before Hayes hit the Beaver State. Chiefly because I'd never done the things you have to do to earn them.

Briefly, thumbnail sketching, as Judy and I saw the two guys: Fred was Dutch-boy blond, majoring in philosophy, and had a tendency to stand with a fishing pole in his hand staring at the water a lot. Hayes was headed for the White House.

"What am I majoring in, Bits? Political science, with minors in a lot of languages. Oh, and I swim, too. I'm very good in the water. I hang around and hunt out the quintessential, I just may help you steal strawberries. Before I'm President, I'm gonna travel the world and pick up bits and pieces—"

"It's the bits and pieces he's mainly interested in. Don't lose sight of that," Fred said from the other side of the fire.

"Why don't you tell the wet young lady over there all about *Magic Mountain*, Freak?" Hayes picked up a small stone and heaved it in Fred's direction. Judy was always falling in the river. She wasn't clumsy, she was just farsighted, and got to thinking about other things while she hopped from rock to rock. Between chapters of *Magic Mountain*, Fred pulled her out. She always dragged an extra pair of jeans along to change into. Her parents thought it was funny.

My mother didn't think anything was funny. She'd been thinking of sending me to boarding school in Portland, so I'd do some studying for a change. I'd talked her out of it—there was something about being sent away from home that would neutralize any studying I'd do. Hayes was going to take the place of boarding school. Obviously.

Hayes's father had been a sculptor ("of some pedantic and overinflated reknown") who'd died just before he'd out-Moore-ed Henry Moore, according to Hayes. Hayes was a family name; in fact, he was a III, although he didn't like it much. That's all he told me about it.

On the Douglas fir: "You know your Doug fir aren't even fir, Bits? It's a pseudo fir, with a Latin name, eight syllables. The cones go down, not up. Did you really not know that?"

He was right about the cones. He wondered why I didn't know any Latin.

I shrugged my shoulders. Again.

And then there was the aurora borealis. By surprise.

We'd stolen a watermelon from the darkened store porch, and Fred and Judy were having a seed-spitting contest on our hay field when the mountain just suddenly lit up.

It lit Goddamn UP.

Streaks, shoots, flares, green, pink, orange, the most outrageous display of color I'd ever seen. Any of us had ever seen. Hayes, Fred, Judy, me. We all stopped in mid-run. Mount Hood was declaring its love for the earth, maybe? Declaring its outrage at not being able to get together with Mount St. Helens all those millions of years ago, in the Indian legend? Declaring *something*, it shot and screamed a magnificence of rainbow colors, and I thought my head was coming off.

I ran to get my mother. I tore her away from the piano, dragged her onto the hay field. She looked. I put my arms around her. She cried. Memories of Daddy, of course.

Wrong.

"Beatrice, you've been drinking!"

"Mother, look at the mountain. It might not do this again for—"

"What would your father say?"

"He'd say look at that wild color, that incredible—"

"Beatrice! You smell like beer!"

She stalked off into the house, her shoes hissing.

I sat down on the damp grass.

"Bitsy, that's incredible. Tell me the truth—did you make that happen?'' Hayes stood over me. I kept my head down. "Hey, come on, I'll confess. I did it. Bitsy. Hey—"

"She used to be so excited about it. I just don't understand. My mother.''

He sat down, bumping my elbow with his knee. "Don't be that way. Here you've got a small demonstration of my princely talents and you're gonna let somebody ruin it for you?''

It wasn't so much a question of letting.

"You want a little poem I reserve for exactly this kind of occasion?''

"Go ahead." I felt him shifting beside me.

> Oh, roar a roar for Nora,
> Nora Alice in the night,
> For she has seen aurora
> Borealis burning bright.
>
> A furor for our Nora
> And applaud aurora seen!
> For where throughout the summer
> Has our borealis been?

I laughed, of course. "Did you make that up?''

"No, that I did not. Walt Kelly made that up, a man of many geniuses and very hard-hitting on basic human matters.''

The boys I knew lent you their letter sweaters on cold nights and took you home from football games, but they wouldn't be caught dead saying something like "basic human matters." And they didn't have rhymes for special occasions. The Hermit Named Dave sufficed for almost everything. Another small laugh came up from inside me.

"You take care of that laugh, now, Bitsy. You feed it just right and it'll grow so big you won't know what to do with it. You know what we're gonna do? We're gonna climb that bastard.''

"What bastard, Hayes?''

"That mountain, the one with the glow on.''

I looked at him. "Not me. Maybe you are—"

"Bits, will you tell me what the hell I'm doing sitting on a wet hay field with a girl who isn't even gonna climb a mountain with me? Hey, Freak, you want to scale a peak?''

Fred and Judy came running over, watermelon rind in their

hands. Fred looked at Hayes, then at the mountain, back at Hayes, and said, ''Mister Hood? Why not?''

Judy and I looked at each other in the dark. When you've known somebody a long time and shared a Flexible Flyer for six winters bought with your pooled strawberry-picking money, you communicate pretty well with very little more than eyebrows. We were prepared to steal watermelons and strawberries, to swim and fish a lot that summer, but we didn't know we were going to climb a mountain. Nor did we know that Hood would suddenly become male.

Hayes put an arm around my shoulders. ''Now, what do we have to do to climb him?''

I thought a minute. ''I think we have to ask my brother to take us.''

''Your brother's a climber?''

''Sure. That's what he does when he's not in college or on top of a tractor. Maybe he will.''

''Good girl, Bits.'' He planted a hay field kiss on me. ''Get your brother in gear.''

''I think she's gonna bench me. I feel it coming on.''

She benched me for a week.

But she was appeased, if not delighted, with my sudden interest in cultured and stimulating, feeding on it when I started saying things like 'peremptory' and 'consanguine' at breakfast.

In the interest of what I conceived in my cock-eyed way to be history, I pulled out a diary somebody'd given me once, a little blue leather thing with a lock which I didn't bother with and started writing in it. And in the interest of what I considered my right to privacy, I didn't tell anyone. Partly, diaries were corny as hell, and partly I was kind of a secret person. It joined the plaster-of-Paris Mozart and the *Life* Magazine photo of Heifetz, the modest collection of things that stayed privately in my bedroom. I kept the diary hidden between the mattress and wooden springs of my bed. It turned out to be a blisteringly accurate historical account.

Things at home seemed to be humming along with a semblance of harmony after a few days, and I worked up the courage to approach my brother to put plan number one into action. Something festive was about to happen; it was going to include the two of us being Bud-and-Betty in "Father Knows Best," arms around each other, double-dating, the whole thing.

I caught him on a blooming bright morning on his way to the barn to get the tractor.

"Beatrice, I'm not taking you up any mountain. No."

My optimistic streak was running high, and I trotted along beside him. "Hey, come on, why not?"

"You're not ready is why not."

"Don't you want to have anything to do with me?"

"I just can't say yes to the mountain this year. Not many fifteen-year-olds can do it anyway. I didn't do it myself 'til I was fifteen. And I'm a guy."

"I'd love to know what the hell difference that makes. I'd just love to know."

"It's a law of nature, that's the difference."

"I think that law stinks."

He stopped abruptly in the shade of the barn door, boots thudding the planks. "How old is he, Beatrice?"

"Twenty."

He concentrated on my nose. "You know what somebody that age sees in a fifteen-year-old kid, don't you?"

"He says he finds me refreshing."

"And you know what that's a euphemism for?"

I hadn't looked that one up. "What?"

He climbed on the tractor seat. The engine roared. "Just be careful, that's all." The tractor moved, he drove out the barn door and off into the orchard.

Hayes had two responses. He said it was damned unbrotherly, and that he was doubly convinced we ought to climb the mountain that had been grinning at him over the apple branches for the better part of a week. Fred agreed, adding that he should get a photograph or two from the top of Mister Hood. With these thoughts in mind we embarked on plan number two.

Plan number two took shape with the aid of the American Legion. The minute the Fourth of July was over they got busy putting together a climb of Mount Hood's south face. My brother maintained that it was a bunch of drunks and greenhorns irresponsibly lurching their half-assed way up the easy side, and made a point of avoiding it. We planned to join the drunks and greenhorns, unknown to my brother.

In the meanwhile, I lamented Debbie Reynolds's departure not one bit, and accepted Casey Parker's invitation to visit Waltzing Matilda, taking three friends along. We just omitted telling Casey. We were ostensibly going to the drive-in.

Hayes and Fred were the first boys we'd ever met who didn't know how to milk a cow. We had to give them lessons in the dark, while Casey and his family conveniently stayed in their house, separated from the barn by lodgepole pines.

From the Parkers' barn we went in the direction of the Benson's strawberry patch. The Bensons were a family of tough-spoken people with three surly sons who drove around in a coupe that had a rumbleseat and backfired a lot. No Mrs. Benson, just a dirty and scowling Mr. Benson. Two surly sons, really. The oldest one, Jimmy Lee, had run away when I was twelve. Nobody had heard from him since. His brother Hank had made a wicked shambles of Sunday school with a stink bomb, a hilarious wreck of the fifth-grade with skunk cabbage on May Day, and was currently giving the truant officers a run for their money. As untantalizing as the Benson family was, their berries were the best in the valley. Mother implied that they weren't our kind of people.

Hayes and Fred liked the challenge of getting into their place. Their house fronted on one end of the patch, and Hayes drove down the deep dusty ruts with no lights, like a pro. We got out, generally uneasy about the one dim light in the Benson house at the far end of the field. The uneasiness lasted maybe fifty seconds, and we'd nearly filled the hallocks we'd found at the ends of the rows when a blast went off.

"He's shooting at us!" Judy was trying not to scream.

We lay down in the dirt, just like the war movies. Two more shots, then nothing. We crawled on our bellies back to the car.

Five miles an hour, no lights, we drove up the side of the field and onto the road, laughing.

Two more gunshots. The back of the car shimmied.

"Christ, he's got a tire!" Fred leaned forward.

We found a turnoff in the woods. It was the first time I'd helped change a tire in the dark.

"You've got lovely neighbors, ladies. That one is an unmitigated horse's ass."

"Not everybody's like that." I handed Hayes the next nut for the hub; he was putting them on by feel. "In fact, you know what

Casey would do if he knew we had his cream? He'd laugh, that's what.''

"I don't think so, Bitsy," Judy said, sitting on a stump. "Just because your family doesn't have a sense of humor, you think everybody else's does. I don't think Casey would laugh."

"I think I'll tell him and find out."

"I don't think it's such a hot idea."

We ate the strawberries and cream beside the river. We were greasy from changing the tire, dirty from crawling in the dirt, and juicy and creamy and gritty. Hayes said it was a radiantly dark picnic. I thought it was a little like Débussy, but I didn't try explaining it.

There were lots of kids who didn't steal strawberries. They tattled on the ones who did. A wistful kind of injustice tended to prevail, though. Judy and I knew that it was the pious tattlers, not the strawberry thieves, who usually ended up pregnant in their senior year in high school, and spent the rest of their lives curdled in a service station somewhere, pumping gas and handing out scenic calendars at Christmas. We didn't know why, but that was the way it was.

By that time, Hayes and Fred had discarded their watches. They wanted to learn the "salubrious mental exercise" (Fred's words) of telling time by the sun.

We borrowed crampons, ice axes and backpacks from some people who promised they wouldn't tell my brother until after the Legion Climb.

With a few days to go before tackling Mister Hood, Hayes and I swam all the way across the Columbia one sunny afternoon. Nobody but Hayes would have done it without a boat going along.

I'd never been in the breathless middle of the river before. In a way it was profoundly scary. I felt like a floating flower. The hills loomed incredibly purple and powerful. If you thought about it, they could close in any minute. Without warning, the Sibelius Violin Concerto came zooming right down out of the sky, the second *largamente*, the one after the cadenza, where it goes sweeping into double-stops in five flats, the way Heifetz played it, as if his violin would split wide open with passion and sweet grandeur.

I was given to dreamy flights once in a while, but I'd never heard music coming right out of the sky like that.

"I don't know why I never did this before, Hayes." I looked up and down the river, whitecaps hitting my ears.

"You know Bits, in three days we're gonna stand up on top of Mister Hood and look down on this very little spot—"

James Joyce, radiantly dark picnics, Sibelius in the middle of the river—I'd never been so cultured and stimulated in my life.

I waited until my brother went away for the weekend to jump plan number two on Mother. Her hands fell in the middle of Chopin. "You're *what*?" The misfired chord bounced off every antique in the living room, rolled off the fireplace.

"You only have to be fourteen to go—"

"Your hands, Beatrice, what if you hurt your hands?"

"I'm not Heifetz, Mother, I borrowed these great gloves—"

"I don't know what to say. Your brother isn't here to help us decide . . . "

I had a sudden clear flash, and decided the guilt feelings that came along with it would dissolve once I got up on the mountain. "Mother, I feel Daddy wanting me to go. It's one of those spiritual feelings. Don't you think I'll be more *religious* if I get up on that peak and see the land the way God laid it out? The way Daddy saw it, the way he wants me to see it? Clouds and forests, and sunshine speckling the snow in the middle of summer? All God's miracles? You *want* me to be more religious, don't you?"

Silence hung against the log walls.

"Beatrice," she said slowly, her thumbs lying together on middle C, "perhaps God *is* a little closer up there. Less remote, you know . . . I'm going to let you—"

"Wow, thank you!" I gave her an enormous hug, hitting two black keys with my elbow. "Wait'll you see the gloves I borrowed, they'll protect my hands like mad!"

I didn't often use God and Daddy that way, because of hurting their feelings. But if they were as loving as Mother said they were, they'd gather a few of the heavenly host together and sing a song of forgiveness. I wanted to play fair with them, and did my best to think reverent thoughts.

But from the moment we left Timberline Lodge with a loosely assembled climbing party sometime before dawn, Hayes made it almost impossible. We hiked along like legitimate climbers for a full five minutes before he started using his ice axe as javelin, baton, shotgun, telescope. Fred whipped out his camera from time to time, catching us in at least a dozen positions of laughing. While we rested and Judy said you couldn't drink while you were mountain climbing, Hayes built a snowman with immense ears. That was what made him abominable, Judy said, and decided to start drinking. Then Hayes decided we'd discard our names. I could be Tenzing Norgay and he'd be Sir Edmund Hillary. We camouflaged each other with sunscreen lotion, and he said the enemy would never recognize us now. And that the whiskey in his flask would go beatifically with melted Hershey bars. As a matter of fact, he was right.

"Have you noticed, Bits, when people's backs hurt, they always say it's the small? It's a very compelling thing, that small of the back. It moves around. Here, have a drink. Pretend you're a St. Bernard."

Starting up again, we told Hayes and Fred about the Saskwatch, the great hairy spectre of the mountains whose chief sustenance was huckleberries, but who once above the timberline (far below us by this time) would nibble on almost anything, especially college boys with big mouths. Hayes said one of the little-known arcaneries of the Saskwatch was that he fed only on sober college boys with big mouths, and he proceeded through half the flask before we got to Crater Rock. By this time we'd followed the ravenous adventures of the Saskwatch through the Andes, the Alps, all the way up and down Mount Kilimanjaro, and major points in the Cascades, and what had begun as a climbing party of fifty greenhorns and drunks had scattered into about eight knots of tired bodies, resting on bare rock patches.

I'd hardly thought about Daddy and God, so I sat myself down, away from everybody else, to rest and have a good concentrated think. We'd been climbing for hours, and were only just over ten thousand feet.

Dear God and dear Daddy, I tried. I felt legs go around me from behind, toboggan-style. "Okay, you can take it into high gear now!"

"Hayes," I said wearily, "please don't. I'm tired, I just want to think little things of my own, before we start the hard part—"

He got up and walked away. Daddy and God were right up there in the sunshine, I could hear Beethoven's Ninth in the sky . . . Good God, I said, please, God and Daddy, don't think I'm crazy just because I hear concertos in the rivers and symphonies on mountains . . .

A body flung itself flat in front of me and started yelling like a tone-deaf boxing referee. "I'm sorry I drowned the baby, sorry I shot you in the leg, take me back—I don't care if you're retarded and toothless, I want you anyway—" Even the crash of rocks falling hundreds of feet above us couldn't drown it out, and most of the climbers convulsed in laughter.

It sounded like a glorious anthem of celebration, the reckless laughs of all those people echoing off the rocks and resonating down the slope we'd just climbed, little giggles bounding in and out of the neat crampon-prints below. Like the whole south face of the mountain just lifting itself out of its grim form for a moment and laughing its head off.

That was what it was about, I think, the willing suspension of disbelief.

We left most of the stuff from our backpacks at Crater Rock. Then, the tying-in—six people looped together at the waist on a hundred feet of rope; one step at a time after awhile, danger charging out of everything that might or might not be a foothold. Sweating in the sun, ankles unsure, little talking, much concern for the climber fore and aft. We were wired in series; the logging-truck driver behind me took a sudden interest in my survival and I in his.

I wasn't surprised that Hayes applied himself with sobriety to the operation; I just wondered how he could do it with all that whiskey. I watched his boot ahead of me at eye-level, where mine would be, two steps into the not-so-sure future. My feet were in the same spots my father had gripped, the same places my brother had stepped. Adrenalin went sprinting around in me in the fear and joy of going up one of God's great miracles.

One crevasse. Deeper than I could think about, so I didn't. Roped together, jumping one after another, eyes straight ahead, the miracle of landing near Hayes's outstretched hands, the logger landing near mine. Up again. And up. And up.

Penultimate? Was that the word? Breathing and heartbeat were too noisy, the wind took every other sound away, I couldn't hear the axes clinking. The only thing I heard was the logger behind me asking for more slack.

We edged over a crest. Ahead of us, parkas huddled together, canteens reflected sun in my eyes. The logger put his hand on my shoulder. "Good girl, Beatrice, you done it—"

Done what? My God, the top! Clouds billowed past, little glimpses of forest in and out of focus like trying to remember an action-packed dream. I staggered ahead a few feet more, dragging the roped logger with me, put my hand on Hayes's arm. "Hey, Sir Edmund, you done it!"

There's nothing at all like being kissed full on the mouth on top of a mountain, tied by the waist to five bodies. Faces that smell like a drugstore, goggles knocking against each other, arms too tired to bow to social niceties like reaching for a shoulder. Noses dripping in the wind, laughter seeping out around dry tongues. Blooooooop, said my stomach.

Judy and Fred were pointing and taking pictures. Saliva blew sideways out of people's mouths as they stuck gloved hands out in all directions. Hooded heads nodded, one guy (drunk or greenhorn or both?) took a breezy leak facing east. Everyone has a personal way of answering the eloquent hello of a wind-dashed mountaintop. I was enchanted, I leaned on my axe and stared out into the sky.

I felt a tug on my rope, Hayes surged forward, taking me and the other four with him into the wind, shouting. "Blow, winds, crack

your cheeks! Tempt me to my worst—avalanche, hurricane—"
He threw his arms high in the air, tugging again on the rest of us, his
gloves climbing into the gusts. "Light from these magic fingers,
that the children of darkness may see the power and the glory
forever!"

His arms dropped, he turned around calmly like someone headed
for a clean pair of socks and sat down, dragging the rope full of us
with him.

"And now, Beatrice," he said in a sock-hunting voice, "we're
gonna have a tiny little nip." And reached into his pack for the
flask. "See the Columbia down there?"

I couldn't think of a thing to say. A fifteen-year-old kid drinking
whiskey at 11,245 feet. Irreverent mouth biting the sleeve of my
parka. Light among the children of darkness. My brother would
have a fit.

three

Big brother had his fit in my bedroom. He had the most self-controlled fits of anybody I'd ever seen.

"Beatrice, wake up. You went on the Legion Climb." It must have been noon. Presbyterians were supposed to get up early.

"I told you you weren't ready. You pulled the wool completely over Mother's eyes and went. Say something."

"I think it's the most incredible fun I ever had. You know that one crevasse? I—"

He sat on my bed. Bud and Betty. "Was the sun shining?"

"Most of the way. You're right about climbing. It's fantastic. Is it always so windy up there?"

"Sure it is. Do you know you could've broken your neck?"

"But I didn't. That's the point, isn't it?"

He was in the doorway. "No, the point is you did it the wrong way. There's something morally amiss about—"

"I wanted to go with you," I said. I meant it.

"I think you'd better haul yourself out of that bed and weed the garden, Beatrice." He walked out the door. That was the allotment. Five full seconds of Bud and Betty, no more.

33

Nipping through the A's later in the afternoon, nails rimmed black from weeding the carrots, I ran into 'austere'. Hayes was still going to take the place of boarding school. Even an austere family was better than none at all.

I decided to ask him, sitting on a log that I'd hauled out of the woods near the tent. "Hayes, would you say my family's the most austere family you've ever met?"

"Maybe. Hey, you know I never had a protegé before?"

Fred handed me a can of Lucky Lager. He did things like that. Handed you a can of beer, or reminded you you'd left your shoes someplace. "Portrait of the artist as a young punk," he said.

Hayes opened the can in his direction, foam chasing him down the bank to where Judy stood fishing.

"You've got this dark impatience, Bitsy, it needs to be fed. Besides, I like your arms."

"You do?" How odd.

"Bits, you know how I like your arms? I like it when you're playing your violin—now, I don't like the violin per se—"

"You don't?" I looked up. "You never told me that."

"Not per se. But I like it when you play and you don't know anybody's watching—"

"When did you see that?"

"I spent four days thinning your apple tress, remember?" They had. They needed bucks, they'd said. "One morning you were playing outside, and besides the shangri-la quality of Bach coming through the branches—"

"I haven't done any Bach all summer, dummy. It was probably Vivaldi—"

"Anyway, that's how I like 'em." He shook his hair back.

"Yeah, well, God did give me okay arms, I guess."

"Oh come on, Bits, there isn't any god. It's a void."

"It is not. There's nebulas and other solar systems and—"

"Sure, there's all that. I mean, as for a little old guy with a long white beard who blows the wind around, there's nobody home."

"What makes you think so?" Then who the hell did that music-in-the-sky business?

"Me makes me think so. The bible is a phony book, written by phony, hysterical morons—"

"That's just not true. I don't care if Jesus was divine or not, but—"

"Come off it, Bits. I don't expect you to flush all your years of religious harassment down the toilet right away, but think about it. Does anything they've taught you make sense?"

"Yes. Let's take the trees and flowers and stuff. God puts blue flowers here and yellow ones there, and tall tress around us and short scraggly tough ones at the timberline, it's all such a neat, lovely pattern!"

He laughed, a leg-bending laugh. "Okay, so he's a landscape architect. Then what do they teach you about people's connection with this cosmic garden party?"

I plugged away. "I don't know if it's what they taught me or not, but I think we're all supposed to do something good, like discover a planet or build a bridge or have babies who do something great before *they* leave."

I didn't know why he kept laughing so much. "Oh, if you can't pull it off yourself, you get extra coupons for your progeny to cash in, at the great redemption center in the sky!"

I said in the direction of his sleeve, "Does 'progeny' mean kids?" A squirrel with a thin scraggly summer tail ran around the end of the log.

"Yes, and we're gonna have lots of them, and give 'em all coupons. We'll stick them on with safety pins, and when the roll is called up yonder they'll all be right out in front, waving their tickets. Come over here." He rolled me off the log.

"Listen," he said in a peace-making voice, "I really do understand that you haven't got around to questioning all the baby jesus jazz yet . . . "

"But I do! I bet nobody's crayoned as many coats-of-many-colors as I have—I've spent years in Sunday school and I've never figured out the point of it. And the Adam and Eve thing, I know that's just symbolic . . . "

"It's all symbolic. Man only lives by symbols—it's the collective unconscious."

"The what?"

"Bitsy, listen to me." He put both hands on my shoulders. That always meant they really wanted you to listen. "All I've got on you is years. Would I be sleeping on the ground, shaving in service stations and walking the roads of this hick town if that weren't true? That and your mountain?" He took his hands down.

"I guess not," I said, feeling very important.

"And now it's poetry time. You in the mood for something lascivious?"

I didn't know whether I was or not. He flipped his hair back.

> There once was a lad named Yorick
> Who could, in times euphoric,
> Produce for inspection
> Three types of erection:
> Ionic, Corinthian and Doric.

Incredible lot of words in there. He went to the tent, unmeshed the dictionary from under everything else, and threw it in my lap, on his way to get two more beers from the immersed TNT case where they kept beer cans and fish in equal numbers.

"I like the Ionic one best," I said when he got back.

"Bitsy, you what?" He sounded surprised.

"Yeah, I do. Those neat little scrolly things, they're like a violin."

He sat down.

"But that other one. Is it a p-h?"

He nodded.

"Here we go, back to the E's." The pages were beer-stained. "Okay, so it's a happy feeling. Euphoric. It's like up on the mountain, all euphoric and windy and high . . . "

"Good, Bitsy, I'm glad you like it." He laughed.

"Well, are you gonna explain it to me?"

He set his beer can on the sand and kissed me on the neck, a private kiss just below my right ear. "Bitsy, I apologize. We're not gonna get to the whole, total explanation just yet." He was talking to my neck.

"Then how're you gonna feed my dark impatience?"

He picked up his beer and started laughing like crazy.

"What in the world is so damn funny?" I asked. "You know what you're doing? Compromising me or patronizing me, I don't know which." I started to walk upstream.

He laughed harder. "Listen, Bitsy—" I heard him get up, beer spilling. I put a good forty feet of sand between us. He'd have to yell if he expected me to hear him. "I'm not patronizing you! Will you turn around for a minute?"

I turned, sun in my eyes. "What *are* you doing then? First you don't like the violin, then suddenly there's no God, then you say some dumb poem and give me a euphoric kiss under my ear, and now you're laughing your head off! You're just weird, that's all!''

We both stood with our feet apart, shouting. "You're a little weird yourself, Bitsy—that beer is spilling all over the place!''

"So is yours!''

"Yeah, but I'm not holding the can upside down!''

I looked. The last dribbles were dotting the sand.

"And you want to know something else?'' I yelled. "You're full of shit sometimes!'' He was really steaming me.

"I know it, Bitsy,'' he laughed. "So are you!''

"And you know what else? I was just going to go and fall in Goddamn *love* with you in another minute or so!'' It just came out, along with the steam.

"Guess what, Bitsy!'' Still laughing.

"What, smarty?''

He threw his beer can straight in the air, sun reflecting off the end of it. "I beat you to it!''

We stared at each other like one of those dreams where they glue your feet to the ground. The can fell in front of him, kerplink on a rock, bounced to a dead stop in the sand.

I don't know how far the world turned while we stood still at those two little points on it.

Fred came out of the woods, downstream, dangling three fish on a piece of line. Judy was behind him with the two poles. They walked between us to the TNT cooler. "You two guys playing statue?'' Fred asked. They both smelled like fish.

My feet unglued themselves. We climbed up the bank and over the sides of Judy's family's jeep. Bushes went by as Fred dug the wheels into the sand.

"Careful, Judy. There's an ominous silence to windward of us,'' he said. "Maybe they're Communists.''

Nobody laughed like Hayes; he had a way of letting it take over his whole body, a funny baritone flexing of shoulders and legs— not convulsive, more like convincing.

Finally he straightened out and said, "What's so damn funny, Bitsy? First you read the dictionary for a while, then you take a hike across the sand and pour a perfectly good can of beer down your jeans, then you holler your head off! You're weird, you are. Hey, did I ever tell you I'm a pacifist?''

Judy chose that night to tell me she thought both guys were very conceited, and educated beyond the level of their intelligence, that I was gullible, that you had to sort out the wheat and chaff in the things they told you, and that I let Hayes push my brain around.

It took her about an hour to tell me all that, before she hunched over on her side of the bed to read. She was reading *Magic Mountain*. I went to sleep. I had an awful lot of figuring out to do.

Falling in love. It wasn't the falling that was hard to figure out. That was something you just did; you had no choice.

It was what you were falling into. Not like a crevasse. You knew that had to end somewhere, you'd eventually hit icy bottom and die. Nor like falling down skiing. Even if you broke a leg, someone would pick you up and put you on a litter and set the bone.

The falling into something like love was crazier. I thought about it a lot. While I held my violin, for instance. I ran my finger around the scroll of it, following the carving, trying to get at the very most inner circle the carver could have had in mind. If you could get your finger on that circle you'd know you had the answer, maybe. The very silent still point where your mind said, Wow, Yes, There it is.

That figuring-out business was something I kept to myself, mostly because I decided I was the only one in the world who hadn't figured it out already.

Meanwhile, nothing was so vastly different since the yelling at the river. Hayes said it "more or less ratified a state of mind that had existed subliminally for some time, awaiting annunciation." I assumed he meant it was no reason to get hysterical.

We probably shouldn't have taken Fred and Hayes to the church supper. We were all much too uncorked. We'd been drinking something made of gin called John the Baptists.

"Bitsy, we've got to work on that regional pronunciation of yours. I told you it's called a John the Bat Piss. Now will you try to remember that?" Hayes was in rare form.

It was raining. Uncorked and not in the mood to try to cook in the rain beside the river, Judy and I changed into skirts and made our unsteady way to the church basement with two tourists. We clearly didn't know what we were doing.

One of the things we didn't know was that Hayes and Fred were going to tell the fat minister they were from China and Afghanistan. Or that Hayes was going to tell him he'd root for him in the levitation contest. Or that when I pointed out Mr. Benson, Hayes was going to go over and shake his hand and ask him how his trusty twelve-gauge was. Or that when the blubbery minister thanked God for the blessed repast, Hayes was going to say You're welcome.

The food was terrific, although I could hardly see it, but just about the time dessert was beginning to look like a brilliant idea, somebody snapped my bra from behind. I turned around, the room twisting sideways. Behind a plate holding about four desserts, an acned face leered at me.

I mouthed silently, "Go to hell," and turned back around. But Hayes of the quick eyes was up out of his chair, nearly knocking the table over, grabbing a shirt front . . . I couldn't look.

The crash of a plate on the concrete floor, a body sailing into the piano, thunder of legs hitting keyboard, people looking up alarmed, I had a feeling I was going to disappear.

Judy grabbed Fred, I slid through a pile of peach cobbler on the floor and hooked Hayes by the sleeve, and we got out of the basement by the back stairs. Hayes and Fred howled.

"Hayes, you've gotta listen to me. You can go back east and play around on the swimming team, but I've gotta live here. You don't understand places like this, you really don't. That's the minister's son."

"Wrong, Bitsy, that's a horse's ass."

They thought it was the funniest thing that had happened in weeks. In a matter of seconds Judy and I did too. It was the most appallingly unholy behavior I'd ever seen.

My mother was beginning to like Hayes less and less.

Hayes was wrong, of course, when he called the church "the little revival show." Presbyterians didn't have revivals. They had self-control. And they did their best to give me some.

Whatever princeliness Hayes had hanging about him baffled me. A pacifist who bashed horses' asses into pianos. A shouter-off-mountaintops who went into long currents of silent, motionless thought, like a tree on a windless day. A big-mouthed college boy who liked people in the abstract and whom I could tell the absolute truth to. Who could be painfully tender and gentle about basic human matters. I was about to discover the tender and the gentle and the pain.

I couldn't find any peanut butter in the tent. But under the dictionary I found Salinger's *Nine Stories*. I grabbed it and scooted out across the sand to where Hayes was sharpening a Boy Scout knife in the sun.

"You didn't tell me!" I grabbed the arm of his sweatshirt.

"Didn't tell you what? That your toe's bleeding?"

My toe sure enough was bleeding. One of Fred's Good House-keeping Rules posted on the front tent pole was: "Bare feet in this hallowed house at all times, no matter how goddamn drunk you are." I obeyed it religiously, but you never knew how many broken bottles you'd run into once you got outside.

"It's okay. You didn't tell me he wrote anything else!"

"I didn't know you hadn't read them, Bits."

"How didn't you know that? Doesn't it show?"

"Now that you mention it, it does. Let's get you a band-aid."

I don't think I ever thanked him for the band-aid. I got no farther than the end of *For Esmé, with Love and Squalor*." More cruelty, more love than I could imagine exploded violently in my face.

I found my way to the other end of the log and put my head on his arm, tears pouring sideways onto his wrist. He must have gone on reading, but I felt his other hand on my head, rubbing it the way you do a baby who can't tell you what's wrong. I luxuriated in the symphony of my own tears and the noise of the river. I felt him reach over to see where my thumb was stuck in the pages. All he said was, "I know, Bits, I know."

There are lots of people who could have dropped by that summer to tell me it was corny to cry over a book. Hayes wasn't one of them.

"How could you not know I hadn't read that? How could you not? I'm completely changed. Clear down to my liver and everything."

"You've gotta believe this, Bits, I understand. You don't get too many times like that in your life, and I just accidentally got put down here on this log with my arm sticking out. Hey," he pointed up. "See that flying squirrel?"

I looked up in time to see it land, dipping a high branch.

It took me days to get back in shape after Esmé.

The day Hayes drove me to my violin lesson he learned what a fermata was, because Mr. Seligmann asked me if I wanted to cheat on the fermatas.

I thought it was a good idea to prepare Hayes for him. "Listen, I really love this man. Please, no horsing around—"

"Christ, Bits, I've been around artists all my life. What do you love about him, anyway?"

"For one thing, he's taught me every little tiny thing I know about the violin, and he also had to get out of Germany terribly fast, couldn't find his wife or anything for a couple of years—"

"How'd he get here?"

"You know what he says? He says he looked all over, and couldn't find anyplace that reminded him so much of Salzburg."

"He may have a point."

"Well, those two reasons, I guess. Mother took me to him when I was in first grade, I'd been crying a lot about Daddy—I guess I was a mess—and the only thing I did was listen to Brahms' First Symphony on the Victrola. I wanted to play the violin like mad. I only came up to his belt buckle."

"Shall I speak German with him?"

"You know German?"

"A little. Mostly about sculpture."

"Don't you sculpt at all?" I couldn't figure out why he didn't at least try.

"Not really, Bits. Do Seligmann's kids play the violin?"

"Oh, God, Hayes, I forgot to tell you. He lost them. I mean *lost* them. Two daughters. In Germany. Jesus."

"The furious hun. No, I won't speak German."

I wasn't doing so well on Mozart's Fourth Concerto. I hadn't been practicing much. Mr. Seligmann asked me if I wanted to cheat on the fermatas in the first movement cadenza.

Integrity loomed up like undigested breakfast. "Mr. Seligmann, I don't want to play it for you until I don't have to cheat on a single fermata."

He turned sideways on the piano bench, with an over-the-glasses glare. "Beatrice, do you *vahnt* to play zis concerto in za recital zis vinter?"

"Yes! Yes I do, I just—today—"

A smile rounded the bend of his mouth, he gestured with his head toward the open door to the next room where Hayes was sitting. Nobody sat in the same room with you while Mr. Seligmann gave you a lesson. "You hahv been busy zis summer, Beatrice?"

"Well, yes, I sort of have . . ."

He gave me a full, glasses-reflecting smile. "Zen you and I do some easy duets for today, vould you like zat?"

I always liked zat. We played duets while his cat dozed on the window seat on top of piles of music; Sevčik and Sibelius looked down at us from photographs on the wall, along with people named Ives and Varese and lots of others I didn't know anything about. When we were finished, I started to make violin case noises, and Hayes came to the doorway.

"She's going to be good vun day, you sink so?" Mr. Seligmann looked up at him.

"Yes, I think she is." He didn't look as if he'd suddenly started to like the violin.

The cat stretched, jumped off the window seat, and rubbed against Hayes's leg. Mr. Seligmann started his standard speech about the cat. "My vun-eyed cat, she sees vat za rest of us don't see. Alvays knows ven rain is coming, alvays knows when pollen is in za air. She sees truce." He meant truth. I wasn't going to argue. It was his cat.

We started out the door. "Beatrice, can you vork on za cadenza some, use some diligence zis veek?"

I said I would. Two western tanagers were dipping around the cherry trees in his yard.

We drove down the hill in one of those silences that Hayes sometimes dug himself into. After a mile or two, he finally opened his mouth. "What's a fermata, Bits?"

"It's when you hold a note for awhile, the music doesn't say how long. You sort of get an agreement in your mind with the composer about it. I use 'em to get my bearings sometimes, but that's cheating."

He looked down at me. "What's wrong with cheating?"

"Not in music, Hayes. You don't do that in music. What kind of music do you like, anyway?"

"Brubeck." And he explained who Dave Brubeck was.

He was quiet for a while longer. Then he said, "You know, your mother should marry Seligmann."

"That's dumb. He's got a wife, I told you."

"Well, she should marry him anyway. They could play sonatas around the fire."

The thought of Mother marrying anybody when she carried Daddy around like a monument was absurd. But I carried him around like a monument too, and I'd marry somebody someday. My brother monumentalized Daddy, too, by being so perfect all the time. My mother marrying my music teacher seemed a little perverted, but I couldn't think why.

Hayes did sculpt a little, with the Boy Scout knife.

"Here it is, Bits. Happy almost birthday." He held it in his hand, Mount Hood from the north side, the pine grain running vertically. "You like it?"

"I love it! But the glacier doesn't slope that much." A fly lit on it. "I'm gonna keep it forever! Hey, maybe you're a real Goddamn prince, Hayes!"

"Watch your mouth, little girl, or I'll wash it out with gin."

I put the pine mountain in my room next to Heifetz and Mozart.

In the general euphoria of being in love, I decided to tell Casey we'd stolen his cream. Judy, Fred and Hayes said I was crazy, and they each bet me two days' worth of firewood-gathering that he wouldn't laugh. I dragged them all to Casey's house one evening, cold sober. He had a very plump wife and a little girl named Penny with long blond hair and long legs. Hayes took one look at her and said she was a potential strawberry thief if he ever saw one. Penny thought it was hysterical when I told Casey.

"Beatrice, I'm proud. Ain't you proud, Mildred? I'm proud that old Matilda's good enough to make you come whippin' in here and steal her cream, and you come all the way up here to tell me about it—" Casey laughed like a windburned hand opening up. The kind of laugh you get when you've been outdoors all your life, I guess.

He even took Fred and Hayes along to help milk Matilda. He told them most city folks didn't know shit from Shinola about cows, and he was proud they appreciated Matilda. And he told them the mountain didn't give a damn about the loggin' business.

It was my way of proving to them that our neighbors weren't all horses' asses. They still thought Mr. Benson was just one rung above the missing link, and they explained the missing link.

Judy said maybe I wasn't such a rotten judge of character after all.

"I've been thinking it over, Bitsy." Hayes straddled the log. It was one of those dark nights with tree-frogs and crickets croaking and scraping their small but important melodies.

"I wondered what you were doing." He hadn't said anything for about twenty minutes.

"Now, are you listening? Because this isn't the kind of suggestion I hand out liberally . . ."

"Sure, I'm listening." I was picking pitch off my jeans.

"And I've decided, of all the available possibilities, I'd probably like it best—are you sure you're listening?"

I put my knee down. "Of course I'm listening. You want my full attention?" I looked straight at him.

"Yes, damn it, Bitsy, I do. I think I'd like it best if you carry a bunch of strawberries when you marry me."

The backs of magazines told all about hot flashes, so I knew exactly what was happening up and down my body.

"Marry you?"

"Sure. Didn't you know that?"

"I don't know whether I did or not. Maybe I did."

"You are gonna marry me someday, aren't you, Bits?"

"Yes, Hayes, I am. I really am." Kids with coupons safety-pinned to their T-shirts. Traveling all over the world. Brahms. Beethoven. Sibelius.

"We'll get married on your lawn, under the dogwood tree, we'll have gallons of capitalistic champagne, we'll all sit around on the grass and get blissfully drunk. I'll get your mother tipsy and dance with her, she'll adore me forever. Bring out the old beast in both of us. 'My men, like satyrs grazing on the lawn, Shall with their goat-feet dance the antic hay.' "

"I don't think I know anything you're talking about," I said.

"You will. We're gonna get you a classical education and a long white dress from Peru or someplace, we'll knock each other out. But I have to know one thing very seriously first." He was talking to my collarbone. "Are you gonna carry those strawberries?"

"God, yes," I said.

"Okay." He was off to the tent, and came back with a bottle of wine. "Bits, we're gonna drink to strawberries and Huxley and mountains and—just don't pour the wine down your ear—"

"Hayes, are you sure, about the dogwood and stuff—"

"Me? Sure I'm sure. Hey, Freak," he called over the dying fire, "you want to celebrate? We're getting married."

Judy and Fred stopped talking about football. There was silence for a moment from across the rocks. Then Fred's voice. "Nice going, Pygmalion. Here and now?"

Another silence. I was looking at Hayes, which is how I know nothing moved on him for a while. Then he laughed. "Maybe. And you can shove your Shaw fetish right up your ass."

Judy rolled from one to the other kissing everybody, we drank toasts in the dark. Fred didn't say much. On the way home I asked Hayes what was up between them.

"It's kind of complicated, Bits, but it's not one of the great issues of the western world, so don't worry your little head about it."

"I don't have a little head. I just want to know about the pig stuff he called you."

"Friends call each other all kinds of names in this elocutionary society, Bitsy. It's a silly delusion of Freak's, it doesn't mean anything."

The pink and red quilt on my bumpy bed was black and white in the moonlight. It occurred to me, looking at my black and white room, that I'd been positively convinced of two things in my life. One, I wanted to play the violin. Two, I wanted to marry Hayes. I don't know when I decided the second part. Probably in the middle of the river, with Sibelius. I was never quite sure.

My mother and brother would think I'd lost my mind. But what they didn't realize was that they could now relax. Rule number one with boys was that the more they cared about you the less they tried to push sex. What a relief.

There were several funny things about my mother. I knew what she was about sex, because I found "ambivalent" not far from "austere." Sex for people was pretty terrible, but sex for animals was great for people. When I was four, she'd tried to have a cocker spaniel mating party in the living room. Our dog was the male, and the female lived higher up on the mountain. Her name was Dinah, ours was Eric the Red. The only trouble was that Eric was about thirteen, and not at all interested, or didn't know he was supposed to be interested. Dinah's family thought the living room was a very odd place, but Mother said she wanted all the children to watch the life process. So we all set chairs around and tried.

Eric was sniffing all the children's feet, and Dinah kept following him with her rear end in the air; the life process had a very hard time of it, and Dinah never did have puppies.

Mother explained "heat" to me later, and said it was a wonderful thing, the business of having babies. I supposed it was. I asked Mother if I'd put my rear end in the air when I wanted to have babies. Mother said no, I wouldn't have to do that. I asked her if she'd invite people to watch, and she said no, she wouldn't do that either. People watched animals, but they didn't watch each other. She said it was private with people. And when I asked her whether my brother had watched her and Daddy having me, she said she'd already explained how private it was with people.

Soon after that my father died, and we never talked much more about sex. Except that when I got my first period she was very solicitous and talked a lot about being a woman. It wasn't so much *my* being a woman as it was *our* being a woman. She managed to convey a solid picture of red, calendared sisterhood. I thought it was rather convivial and nice.

The closer I got to boys, the more she indicated that I wasn't ready for the private act of having babies, regardless of how red and calendared I was. By the time Hayes appeared on the scene with his beer and his irreverent mouth, I think she lived with the pulsating suspicion that he was going to present her with a grandchild before she could turn around. And I think it scared her to death.

"Bitsy," Hayes said one dark night on the way back from the Columbia, "have you noticed that I'm a boy and you're a girl?" The bruise on Fred's face had healed, and I hadn't asked whether it was related to the pig stuff.

"Yeah, Hayes, I've sure noticed that."

"And do you know what boys and girls do when they love each other?"

I leaned my head to the left a little. "Yeah, Hayes, they get married."

"Good, Bitsy. So far, you get an A-minus, but—"

"My mother'll be delighted. She'll be glad you're so stimulating."

"The discussion has very little to do with your mother from this point on. In fact, it has quite specifically nothing to do with her." He was getting to be a terrific mountain-road-driver. "These boys and these girls we mentioned—"

I got up on my knees and kissed him on the front of the throat, right above the T-shirt, low enough so he could keep on driving and not hit the guardrail.

"Bitsy, goddamn it, that's frustrating, for christ's—"

"I'm sorry." I sat down, feeling very short.

"It's precisely that sort of thing I'm talking about. That kind of neck-kissing when I'm driving a car, and then flying off down the side of my arm purring. Am I getting through to you?"

"I'm not sure, Hayes."

"Okay, I'll try to simplify it. And would you mind not hanging your hair down my chest while I'm talking to you? There's a sixty-foot drop right out there."

I moved over. I hadn't found an intact rubber band for days.

"Listen. I like your hair. It's nice hair. But I'm trying to drive, and I don't think you understand what I'm trying to tell you." He looked sideways at me. "And you don't have to sit all the way over on the other side of the car like that, and sometimes I think you're either dense—or something, and—here it is *August*, for christ's sake!"

"What do you want, then? I'm not supposed to kiss you while you're driving, I'm not supposed to sit way over here, what the hell do you want?" I put my elbow out the window.

He stiffened his back against the torn Chevy seat. "Bitsy, I'll tell you what I want. You have this dim idea that love is from the shoulderblades up. It's not. What I want is to make violent love to you and—"

"You mean *do* it?" I knew I was squeaking.

He didn't take his eyes off the road. "Yes, and don't interrupt me 'til I'm finished talking. I want to make earthshaking love to you, and not stop 'til you've gone shooting out to the end of the stars and back—and I'll bring you back safe and sound. That's a promise."

We turned in at my driveway. He stopped the car, letting it idle noisily in neutral. I pulled a strand of hair out of my mouth and held onto it. Only one or two guys had ever suggested it to me before, and certainly not with that end-of-the-stars business attached. "No."

He hung an elbow on the steering wheel. "No?"

"No. I—I haven't figured out what love is when you fall into it, Hayes. When I figure that out . . ."

"Why not?"

"Because I'm not ready."

I watched him thinking. Hayes was a very smart person, and he knew meaningless dialogue when he saw it. He pushed the flying lock of hair back, took a deep breath and scraped the gears. At my house I took my bathing suit and towel, got out, and hung halfway in the door of the car.

"Good night, Bitsy. It's late." He looked as if he'd rather be almost anyplace than in my backyard.

"Okay. Good night, Hayes."

I didn't see him for about five days. By the time he reappeared, I'd memorized the first movement of the Mozart.

"Hi, Bits. Want to fry some fish?"

"Sure." It was a golden August afternoon.

The Chevy ashtray was filled, overflowing, with lipstick-stained filtertips. On display. "Nice ashtray you've got there, Hayes." I knew very well I didn't have to say that.

He glanced at it, gave me a look that was supposed to take the place of a couple of paragraphs, and started the car. "Look, Bitsy, I accept your conditions. I love you, that's why you're in my car today—oh hell. Seen much of the minister's son lately?"

"Hayes, that's a very dopey thing to say. Screw the minister's son."

"No, thank you. Let's go fry fish."

"You're not mad at me then, Hayes?"

"It's not a question of being mad. Let's not ask questions today, all right?"

"All right."

It wasn't with undiluted joy that Hayes accepted my conditions, but he accepted them. Red filtertips turned up from time to time, plus about a dozen unstrung dime-store pearls scattered around the back seat. And one rusty earring, for a pierced ear. I didn't go around looking for someone with an infected earlobe. And I didn't mention it to Hayes, because there was very little point in being sarcastic with someone you loved. In fact, no point at all.

It was quite obvious, if you looked around very much, that guys were going to have sex with some girls and marry others. Hayes was going to have sex with a bunch of rusty earlobes and marry me.

Judy said the Chevy had had that kind of leftover stuff in it all summer. I just hadn't noticed. I asked her whether she and Fred had had the sex discussion.

"You mean whether to do it or not? Sure, we had it." We were washing dishes at her house.

"When?"

"On the way back from climbing the mountain."

Hayes was right. I was dense. "What did you say?"

"I said no, then maybe, then no."

"Judy, why'd you say maybe in the middle?"

She held a glass up to the light and put it back in the sink for me to wash again. "I'm not sure. I think I said it because I might never see him again after this summer, and he's one of the most genuinely fair people I ever met. I guess that's why he let me say maybe and then no again. Most guys would be furious if you did that."

"Boy, if I thought I'd never see Hayes again after this summer, I'd—Why do you think Fred's so genuinely fair?"

"Because while we were talking about it, he said there's enough fighting going on in this world without us fighting about something like doing it together. And he also explains parts of *Magic Mountain* that I don't understand."

"Like what?"

"Well, it's really about life and death, and he says you define your life in the way you feel about death. If you think about it, it's true. Maybe I'll be a doctor."

"A doctor? Wow. You know how I feel about death? I don't want to have anything to do with it."

She stacked plates in a cupboard. "Anyway, that's why I think he's fair."

"I thought you thought they were educated beyond the level of their intelligence."

"I do. I still think he's fair."

"Do you think he's doing it with anybody?"

"Sure, probably. Guys have to do it with somebody. Mother and Daddy told me that. That's the way it is."

With the apples ripening, the days getting just the tiniest bit shorter, and with roadmaps beginning to make their appearance as Fred and Hayes figured out their route back east, there was much more to do than worry about whose filtertips were whose. I hardly gave them a thought.

There were no tire tracks in the dirt road to Wahtum Lake. The jeep bumped around, obscuring everything behind us in yellow dust. When the road got too rough, we parked and walked through the woods. Spongy pine-needle turf invited bare feet, but there was the matter of random fishhooks, so we kept our shoes on. The Doug fir shade thinned out gradually, easing into purple fireweed, sunshine and dead white trees at the edge of the stick-filled water. Trees and bees made the only sounds. The sky was unmitigated blue. Someone had left a raft of eight or nine planks nailed together, which drifted among the dead timber.

Hayes and I waded around black and orange waterdogs, which he said were newts. I knew he was just being regional about it. We got on the raft, splinters grazing our legs. Somebody's airplane flew over, saw us hand-paddling in the middle of the lake, and dipped its wings. We waved. The sun was glorious, "ebullient," Hayes called it.

"Listen, we've got serious stuff to talk about. What if you don't get back here next summer? What if you really can't stand the violin."

"For christ's sake, Bitsy, I may not get back here next summer. But you know what we'll do? We'll build an incredible house somewhere, in Switzerland or maybe China, right beside a lake, walls all made of glass; we'll put a practice room on one end, all insulated. Egg cartons all over the connecting wall, I won't have to listen to you unless I feel like it. If I get into some fat book, we'll close the door, you just play away. Along about sunset I'll haul myself out of my chair, slip you a cold beer, you'll say thank you very much, we'll go swimming nude in our own little lake, the kids all hollering and splashing around." He backwatered, changing the direction of the raft.

We lay on our sides, grinning at a dragonfly picking its way along the middle plank of the raft.

"You know what, Hayes? Maybe I'm not smart enough for you. Did you ever think of that?"

He looked at the blue spot on my neck and didn't answer me.

"Sometimes I think I don't know anything." I looked at the crescent of dead timber across the lake.

"That proves it. That's the mark of the truly transcendent mind."

"Horseshit, Hayes."

"One too many of those, Bits." He put one hand on my shoulder, I went backwards into the lake. I swam under the raft, everything was green, I got his ankle, pulled him in. Every time we splashed, water showed blue like a shower of ice drops.

"Hey, how do you know that about the egg cartons?" We were kicking the raft toward shore to get the food.

"I don't know. It just seems like a good idea."

We took green apples and salami and four cans of beer out on the second trip. I lay on my back shoving an apple into my mouth. Hayes sat amidships. An ebullient blue and golden day if I ever saw one.

It hadn't occurred to me before to wonder whether Hayes was handsome. He was.

"Hayes, what kind of eyes are our kids gonna have, with your green and my blue?"

"Well, Bits, it has to do with dominant and recessive genes—"

"No, I mean their eyes. What color are their eyes gonna be? Not their jeans."

He laughed into his beer can. "Bitsy, I can't believe that. The schools around here must be lousy—"

"What did I say that's so dumb this time?"

"It's not so dumb, I just never thought about it—recessive jeans, that's what they're gonna wear—"

"Damn it, will you tell me what you're talking about?" I turned over on my stomach.

He was still laughing. "A vast wardrobe of recessive jeans—"

When he explained it to me I remembered something about it from biology, I'd just forgotten the name. The schools weren't lousy, I simply looked out the window a lot. The teachers were always telling me how precocious my brother was, and how they expected precocious things from me. Mostly I looked out the window.

No more. The teachers would jump out of their clothes when they found out I knew things like "ostensibly" and "ambivalent" and "Corinthian."

"I have to add that to my collection, Bits."

"What?" I looked up from the raft boards.

"Recessive jeans. It goes in my collection of your whimsical interpretations of the ineluctible realities of science and fact."

"Holy shit, Hayes. Here you are, all euphoric and suntanned, I'm taking you seriously, will you please just maybe return the favor?"

He leaned toward the fourth can of beer near my feet, and licked the back of my knee on the way. No boy had ever licked the back of my knee before.

"And not tip the *raft* over?"

four

Every once in a while I light up a Lucky Strike outside in the wind somewhere and it tastes just like the breezes that swooped eastward up the Columbia and rattled the cottonwood branches around in the dark.

The matter of three missing hubcaps had been dealt with. I knew perfectly well that the scrofulous minister's son had them. One each for the father, son, and holy ghost, as Hayes said.

We sat around the fire on the beach, watching our windbreak of beer cans grow taller. Fred was the fairest of us all. I watched his blond head as he reached across Hayes's jeans lying on the sand to use the churchkey on the leather thong. Late August was the warmest for swimming in the cove; an exquisitely quiet peace lay over the night, like Vivaldi's "Summer," the Adagio. The only trouble with that movement is that it's very short.

I didn't know Fred had had a guitar in the trunk of the Chevy all summer long, or I'd have asked him to teach me something about it. He pulled it out along with the Army blanket that gentle August night and sat strumming unobtrusively on the other side of Hayes's jeans. He started to sing.

Mountain strong
Mountain grim
Mountain don't care if the moon goes dim.

Mountain blue
Mountain white
Aurora borealis in the middle of the night.

Mountain cold
Mountain high
Mountain's gonna watch me when I die.

Mountain sits
Mountain is
Don't give a damn about the loggin' biz.

The last words drifted away like sparks over the water, where reeds waved like drum brushes.

"And that, ladies, is the definitive lyric of Mister Hood." He put the guitar on the blanket and looked up at the stars.

It was clearly time to go swimming. I kept up with Hayes's swimming team crawl for about ten strokes, no more. We stopped, shook water out of our ears, let the waves swirl around us.

"The really amazing thing," he said, "is that the universe is there at all." The fire lit his face orange above the black water. "I mean, considering the incredible possibilities, the accident of the universe just knocks you out."

I nodded, thinking to the end of the stars, then doubling it, trying to double it again before my brain gave out. I'd been doing that impossible mathematical stunt ever since I could remember.

"Let's take off our suits," he said.

"Oh, come on, you're kidding. I've never done it in mixed company . . ." Judy and I'd done it in April in a millpond, just to be the first ones in the water that year.

"Bitsy, you are one of the most exasperating people—"

"Hayes, my mother!"

"She is *not* here right now, Bits. Let's just go skinny-dipping and break another cultural barrier."

"Another what?" I knew intuitively that skinny-dipping wasn't sex, especially in the dark, and that only by the most tiresome stretch of the imagination could you call it that, but I stalled anyway. I kept hearing the Vivaldi Adagio and Fred's mountain song. Mother would think that was all very nice.

We took off our suits in eight feet of water and threw them on the moonlit sand. Mother would jump out a window.

We swam some more.

"Hey, this is terrific! Can we do this all the time?"

"I told you we will. Let's go to the rocks."

The cliffs were basalt, enormous hexagons that rose to about seventy feet above the water. I guessed they were a million years old; the Columbia had trickled and washed them down, long before the Indians, probably even long before the fish. People, mostly crazy people, talked about diving off. Nobody I knew ever did it. There was a wicked backwash.

Judy and Fred had gone somewhere, which was just fine. I didn't want to discuss why I had no suit on. As we got closer to the rocks, we saw a silhouette moving around the north edge about twenty feet up, a pair of long legs and bent arms, knees tense against the sky.

"Hey, look, somebody's gonna dive off." I pointed up.

We stopped swimming and watched. He did a very sloppy dive, went in about three yards in front of us. I wanted to be the first to congratulate him when he came up, for foolhardiness alone. We waited.

"Shouldn't he be up by now?" I asked the empty space where Hayes had been. Damn him. Playing games, I was stark naked, two guys were about to surface right under me. I moved back.

There was Hayes, where was the other one? The moon spilled like cream across the water. Hayes didn't say anything, just took a huge breath and went down again, leaving rings in front of me.

The cold truth lay on my brain like scales. I counted twenty seconds. Hayes came up, moved out toward the middle of the river and went down again. I couldn't count the seconds. My eyes got caught in the circles.

Two heads. One with black muck on it. Hayes's arm around its chest. His voice came puffing across at me. "Get a towel, hang on to it. No—wad it up. Just stay on the sand."

I swam past them to the shore, ran up the gray sand on all fours to the nearest towel, wadded it up and turned around.

They were only about halfway, I could see the two heads

together in a French kiss. I couldn't decide what to do, so I yelled to Fred and Judy to build up the fire, wherever they were.

I shivered and watched Hayes drag the guy up onto the sand, lay him on his side, hit him hard on the back, then turn him over, chest up.

"Put it under his neck—"

The towel. I did. The guy was lying between us. Hayes had his mouth over the other's, pinching the nose with one hand. I'd never seen anything like it in my life. He blew in, lifted his head, looked at the chest and blew in again, over and over, I couldn't tell how much time was going by.

I didn't know whether I was bending over a corpse or not.

Fred appeared with the Army blanket and put it over the legs. I grabbed a towel and started wiping the head. Hayes kept on blowing, Judy brought a burning stick to look for the cut. We found the gash in his hair, Hayes kept blowing into the mouth. The lock of hair kept swinging back and forth in front of my face.

The body suddenly shivered and vomited. Hayes kept blowing in, and the same thing happened again. I saw the chest lift, like a hill waking up. A puke-and-blood-spattered arm moved.

"Holy shit," Hayes whispered. He leaned back and closed his eyes. I watched the chest go up and down. Across it I'd have had my first look at a naked man if I'd been paying attention.

"Jesus Christ, what time is it?" the guy muttered.

The four of us started laughing like crazy fools; Judy stroked his pukey arm.

"What the hell happened to my head?"

Hayes opened his eyes. "You hit it, man, you're bleeding—'

"Somebody got a band-aid? What the hell time is it?"

We laughed again. He started lifting his head, but it fell back down like a bad idea. He looked mad.

"Calm down," Fred said. "You're gonna have to have stitches or something. Just relax."

Judy threw the glowing stick away and ran for the car to get the first-aid kit. The guy wouldn't stop asking what time it was. I told him I thought it was about eleven. Hayes rolled over on his stomach and went to sleep.

"I gotta get outa here. I gotta date." The guy got himself up on one elbow. He looked at me. "Jeez, honey, you're gonna freeze your ass without your snowsuit."

"What's your name, anyway?" I asked as Judy came running back with the first-aid kit.

"What's it to you? Jimmy Lee."

Jimmy Lee Benson. There weren't two Jimmy Lees. Judy and Fred wound a bunch of gauze around his head while she and I had hysterics and tried to keep from kicking sand all over him. We finally got control of ourselves and told Fred. The guy had staggered away, and Fred and Judy and I had a royal howl, with Fred taking time out to holler to him that he should go to the hospital.

Hayes slept through the whole thing.

In the car, Judy curled up on the front seat, the fully-clad Hayes sleeping with his head on my fully-clad lap in the back. I knew Jimmy Lee wouldn't go to the hospital. When you live around mountains you're not supposed to go to hospitals. I never knew why.

A doe ran across the road in front of us, terrified in the headlights. Fred swerved to avoid her. "Poor simple-minded thing, isn't ready for us to come fouling up her life . . ." he said. The air was getting colder as we climbed.

The night animals were out all around us. Raccoons, deer, even a porcupine. Judy and Hayes were missing them. "You get born alone, you die alone—what a strange, unfriendly arrangement," Fred said. The mountain was silver gashed with black.

"Wow, yes," I said, trying not to breathe against Hayes's head.

"You know, Bitsy, you're a big laugher, but you take things awfully seriously—"

"So do you—"

"I wonder if you could tell me, what do you think of all this?"

"All what, Fred? You mean Jimmy Lee and everything? I loved your song, I really did, it's gonna be nice to—"

"I mean, what do you think about my friend back there?"

"That's a very long question."

"I meant it that way. Do you think you have it straight?"

"Have what straight? This hero with his head in my lap? I think so."

"That's what I thought. He comes from a long line of sculptors, Bitsy. Just don't—you know, you're fifteen—"

"Sixteen tomorrow."

"Sixteen tomorrow. What I mean is, he's twenty, it's a wheat

and chaff kind of thing, we're leaving in a couple of days, just
don't—''

Hayes moved his head. ''Just don't take a wrong turn and hurtle
us over the guardrail, you pensive bastard,'' he said sleepily.
''Boy, these recessive jeans . . .''

''End of sentence. Well, I hope your birthday's a triumph,
Bitsy.'' He drove the rest of the way in silence. I put my head out
the window, smelling the Doug fir.

Old Fred and his blond skepticism. On that breezy mountain
evening, I didn't know I was underestimating him.

I dried my hair with a towel and sat down on my squeaky bed
with the diary. I tried to get the whole thing on one page, but it ran
over. I couldn't decide whether something that was almost a
tragedy was funny or not.

By the time I finished writing it was my birthday. Happy birthday to me. I turned off the light; Mozart, Heifetz and the pine
mountain carving went gray against the wall.

At about ten the next morning Mother wished me a happy
birthday with a new volume of Handel sonatas, and we started them
then and there. She was almost always willing to stop whatever she
was doing to play. The day was beginning as a triumph.

We were coming down the home stretch of the sixth sonata when
the lifesaver pulled up in a cloud of dust. Mother greeted him in her
finishing-school voice and marched kitchenward to do the birthday
baking. We headed for the orchard.

Lots of people have given me Pogo books, but nobody else ever
gave me *Uncle Pogo's Book of So-So Stories.* We read it and
laughed in the yellow mustard and purple vetch of the pear orchard.
We talked about euphoric things like dogwood tree weddings, how
big the pears were getting, climbing the north side of Mister Hood
someday.

He left to return the car to Fred and get the oil checked, saying
he'd come back for birthday cake and ice cream.

I walked in the front door that my father had ordered from
Portland, the huge window getting my seventieth finger smudge of
the summer. It had remained unbroken all those years. Something
about our family kept things unchanged, intact. New things like a
different window didn't fit us.

Before I heard the iron door latch close I had a sense of something terribly wrong. Fiddle had broken her leg. My brother was poisoned with malathion spray.

Mother stood by the dining room table, her hair wild, her face swollen. Crying had ravaged her; this had every earmark of a genuine tragedy.

"What happened?" I hoped she wouldn't tell me.

The sun shone in through the red cranberry glass in the window, giving the room the color of an open heart. Nothing moved except a bowl of chrysanthemums on the dining room table, shaking from the weight of Mother's hand. The President was dead. The pricks and horses' asses had declared war again. She was selling the ranch.

I went toward her hand. People always reach for other people's hands at times like that. I don't know why. The house smelled like birthday cake. Her hand moved a little, with it a small blue book. The diary.

"Oh boy," I breathed. Fiddle trotted away, the President and my brother took up their beds and walked, the horses' asses signed a quick truce and we'd keep the ranch.

"Oh *boy!*" she echoed, a deep scream boiling up from some inner molten fury where her insides used to be. "I found *this.*" She made the word sound slimy. "Under your mattress." Mother the diligent mattress-turner.

"And?" I waited.

"*And!*" Her fist came down on the table like a bird falling out of the sky, plunk. Water spilled out of the chrysanthemum bowl. "And I found what you've been doing with your time! All that liquor! With boys! Swimming naked in the river with them! Oh, I'm sick. You've made me ill."

"Do you know he even—"

"Your father would be so ashamed! Naked in the river!"

"Mother, I don't see what you're so excited about."

She exhaled a long time, veins standing out wherever she had them. Then very quietly, "You don't see what I'm excited about. You don't see. Why didn't you tell me the *truth*?"

"Because you didn't want me to. That's all. I haven't done anything bad. Don't you see me standing here, just the way I was yesterday? I'm not ruined."

"And yesterday you were making plans to swim naked with boys."

"I was not. It just happened."

"*What* happened?" More water spilled.

"You read it. A big ten minutes in the water. In the dark. Then Hayes just happened to save Jimmy Lee's life. I didn't even know he'd come home."

She pulled a chair out and sat down as if she were getting ready to die. "I'm shaken. Absolutely crushed. What were you *planning* to do?"

Her desperate humorlessness succeeded in making me mad. "Holy shit, what is this, anyway? First you read my own private diary, then you don't even believe it? What *are* you?" If I hadn't started screaming and swearing, she might not have gone to pieces.

"You're revolting. You've deceived me. You're a bad nasty girl. You're going to be punished."

"What are you going to do?" I tried pretending it was someone else. I'd never figured on being bad. Bad? Really?

"We're going to start by not seeing that college boy again."

I sat down. "Mother, you can't do that." Somebody else.

"Of course I can. You are not going to see him. That is a beginning." The room flooded redder as the sun made its way between two Douglas pseudo firs through the cranberry glass. Shadrach, Meshach, and Abed-nego. I had a feeling she meant it.

Tears dripped scalding down my chin. "Please, Mother, don't do that. I'll do whatever you want. I'll apologize." Pull out your eyes, apologize. *Portrait of the Artist* was two weeks overdue at the library.

"That is my decision. You will not see him again."

My voice seemed to come from my knees. "Mother, they're leaving tomorrow. That's my life we're talking about."

All of a sudden I was asking her to do what she couldn't. I was asking a woman who hadn't had a brush with passion in ten years to grasp compassion by the throat and fling it sweetly around the bleeding living room. Damned impossible trick, so I gave up.

My brother stood in the doorway. He knew what was going on. There was one small thing in my favor. As dumb and empty-headed as he thought I was, he thought Mother could be pretty dumb too. He waited until he had our attention. Perfect, unflawed. I thought I hated him.

And then I didn't.

"Oh, Mother, let her see him one more time. She can explain. Maybe it'll be a sobering experience."

We'd come, in our austere and demented way, to depend on his authority.

"All right, he may come here." I hadn't seen her defy him since he'd refused to wear his parka to school one March day when he was in the seventh grade.

Mother and I sat, the offending little book between us.

"I am sending you to St. Margaret's Hall."

"Okay," I said. It could have been somebody else.

"We'll go tomorrow. It's settled."

"Okay." I'd never been called bad before.

"Are we gonna have any dinner, or shall I go fishing?" my brother asked.

I wanted my father to walk in the door, laugh and say he'd gone skinny-dipping too, be proud that his daughter had been able to climb the mountain, proud that her own true love could save somebody's life; say he wanted to shake that young man's hand and tell him he was glad his daughter could love somebody so brave and clever and funny. He didn't.

"I suppose you'd better go fishing. I'm going to lie down." The migraine always managed to surface when there was trouble. I never got them. I must have been a carrier.

"Could I go?" I asked him.

"Maybe you could have a little talk with her," Mother suggested. It sounded as if I'd inched back toward the family bosom. It wasn't a very inviting one, but it was all we had.

He eyed me skeptically for a second or two, said with cold neutrality, "Come on, then."

I followed him out the back door.

We drove off in the Ford, not talking.

His spot was about three miles above Hayes' and Fred's campsite. We climbed down to a bunch of huge rocks, the kind that Daddy had used to build our fireplace. I sat on one. He baited his line.

"Oughta be some fine fish here," he said, eye on a lure.

I didn't want him to catch one just then. I felt like one, with a hook caught in the roof of my mouth.

"That boyfriend of yours catch any?"

"Some." Hook in my mouth, I gasped for breath.

"What's he think of our fine countryside?"

"He says if you take the long view it's not without redeeming qualities, the quintessential grandeur of the mountain being one."

"He does, does he?" One eyebrow lifted.

He cast into a little pool upstream from white water. I was still trying to pretend it was somebody else.

"Beatrice, what are you doing with your life?"

"What do you mean?" A chipmunk dashed by.

He reeled in, studied the baited hook and cast again. "Are you letting this guy change you?"

"Yes." I was turning into someone else, right on the rock.

"Listen, I'm not trying to sound like a father, but we haven't got one and I'm your next of kin. I'm trying to help you."

"Where were you before? I don't even think I want your—"

"Well, damn it, you're gonna need it before Mother's through with you."

"I thought you made the decisions around here. We just—"

"Listen, how can I talk with you if you won't—look, you've got a multiple choice here; take road A or road B or road C." He drew a diagram in the sand with the end of the fishing pole. "Road A is keep on being nasty and cause yourself and Mother a whole lot of unnecessary pain, and regret it later. B, listen to me, think about it, then ignore my advice. C, consider my advice and follow it. Which are you gonna do?"

"It depends on your advice."

My brother bristled with strength of character. I think it kept him from going through adolescence. When he was fourteen he carried a guy with a broken leg two miles out of a forest. And when he was eleven he ran barefoot one morning in his pajamas over two feet of crusted snow to the end of the lawn and back. Foolhardy, but with the moral fiber of John the Baptist.

"Well, first, you could stop being so hard on Mother. That means learning a little bit about simple Christian thoughtfulness." He sat on a rock a few feet away.

"Oh, for Christ's sake, can we leave Christ out of this for a while? Do you even know this is the Goddamn Bible Belt?"

"Not strictly speaking. We're too far west."

"We're smack in the western extension of it. Hayes told me.

You know what that means? It means there're other belts, this isn't the center of the world, there's stuff out there you and I don't even know about—''

"In all those other belts, eh?" Patronizing. Boy, was I glad I'd looked that one up. "I'm not talking theology, I'm talking morality. Here you are, just sixteen, already you're skinny-dipping with boys. By the time you're twenty, what'll you have left to do?"

"How the hell do I know? Maybe I'm gonna be splattered all over the highway by next week. What then?"

"Beatrice, it's a question of separating the wheat from the chaff . . ."

"Everybody's always talking about wheat and chaff—I'm *surrounded* by people who think they know the almighty difference! I've never seen such a bunch of human threshers in my life. You know what I think? I think everybody's full of shit sometimes!"

He looked at me with strength of character. "Beatrice," he said, "don't you think you're overeager and indiscriminate?"

If I'd been undereager and discriminate I wouldn't be going to boarding school. But I wouldn't have climbed the mountain either. I might not even have met Hayes.

"Well, if you won't answer that, maybe you'll answer this one. Do you think you're in love with him?" My brother wouldn't do anything as terrible as read somebody's private diary, but he'd ask, in that calm, quiet voice, as if he wanted to know whether we could save the dog's injured leg.

If I told him the truth, he'd start talking about strength of character. So I said, "I don't ask you that stuff, do I?"

"No, you don't." He had a way of being supremely fair.

"And you wouldn't tell me if I did ask, would you?"

"No," he answered, prying a chunk of dried mud off his boot. "No, I wouldn't."

I wanted to ask why he'd taken the flashlight and all the Mickey Spillane books out of the hayloft, but I knew I'd get an answer so full of moral fiber that I'd throw up listening to it.

I sat there trying to love everybody at the same time, but I ended up just pretending it was somebody else getting sent to boarding school, and trying to figure out whether I was bad.

He put the fishing things away. No fish. We climbed to the car.

"What are you gonna do, Beatrice?" he asked, awfully fairly for somebody who was trying to be brother and father at the same time.

"I don't know. I guess I'm gonna go to that school and wear a uniform and get out of Mother's hair."

Later, I waited for Hayes on the front porch, in the dark. Nobody said anything about birthday cake, but I knew it was sitting in the kitchen, frosted at about noon before everything started happening.

He pulled up, I ran to the car and yanked the door open.

"Jesus, Bitsy, what's happened to—"

"Don't say anything, just come on over here—" We walked around the mammoth dogwood tree and sat down in the dark on the far side, away from the log house.

"Listen, Hayes, I cried all over you once—this is gonna make twice—it's not pretty or noble—I got a little birthday present today—"

"Hold it, Bits, calm down—"

"I didn't tell you—it's so insanely dumb I can't stand what a horse's ass I am—I kept a diary from the day you walked in here and—my mother found it."

"So?"

"So, picture her reading about the creeping jesus and the end of the stars and back and—about last night—"

"You'll have to be clearer than that, all the snuffling—"

"She's sending me to boarding school. Because I'm bad."

"She's what? You're *what*?"

"No more chances this time. I've used 'em up."

He looked at the moon rising over the east hills. "Bits, if there's any goddamn thing you're definitely *not*, it's bad. Don't give it another thought."

I tried believing him.

"Hayes, do you know that school is full of Episcopalians? They get down on their knees all the time—"

"Holy shit, Bitsy, that *is*—jesus, I don't know *what* it is—"

"It's different with Mr. Seligmann; he didn't *want* to lose his daughters, he went around hunting for them, and here she is sending a perfectly healthy one away—you don't do that to somebody you love, do you?"

He didn't say anything.

"That's what I thought. I'm not very smart, maybe, but I know that much. It's very weird, but I feel like I want to die."

And then I didn't. He had lovely arms, and a lovely mouth, the kind you want to live a long time and grow old with, get gray hair with, have every tooth in your mouth filled with gold, play the violin with old craggy fingers that got stuck in fourth position while he read some fat book for the seventh time, eventually walk with a cane down to the lake at sunset in Switzerland or maybe China, put your funny old arms around each other and have a royal howl, maybe you'd still be able to get a little sexy, and when you were in your nineties you'd still laugh your heads off about something like climbing a mountain together.

"Bitsy, I've got some forceful concluding remarks. These things don't happen to just anybody. Special people get specially-designed events. Sometimes they're great and sometimes they're shitty. Now, keep listening, because this is important. Whatever they try to put in your brain at that church place, think just the opposite. Take the Latin and the geometry like the art forms they are, but the religious stuff—leave that alone. Don't let it into your mind to do its damage. Don't—*don't* let them put a rod up your ass. When I marry you I want you to be pure and full of truth, not bent out of shape by prelates and scriptural garbage. Will you do that?"

"Yes. I mean no. Whatever it is. I'll try." I'd had an awful lot of instructions that day. I was getting dizzy.

"The nearest you should let yourself get to their spiritual harangue is Bach. You can play a Mass now and then, but don't get any closer than that. Okay?"

"Okay, I'll—do you know this is the second biggest dogwood tree in Oregon?"

"It's damn big."

"My father planted it. It's got eleven trunks."

"I know. I counted them while I was working up the nerve to tread on your virginal front porch after you—"

"I don't want to go to boarding school. If there's any way to say *don't want to*, that's what I mean."

"I know, Bits. Are you afraid of it?"

I wasn't afraid of going off to Switzerland or maybe China, how could I be afraid of going to Portland? "No, I'm not afraid, exactly—"

"Bits, you know what else I like about you? Things you don't even know you have. Guts, for instance. You just lead with your guts—and listen to this." He put his hand on my chin. "Not everybody likes people with guts. But go right ahead and lead with 'em. Starting with boarding school. Now, can we have some cake?"

"You're kidding. Are you ready to face my mother? She's in that house and I think she's out to get you."

"Sure. I'm ready." He pulled me up by the hand. If I'd been Hayes, I wouldn't have gone near her.

The birthday cake was good. Maybe that's why Mother hadn't thrown it out when the shit hit the fan. We stood in the kitchen, laughing, crumbs falling all over the floor. She came marching in from the dining room.

"Hayes, this is too bad. Too bad. It could have been such a nice friendship." She sounded like a nun.

He turned to face her, crumbs falling out of his mouth. "You may have trouble believing this, but it was. Is. I—"

"I'm so ashamed—" She started to leave the room like a funeral procession of one.

Hayes took half a step in her direction. "Just a minute. Wait just a minute! I have not raped your daughter. The idea never crossed my mind!"

She looked as if somebody had just opened a ten-year-old coffin and left the room.

I think it was in those electric seconds in the kitchen that Hayes taught me how to face people who are out to get you.

I'd never had anybody swoop into my life like that. Never fallen in love before. Never thought about not seeing them for a whole year, or maybe even, God forbid, longer than than. These weighty considerations may account for the ineptness with which I handled the whole ceremony of being unceremonious when it came time for Hayes to get himself gone.

"Here's the plan, Bits." He stood with his feet apart on the front porch, moonlight whitening his jeans. "You listening?"

"I'm listening." I held onto his side belt loops, my right thumb lying against the leather churchkey thong.

"You've gotta look at me, too. That's the way it's done."

I lifted my chin, my eyes went right along with it, like zipping a parka against the cold.

"That's better. We don't say anything remotely like good-bye. Got that?" The irreverent mouth curved in roughly a third of a smile.

"I've got that."

"I'm gonna go to my school and you're gonna go to your nunnery, and—Bits, if you cry another tear today your eyes are gonna fall out—"

"I'm not, Hayes, I'm really not—"

"And every time I see a mountain, or even a hill, I'm gonna lift my glass and drink a euphoric toast to a fine little climber, okay?"

"Okay."

"And I think now is as good a time as any to tell you I didn't lie to your mother in the kitchen."

"Hayes, I've lied to her in every room in the house."

"I really never thought about actually raping you—"

"Will you do me a favor, Hayes, before you go?"

"What?"

"Say something with lots of *s*'s in it."

"Why?"

"Because you say them like José Ferrer."

"Sonofabitch. Nobody ever told me that before."

"That hasn't got enough *s*'s in it."

"Okay. Uh—okay. Here we go. Quintessential sensuosity staggers Bitsy, spirituality is stifling her somnambulent sex life— someday she's gonna sense what she's missing. And—wait— don't laugh. And solemnly say she's sorry she spent her sixteenth summer sublimating."

"Thanks," I laughed.

"For my handy instant analysis?"

"No, for your *s*'s. Besides, I was fifteen most of the summer."

"You know, Bits, sometimes you make a strange kind of sense."

I thumbed the belt loops and leather thong. I was going to want to remember what they felt like. "Well, I guess it's time—" An icy, glacial despair hit my stomach, like winter suddenly throwing itself at you in August. "Hey, can I go with you? I don't think—please, can I? Mother's sending me away anyway—"

The flying lock wasn't even moving, he was shaking his head so slowly.

"Listen, Hayes, you're so smart, you've gotta understand—"

"No, Bits, you can't."

I had the belt loops in both fists. "Oh, my God, Hayes, you've gotta—you're the only person that loves me, I've—"

"No. If you think about it for a few minutes, you'll see—"

"I'm tired of thinking, I can't think another thing, I don't even know who it is doing the thinking—"

"What about those guts of yours, Bits? What about—"

"That's where I hurt, Hayes, right in my guts."

I had no way of knowing the look he was giving me was growing me up. "No, for a little while you're on your own. It's not so bad, being on your own, it's not forever."

"I know that, I just—"

"No. Now, I want to leave you laughing. Let's see—Benson and his shotgun?"

I shook my head.

"Saskwatch full of huckleberries?"

Nothing.

"Hey, how about the look on your mother's face when we tell her no bible-toting fat man is gonna marry us under the—"

Some people I know would've laughed outright when Mother produced the diary. I laughed, several hours late.

"Good girl, Bits, that's just fine. And now I'm gonna get in my Chevy and—oh *shit*!"

My mouth was accidentally squished against his throat. "It's okay, Hayes, it's okay." If you had your mouth a certain way you could feel somebody's heart beating, right in his throat.

"Happy birthday, Bits," he whispered.

"Thanks. Now you get in your car—"

"Okay. No good-byes." He backed away.

'Right. Now, just turn around and walk straight to that little one-hubcap Chevy—"

"Remember," he put his hand on my cheek, "just the opposite."

"I'll try."

"See you, Bits." The lock of hair flipped toward me, he turned and took his long legs off the porch.

After the car rounded the ponderosa at the bend of the road, I sat on the half-log step and lit up a Lucky Strike. Right there at my own house. Waving pine branches drowned out the sound of the car going down the hill. The breeze felt like fall. I put my bare feet in the bed of johnny jump-ups that my father and I had transplanted from the creek when I was four years old. I was too exhausted, too defeated, too empty to go to bed.

Two days later Judy and I sat on the log beside the East Fork, drinking the last two cans of Olympia from the cooler. The sun was shining, squirrels ran around. We were there ostensibly to clean up the garbage. Holes from the tent stakes and a stray muddy sock were all that remained. Except the mayonnaise jar that we'd found floating next to the beer, with a note inside.

Ladies:
　　　The sculptor's son is sculpting a pile of damp tent and crap in the trunk, clearly in no condition to apply his hand to paper at five A.M. *It falls to me to give the valedictory address.*
　　　Womenfolk, it's been more than invigorating touring your countryside, fishing your fish, scaling your peak, eating your strawberries.
　　　Bitsy, I hear you're off to church. Take it easy. Do me a favor and read Pygmalion *by George Bernard Shaw.*
　　　Judy my fisherwoman, maybe we'll run into each other one day. Against that fortuitous time, take care of those extra jeans. And drop me a line now and then.
　　　　　　　　　　　　　　　　　　about to take off,
　　　　　　　　　　　　　　　　　　　　Fred
P.S. We had a feeling you'd drop by for a beer. Here's two. Can't get uncorked on that, but we need some to start the trip off right.

"Do you think she'd have done it if you hadn't taken your bathing suit off?" Judy folded the note and put it in her pocket.

"I don't know. I don't know anything."

"Are you gonna write to me?"

"Of course I'm gonna write to you. This is all very weird. You think we can still be best friends? That's childish as hell, I guess—"

"Sure, for a while. You know, you meet other people, things happen. Nobody expects—it's like the river, it just goes on, you don't have to push it, we'll lose track of each other. Probably."

"Hey, Judy, you might just possibly say something a little more optimistic than that when I've just been royally bounced out of my family bosom—''

''You're right. I could. My family bosom wasn't too delirious with joy either.''

''But I bet they eventually laughed, didn't they?''

''Bitsy, I hate to hurt your feelings, but they did.''

''I told you so.''

''Hey, let's take the cooler. I'll use it for something.''

We dislodged it, carried it up the bank to the jeep. She kicked the muddy sock out of the way. Neither of us looked back as she started the jeep. She had to iron her cheerleading costume, I had a diary to burn and a suitcase to pack.

five

When Mother cut the queasy gash in the apron strings that August, I did the same thing to my hair—and found out I needed glasses.

I tried getting a good-bye at the ranch on the sunny September morning when we piled me into the car with my suitcase and violin and drove past the ponderosa and stacks of pear lugs ready for early harvest. But it was hard to come up with one.

All I knew was that there was a kind of Thursday evening we'd never have again. Mother would be making applesauce, pork chops would be simmering with the tiniest clink of the lid steaming up. The month would be October; it would be already dark. I'd be finishing up some homework, and the fire my brother built would crackle over the andirons in the stone fireplace. Brahms's First Symphony or something would be on the record player, and my brother would be just home from football practice. We'd be almost ready for dinner and, in the time before setting the table, I could see how Li'l Abner and B.O. Plenty had fared that day, the *Oregonian* crumpled on my crossed legs in front of the fire.

A son in college, a former daughter in boarding school, what was Mother going to do with herself?

Maybe it was like the D.A.R. scholarship somebody always got; you weren't supposed to understand it, you were just supposed to say thank you very much.

And I knew we wouldn't make cider together again. We'd done it until I was twelve. By the back-porch light the press would grind away; my job was to throw bruised apples into the chute, and my brother's to turn the crank while they sputtered and fought to get out of the chopper. Then we screwed the press down on the pulp with a broomstick, our hands wet and cold in the October chill, juice squirting out at us and never hitting the same place twice. We strained the cider through cheesecloth, funneled it into jugs and left it on the back porch for the night. My brother always set one jug aside to get hard; we would sneak down to the dirt cellar and drink it in about January, pretending we were getting drunk while Mother was at choir practice. I knew it was the last conspiracy we'd ever have.

Neither of those seemed like a good-bye, but they'd have to do. Those and the fact that cinnamon always smelled like October.

Mother and I drove most of the way to Portland without talking. She did tell me to look up at the beautiful gorge made by God's own great hands, and if I hadn't been such a rotten kid I'd have said something nice in return. Like purple mountain majesty. I kept thinking of microscopic bits of Jimmy Lee's blood in the river, how you'd never be able to tell, even if you took a water sample. And whether our car was going as fast as the river.

Portland postcards have a nice view of Mount Hood. St. Margaret's didn't. It had a view of houses and a parking lot. We unloaded me at the dorm. Mother reminded me to call the violin teacher that Mr. Seligmann was turning me over to, gave me a melancholy kiss and money to buy a watch, had a brief, whispered talk with the housemother, and went home.

I wouldn't be playing za Mozart in za recital zis vinter. Or skiing. Not to mention the cinnamon smell or the cider press. I decided it was kind of like puberty. It hit you by red, calendared surprise, but in the long run you adjusted gears and went with it.

The thoughts weren't lofty, but I armed myself with them anyway and mounted the stairs to a room that had my name on it. My real name.

In the middle of the room stood a girl with long straight red hair and sweat socks. Except for those she was naked. She was an authentic redhead. I felt like Mickey Spillane.

Two people were going to spend an indefinite amount of time breathing on each other in twin beds. They were careful about first impressions.

A smile grew out of her face like the kind of perennial plant that grows predictably in the same place every year. I wondered why she plucked her eyebrows. And she had something I didn't know existed. Straight pubic hair. Straight. I was sure there were people who just went to boarding school without being kicked out of their families, I just wondered how you told them from the others. I also didn't know how much of flunking Family was stigma and how much was rotten luck.

She looked my violin case and me over and stuck a thumbnail in her mouth. I had a feeling she was wondering who would get the bed by the window.

"Beatrice. You've got the shortest hair I've ever seen. Who cut it?"

"I did. I'd like you to call me Bitsy, if you don't think it's too dumb. Did you go here last year?"

"How long was your hair before?"

It hung down onto my diary in bed, was long enough to blow across Hayes's face while he maneuvered the Chevy up and down the mountain roads, long enough so that it obscured part of Fred's guitar when he sang beside the Columbia, long enough to get in Hayes's way while he was bringing Jimmy Lee back to life. "I don't know. Long enough. Not quite two feet. What's your name?"

"You really have a nickname like Bitsy? It sounds like somebody who goes pouring martinis down people's cravats. My name's Beth. Red-haired Beth. My daddy's a doctor, in case you get sick or pregnant. I have six charge-a-plates, and I play the piano. Not well. No, I didn't go here last year. Are you a virgin?"

"Sure." I put the violin down and took the bed without a window.

"Are you just barely a virgin, or all the way?"

I thought you either were a virgin or you weren't. "I'm all the way a virgin, Beth. Why are you here?"

"Oh, my mother and daddy want me to take Latin and get poise. And study piano with this fabulous teacher. I've had my first lesson. I have to learn every minor scale there is by next week." She piled about nine sweaters in a drawer. "I'm a virgin too."

"Are they gonna make us pray all the time?"

"I don't know. Nobody makes you pray, you do it if you want to. I was just going to take a shower. Do I look like Lady Godiva?"

"A little."

"Oh, yeah, there's a letter here for you. Who's *H* that sends letters in pencil?" She picked up an envelope and threw it to me. It landed against my belly.

"Beth, it's a long and mysterious story." She shook her long red hair.

"Is it the kind of mysterious story you tell over a martini?"

"I don't know what a martini is." I tore the envelope across the front by accident, right between my name and the address. I heard the door closing, then bottles, spoons, and glasses rattling.

Dear Bitsy,

I love you^{8000}. There now. I feel better. They teach you about exponents yet?

Three new hubcaps joined us in Chicago.

This place is drear and depraved. How green were your valley?

I've noticed in the amorphous process of unpacking that you must still have the Nine Stories. *Keep them. No fine for overdue books.*

Want to go to Victoria Falls? I do.

Freak is getting his pictures developed. And I'm going to develop a fast summa cum laude. *Take Latin.*

Do you see, little one, how absurd it would have been to try to come with us? It's also illegal, by the way. State troopers have a nasty, idiosyncratic habit of yanking young girls out of lusty young men's Chevy's and sending them packing home-ward. Not that it wasn't a compelling idea to tuck you between Freak and me. You could have been in charge of changing radio stations. You also would have parted company with your precious virginity by the time we reached Colorado.

Remember, think just the opposite. I love you several million times.

Dysphemistic expressions of ardor,
H

"Beth, this is a martini? Are you serious?"

"Sure. My daddy taught me how to mix it. You like it? Who's *H* that made you run to my dictionary?"

"Somebody who knows words that aren't even in it."

By the time Beth had heard the high points of the mysterious *H*, we were both mildly uncorked. When I found my schedule card, Latin was already on it. And chemistry.

Beth didn't think it was so terrible to get kicked out of a family. She said we should both go to Stanford. I never heard of anybody teaching their daughter how to mix martinis. She said she was Episcopalian, and she explained what a charge-a-plate was.

I took one look at the chaplain a day or so later and decided he was an unctuous buffoon. He had a receding hairline, wide brown eyes, and a mouth that kept opening, about to say something, and closing again, swallowing it. We had chapel twice a day. The only part I paid attention to was the music. Father Payre had the feeling we should sing all the responses, and got us into two parts. He did the third. I thought it was lovely, but it didn't make me listen to the rest of it.

He wore long robes for chapel and throttled himself from place to place like a jet-propelled French horn. I decided his church history class was a pile of muck, and wrote large *H*'s up and down the margin of the textbook.

The Latin teacher looked as though she'd wet-nursed Caesar. That was the way Beth put it. Every night we leaned out the window, lying on Beth's bed, conjugating Latin verbs and smoking an illicit cigarette. Then Beth rolled the butt Army-style (her term) and tossed it two stories down to the ground.

I don't even remember the World Series that year. At home, the teachers would bring their radios to school and keep them low during class, with one kid selected to sit near the radio and tell the class when something happened. We'd all cheer some team we'd never seen play, yell for someone we'd never seen hit a ball. It was crazy, in a way, but kind of nice, too. No one at St. Maggie's seemed interested, and I sort of forgot about it. Along about November I got around to asking who won.

Of course I missed the kids at home. The guys with the letter sweaters, always coming up and throwing a football arm around you in the hall, hanging on your locker door figuring out ways to get out of biology. You did it by convincing the principal that you were the only one responsible enough to carry a meaningless set of three-by-five cards from his office to the cafeteria manager, get the manager's signature and take it back to the principal. That could take a good twenty minutes, and by the time you got to biology they'd be past chordata forever and you'd never have to learn it. I supposed that was how I'd escaped recessive genes. I didn't regret that one; having Hayes explain it on the raft was far better than watching the coach who doubled as biology teacher telling us about heredity while he had his mind fatuously on his own good looks.

I missed the pious tattlers, too. They had been nice to hang around with, even if they had their lower lips sucked in pretty permanently, ready to gasp at the horror of whatever you'd done lately. The tattlers were part of the quite peaceful landscape with the mountain looming over the football field. I missed it all.

There was that almighty difference, though. Between Hayes and the kids at home. I couldn't have explained it, but it amounted to strangely specific things. I could see him striding in and saying to our kids, "Look, little ones, about this indecorous matter of farting in the dining room . . . " And the little ones, up to their ears in *Mad* comics, would laugh and throw their arms around their daddy because he was such a terrific guy. I had to agree with them.

And there was that odd and unclear relationship between Hayes and St. Maggie's. If I was going to be so finely educated, St. Maggie's had some very important part in it, I guessed.

Dormitory life was exotic, in sketchy sorts of ways. I'd never known a roll of toilet paper could go so fast. Sometime about mid-autumn I stood in the shower watching my tan peel off, watching the tadpole-shaped drops of water converge in a big puddle in the middle of the tub. Like the animated sperm they used to show us in the movies about what hysterical fun it was going to be to menstruate. I had the feeling I'd made a jump of some sort. From going to seed with Debbie Reynolds to Latin verbs via Hayes in a few short weeks. I'd traded in my family and a full-fledged daily view of the mountain over the shoulders of the letter sweaters for Hayes and a gritty eyeful of the parking lot that edged weedily into St. Maggie's.

It felt very strange to wear glasses and a watch. I got used to the rim around my vision within a few days and stopped checking for the dark line on the side of the picture. And the presence of a ticking chain around my wrist jarred things for only about a week. It was helpful, in the long run. It was no damn good trying to tell time by the sun when I always had four walls around me.

St. Margaret's had certain automatic traditions. For one, the night before any test at all there was a lot of pajama'd wailing. "I'm gonna flunk, I'm gonna flunk, I don't know anything!" It seemed a dumb thing to do but I did it a couple of times anyway. Then, the morning after I'd aced my second geometry test, a girl once and a half my size grabbed me by the front of my uniform outside chapel, knocking my glasses sideways and flattening my shoulderblades against the framed class of 1924.

"Bitsy, you asshole," she whispered hoarsely an inch from my forehead, "if you're gonna flunk a test, you flunk a test. If you're not, you pass it and shut the hell up! No in-between, understand?" She smelled like bacon.

I whispered back, "God, yes, Sandra. I understand. Let go, will you? That's my neck under there!" We got away from the wall, crowded into the line and walked down the stairs like partners, partners who weren't speaking.

I couldn't argue with her views on hypocrisy; in fact, I was with her all the way. Especially if she was going to throw me against a wall. But Beth thought it was a good idea to stretch Saranwrap over the toilet bowl, because big Sandra always got up in the middle of the night to go to the bathroom. So we did. About midnight Sandra screamed and woke everybody up.

Another tradition was hating the uniform. I'd never in my life worn a maroon gabardine jumper with open sides over a white blouse with a round collar; not even once, let alone five days a week. I'd never had a blazer at all, certainly not a maroon wool one with a gold cross marked H, flanked with S and M, on the pocket over my heart. If left to my own opinions, I'd have liked it. But after a couple of months I saw the point and began spilling macaroni and cheese down the front of it along with the rest of the Christian soldiers who'd taken up residence at St. Maggie's for one reason or another.

The English teacher was one of the strangest people I'd ever seen. Enormously tall. Rhinestone glasses, a long cigarette holder, shoes with straps. She came into a room like a fleet of Marines.

She'd been a WAVE. In her brown leather briefcase she carried things like torn-out pages of *The New Yorker*, whatever that was, ballet programs, college catalogues, packs of Pall Malls, about eleven ballpoint pens, and a copy of *Pygmalion*. By George Bernard Shaw. I know, because the whole briefcase spilled in front of my desk one day before class. I picked up *Pygmalion*.

"Bitseh, would you like to read that stunning little play? I've considered exposing the entire class to it. One wonders if it wouldn't be good for your fledgling minds . . . this little affair . . . "

I thought it was a great idea, this little affair notwithstanding. This little affair found its way into almost everything she said, and you never knew what she meant by it. I would read it and see about Freak's delusion.

"Sure, Miss Montgomery. Somebody told me to read it anyway."

"Who would that be, Bitseh?"

"Oh, a college boy I know."

She tossed a Stanford University catalogue back and forth between her huge hands and said, "I had an idea you'd been keeping literate company. Take my copy then. I'll just put my name in it, you return it when you're finished." She pressed hard on my desk while she wrote.

She was funny about names. She called me Bitseh, she signed her own name M3. For Marion Monroe Montgomery. I wondered if I should shorten my name even more. Having shortened my homelife, my hair and my eyesight, it seemed appropriate. But I couldn't think of anything shorter than Bitsy.

She was funny in the way she talked, too. Her voice sort of crept out of the side of her throat. And that thing about my keeping literate company. As if I shouldn't be keeping that kind of company. But people had all kinds of quirks. Hayes had his, Mother had hers, M3 had hers. I threw 'Corinthian' at her one day and she caught it. I quite openly liked her. I stashed *Pygmalion* away for a rainy afternoon and got to work on more pressing matters.

For one thing, we were finding out all about Sam Coleridge. It was kind of like being ambidextrous, thinking just the opposite while I read him, but I did my best. Another thing I caught from M3 came in very handy. When you wrote exams or papers you called yourself 'one.' It looked like a hell of a good idea.

ENGLISH EXAMINATION: THE ROMANTICS

Discuss Samuel Taylor Coleridge as a Romantic poet, with special attention to the merger of wonder and irony in *The Rime of the Ancient Mariner*. Use only one side of the page.

When one considers Sam Coleridge's marked fervor for the improbable, his merger of wonder and irony is less enigmatic than it seems at first. It is quite like hearing a mountain laughing its head off in the sunshine. One suspends one's disbelief. But where others are aposiopetic, Sam speaks. Thus in the salvation-ridden but enchanting "Rime of the Ancient Mariner" one is swept along by . . .

> Bitsy: You express vivid feeling for 'the willing suspension of disbelief,' an arresting approach to the Romantics in general. However, two marks against you this time: 'Salvation-ridden' is a very strong and cavalier phrase, and in future do not refer to the poet Coleridge as 'Sam.'
>
> A-minus

St. Maggie's taught me what an antiphonal choir was. Rather, what antiphonal choirs were. It had to be a two-part thing. You could sing a lot about the redemption of sins and stuff on one side, and the other choir would answer you. They didn't really answer—that is, they didn't explain anything about sin or redemption, but they sang back at you. I thought it was a really nice thing, and decided that the perfectly quintessential antiphonal choir would be set up on two mountaintops. They'd sing back and forth across the valley to each other, maybe the last part of Beethoven's Ninth Symphony, like what I heard at Crater Rock. And everybody down in the valley—all the loggers and service station guys, all the people in the letter sweaters, all the teachers and housemothers and everybody would stand there in the valley and say, "Holy shit, that's terrific!"

Beth said she sort of understood what I meant, but concluded that I was drunk. She was right. We were out the window, doing *induco, inducere, induxi, inductus*, having sneaked orange juice from breakfast and drunk it with gin before Latin verbs.

I learned a whole lot of new words that year. "Toady" and "booby" were two. A toady was a girl's crotch, a booby was a breast. I didn't see why you had to have nicknames for them, but so long as I was a uniformed St. Maggie, I might as well use the regionalisms.

Even our housemother used them now and then. She had terrific, graceful, curly gray hair and the best posture I'd ever seen. And a nice contralto laugh. The laugh was what got to Beth and me, when she called us into her sitting room one afternoon. I'd just got back from a violin lesson with my new teacher, who lived with about seventeen begonias and was blissfully unaware that I had anything to do besides practice her unusual approach to bowing, an ungainly wrist flip that Mr. Seligmann must not have known about and that I never came to terms with.

I started up the stairs; Mrs. Martin called to me. I headed for the powder-blue sitting room. Beth was already there, flipping through *Time* magazine.

Mrs. Martin closed the door softly. She did everything softly. "Now, you two sweet little sneaks, the time's come to make ourselves clear. I'm talking—" she began to laugh—"—about the smoking . . . " She sang the words like "schooldays."

Beth and I looked at each other and registered the mutual idea that things could be worse and that Beth would speak for us both, since she had a better track record with grown-ups than I did.

"Mrs. Martin, you're the most understanding person I can imagine, to just say it like that, and not tell us how bad we are—"

"Bad, Beth? No, you must never say that about yourselves, you girls are about to have a lesson in semantics." She sat in a cushy blue chair. "The word is not 'bad.' The word is 'naughty.' You are two naughty girls. Do you see the distinction?"

I saw it. Immediately. Gratefully.

"And I must ask you to understand my position."

"We do," Beth said, nodding her red hair. "You don't even have to tell us. Does she, Bitsy?"

"No, you don't, Mrs. Martin. We—"

"Bitsy, I know you've come to us under rather uncomfortable circumstances—you may think of St. Margaret's as a punishment—try to understand, dear, I'm trying to make it easier for you, not more difficult.''

"I see what you mean, Mrs. Martin, believe me, I do."

"And now, girls, get your little toadies up the stairs and get rid of the cigarettes. Please.'' She smiled at us.

We did. All except one pack. I still wondered if I was bad.

Mrs. Martin was great. M3 was fascinating. Father Payre was pathetic.

"Now, class, you must understand," he rolled his big eyes around, "St. Paul was no mere toady—"

The church history class collapsed. He opened his mouth and closed it again.

"Oops!" he apologized. "Did I pull a booby?"

That is exactly what he said. Pathetic Father Payre with his flowing robes and vast innocence. Watching twenty girls trying to keep from falling out of their chairs.

> *Dear Bitsy,*
>
> *I'm rereading Marx and old Dr. Freud, and swimming a lot. Won the freestyle in the last meet. Shall I teach you a flip-turn next summer?*
>
> *People get horny, an inner voice cries out, "Go west, young man!"*
>
> *The aforementioned people being horny, they deem it wise to state their positions. And so I do. Sex as a gloriously invigorating sport, pastime and persuasion has fallen into squalid disrepute. The so-called moralists with their warped, ascetic minds and distorted consciences have thrust their quaint fairy stories at us, neatly bound in a volume called bible, and perverted the species accordingly. I'm going to become a professional revolutionary in the fight to restore sex as a way of life, a redeeming force in the accidental universe. I shall start by seducing (or raping, if necessary) you.*
>
> *That's before I'm President. What do you think of it as an election platform? I suggest you grow your hair long again so you can hide behind it when you stand next to me during campaign speeches.*
>
> *I have a fanatically overexposed snapshot of you drinking from a flask on top of some mountain or other. Right here in front of me.*
>
> *Arm yourself for my arrival. In late June.*
>
> *Love,*
> *H*

I was keeping literate company, all right. That was about the time Mother began sending me articles torn from *Reader's Digest*, exclusively on the subject of sex. How to avoid it.

I stuffed Hayes's letters into drawers and Mother's articles into the wastebasket. I never was crazy about receiving clippings in the mail, regardless of the motivation of the sender. Beth always found the clippings. One of them warned in italics: *Sex is like liquor—take a little, you'll want a little more!* She deemed it a riot and passed it around the dorm. People whispered it to me when I left on dates, somebody crayoned it on a piece of cardboard and placed it in the center of the rug in the greeting room just before a board of directors' meeting.

I didn't have a period for months after I hit St. Maggie's. I decided it was the thing in the puberty movies, where you could miss periods for a while if you were emotionally upset. I'd been that, all right. It just plain wasn't the easiest thing in the world to watch one part of your life drive off in a Chevy and the other part kick you into boarding school. No great tragedy, not like war or anything, but no big laugh, either.

Beth asked her father for me and he said yes, it was quite possible to miss a few periods in that sort of situation, but I should drop in on a doctor if it went on very long. It was just as well, I wasn't crazy about bleeding all over the place anyway. I didn't actually *mind* the gushing and dripping, but quite honestly the thrill had worn off after about age fourteen.

One day, on the floor of the study hall, M3 found a letter I hadn't finished. She held it between her index finger and the next one, (first and second, for a violinist) pointing it at me. In a very loud voice, she said, "Bitseh, is this unpolished gem yours?"

> *Dear H,*
>
> *First of all, I love your whole six-foot one-half-inch sta-ture. I never said it to anybody before you. I never felt like saying it to anybody else. I never loved anybody so much since I was born. I never got around to asking you this question; what made you think of licking the back of my knee on the raft? I have a feeling it was a very sexy thing to do. Will you do it next summer? I guess there's a lot I don't know. Beth wonders why I'm shrugging my shoulders. I think it's because I wrote "never" 4 times in one paragraph.*
>
> *I've been to chapel 2^6 times since I got here. I'm trying to*

think just the opposite. Latin is okay, and I like the English teacher. She knows a lot about Sam's marked fervor. I still don't think he's a snotnose.

Wearing glasses is all right. My mother is speaking to me a little bit—I mean she's writing letters—but I'm still not sure whether I'm supposed to feel guilty or angry. What do you

It hadn't looked so grotesquely pukey when I wrote it. I tried to climb into my social studies book. We were on John Winthrop. "I don't know, Miss Montgomery. I don't remember if it's mine—"

I thought she'd suddenly save us both by causing it to disappear, or remembering it was someone else's. She didn't. Her rhinestones glowed at me. My eyelids were hot all over the insides.

"Yes, it's mine." My hands felt like lime jell-o.

"I'm sure someone will be delighted to know you appreciate the *attentions*—"

I took it and made my panicked way to the bathroom, tore it in shreds and threw it past the swinging metal lid of the trash can. The bathroom had two smells: phony pine deodorant and human crap, always fighting each other for supremacy. For as long as I was at St. Maggie's, the fight ended in a draw.

And I tried to make my letters the kind M3 could read to the chaplain or the board of directors.

The begonia-ridden violin teacher, while she was hell on wheels about the bowing, threw me into a new and noisy glory. An orchestra. It was a very sexy experience, sitting among all those hot college musicians, learning how to get the conductor in my peripheral vision. Hot stuff indeed. We played things I'd heard on records, oboes and flutes and French horns tweeting and trilling and honking to my left. Once a week for three hours we tried to match bowings and *attacas* and listened to the conductor hum "dayim, dayihm!" with his thumb pressing all four fingers in the air. At intermission the college kids talked about the French Revolution and Nietzsche and getting drunk. The joke that year was:

> I wanna do something big, something clean!
> Then why don't you go scrub an elephant?

St. Maggie's wouldn't let me wear jeans to rehearsals, but they didn't make me wear the barfy uniform, either. That is, after I wore it the first time and came back and told Mrs. Martin that the guy sitting next to me said I looked like a horror show. Mrs. Martin let me go to rehearsals in civilian clothes, but said it would be our little secret. It was.

And then I discovered the Gnostics. By accident. Either because I got tired of H-ing my church history book or because they were in italics, they seduced me.

Now, as heretics go, these Gnostics who menaced the early Christian church with their wild arguments about the unknowable God—actually, there were two Gods, one was a fraud—the dueling of light and darkness, with their secret sacraments and furious inquiry about the nature of existence, these guys were the first troublesome religious philosophers that I heard about. They went around making everybody angry, because they asked such damn basic questions. Like, does God give a damn? And, are you *sure* that's the way to run your life? And, which God do you know, the real one or the phony one? And, who's gonna win, light or darkness? Then, in the middle of the questions, they split. Part of them became ascetic, a very few of them got sexy as hell. Libertine. They were around before Christianity even got started. They knocked me out.

"Bitsy, I believe you've come upon a metaphysical dualism." Father Payre leaned back in his squeaky, unoiled chair. I'd been sitting in his office with him for about half an hour, playing with the wrinkled pleats on my uniform.

"You can say that again! Boy, I'd love to be a Gnostic!"

"Would you? I suppose you could try to be one, within certain restrictive—"

"I think it's their loud indecision about God. Whether He's good or bad, whether He cares or not—I wonder that stuff all the time, Father Payre. Don't you?"

His mouth reminded me of a Mason jar. "No, Bitsy, I don't."

"Well, then, do you think the Gnostics were wrong or right?"

"I don't think it's so much a wrong-or-right issue. We actually owe them a debt. In their inquiry they climbed to great heights of religious thought. Tell me, Bitsy, what kind of Gnostic do you think you'd like to be?"

"You mean the ascetic ones or the sexy ones? I don't know. Maybe both together. Can you do that?"

He laughed. "I think some of us have tried. I have a feeling it doesn't make for an easy existence."

"Is existence supposed to be easy? Is it, Father Payre?"

"No, Bitsy, it's not. Not ever."

"You know another thing I like about them? That part about Jesus not suffering on the cross at all, but making off laughing. Well, anyway, they knock me out."

"Let me know when you find another heresy you like, Bitsy."

"I like this one just fine, Father Payre."

"Go on, Bitsy, you'll be late for dinner."

Father Payre stopped being an unctuous buffoon. I even tried tuning in to his sermons occasionally, but they weren't so hot most of the time. Religion wasn't such hot stuff in general, but I liked the Gnostics.

Episcopalian self-control before God wasn't like Presbyterian self-control. Episcopalians didn't literally sweat, but there was a mild excitement about them. Music in three parts, prayers that got sung, considerable getting up and down from rear end to feet to knees to rear end again. They seemed to attach some importance to exercise. And swinging, smoky incense and long lacy robes with a lot of priestly hiking around in front of the altar. Kind of like a movie.

St. Maggie's let us take our pick of churches in Portland on Sundays. I knew I needed the exercise, and I went with Beth and the other Episcopalians. The mild excitement was sort of a well-dressed one. Hats, perfume and charm bracelets. I knew what the *New Yorker* magazine was by then and the Episcopalians looked something like that.

They had a parade up the center aisle. A cross went by, and you were supposed to bow your head when it got even with your pew. An altar boy in lace carried it. I went out with one of the altar boys, who didn't think it was unctuous to carry a tall cross around. I asked him if it made him feel funny, like Calvary or something. He said no, it didn't make him feel funny at all. I decided that either he was strange or I was strange.

The Episcopalians had real wine for communion, not grape juice. I didn't take communion, because I wasn't one of them. In fact, after leaving the fold of the Presbyterians I never took communion again. My reasoning was quite simple. After Hayes drove off in the Chevy and Mother drove off from St. Maggie's in the Ford, my religion was mostly between God and me. You couldn't take communion with a lot of other people if you didn't feel you were communing with them.

I didn't think it was as simple as Hayes said, although I knew he had my best interests at heart when he told me to think just the opposite. The difference was, Hayes wanted me to skip all the middle steps—the steps of why and how to think the opposite. I just couldn't do it suddenly like that. I decided that if I were smarter, I'd be able to figure it out faster. Beth said I made things too complicated. I told her I didn't make things complicated, they came that way.

> *Dear Bitsy,*
>
> *I'm glad you're taking Latin. I don't know why, it just seems like a good idea. There's this guy in* Magic Mountain *who says about some other guy:*
>
>> *He is an ass, of course; but at*
>> *least he knows some Latin.*
>
> *How is yours? Your ass, that is. I must run and get mine in gear to do its cheerleading part for the Mountaineers.*
>
> *Lots of kids think you went away because you were preggers. You'd better show up at Christmas flat-bellied so they'll know you're not.*
>
>> *Love,*
>> *Judy*

That wasn't the last letter I ever got from her, but she did tend to be silent as all hell.

Beth and I treated the whole school to an *Ave Maria* near Christmas. Beth at the organ, me at the violin, both uncorked because we'd gotten nervous and hauled out her gin bottle a half-hour before the vespers service. Awful, terrible, but everybody said they'd almost cried, it was so sweet.

M3 cornered me on the way out of the chapel after we'd played, smiling her enigmatic smile. "So, Bitseh, our girl who likes swimming in the nude also likes the *Ave Maria*. You may be a Renaissance woman yet." She changed her briefcase to the other hand and walked down the hall on her gigantic feet. I was too drunk to know whether I was angry or not.

Beth and I kissed goodbye and took trains in opposite directions for Christmas.

Mother met me at the station. "Beatrice, how is your violin going?" Same melancholy kiss. We got in the car. How's your loneliness, ma?

"It's all right. Beth and I played an *Ave Maria* last week. Wow, the snow's deep!"

"Yes, Fiddle-Faddle looks so forlorn standing in the corral, up to her knees in drifts." You look a little forlorn yourself, Ma.

"I'm getting some good grades, Mother."

"That's nice. Both Judy and the minister's son have called. Your brother got us such a lovely tree yesterday." Dear God. Well, anyway, there was snow for skiing and I'd see what was up with Judy the non-letter-writer.

"And Mr. Seligmann wants to see you, of course."

"Sure, Mother. Boy, what a teacher he is. This new lady stinks. But the orchestra is—do you know what it's like to have oboes and cellos and French horns right next to you? It's terrific, that's what it is."

She was glad it was terrific.

I don't know why I told her about missing all those menstrual periods. (Beth called them my "wandering minstrel periods" and told me they'd come home, wagging their tails and whatnot.) It turned out to be not such a hot idea.

"You haven't *what*?"

"Watch it, Mother, there's the guardrail—" She straightened out the car, flourishing the steering wheel with a sort of widowed strength. The icy West Fork wound a hundred feet below us.

"Beatrice, you—I don't know what to say—"

"What do you mean, Mother?" I should have known.

"That college boy, you had inter—"

"Oh, don't be silly, Mother. I'm sixteen, for heaven's sake."

"I *trusted* you, Beatrice."

"You're kidding, Mother. Don't you think I'd *look* different if I'd done anything? Don't you?" Wouldn't I?

"You've lied to me, You've . . ."

"But I'm not. I wouldn't just go and do something like that."

She didn't believe me. I cried. And I made a big decision. Those kids Hayes and I'd have would never have to lie. So that when something important happened we'd just believe each other. If you thought about it, it was brilliantly simple. They could go ahead and read dirty words and smoke cigarettes and skinny-dip and tell us all about it and we'd laugh and say we'd done that stuff, too. We'd show them how to mix martinis if that's what they wanted, and eventually they'd have great big colorful coupons safety-pinned on their T-shirts with pictures of Alfred E. Newman or whatever they wanted on the coupons. The decision didn't look at all over-eager to me. Even when I was sixteen I guess I didn't subscribe to the I-wouldn't-beat-you-so-hard-if-I-didn't-love-you-so-much philosophy of child-rearing.

I only saw Mr. Seligmann for about two minutes the whole vacation. His wife was terribly ill with something or other; I took him a box of fudge (Judy and I used brandy instead of vanilla—her house, not mine) and left. He looked awfully weary from dishing out Vicks and aspirin and things. Judy was taking double chemistry.

My brother liked the Gnostics. He said it looked as if I were letting the Bible Belt out a notch or two.

Judy and I went skiing and she made me go to a school party, just to show everybody I wasn't pregnant. I refused to let the warped minister's son take me home from the party, and rode home instead with Casey Parker when he took Penny home.

"Why'd you go away, Beatrice?" Penny was squeezed between us in their pickup. Cold air came in around our legs.

"Penny, it's hard to describe. Mother thought I needed an education. You know. How's school?"

"It's okay. Hank Benson drove his coupe right into the flag-pole." I looked across her at Casey.

"You know Jimmy Lee come back? Just about the time you left. Come back a little crazy, but he come back." Casey laughed.

"Yes, I knew he came back."

"Come into town, all bandaged up, all over his head, said some guy tried to beat him up—"

"That's not true, Mr. Parker, that's a dirty rotten lie—"

"Whatcha gettin' so excited about, Beatrice?" I never did explain it to Casey. Some people were crazy.

My mother had a need for the poor, especially at Christmas. Halt and lame helped, but poor would do. Every year our Christmas dinner table (arch with cedar branches, alder cones, candles and wooden shepherds) stretched to take in two or three elderly and crumpled people with stringy hands and a tendency to spill cranberry sauce down their linty sweaters. There were still a few shepherds around, and one year we had a real one. I remember he smelled like lanolin.

By the time I had got to St. Maggie's, I was fairly sure Currier and Ives (in the hallway outside my log bedroom) had never really existed, and our austere yuletide gatherings offered a simpleminded proof. The talk centered around rheumatism and whoever had recently died, with long narratives of hospitals and failing hearts creaking back and forth across the six-inch Virgin Mary from Germany with her two-inch baby who always had a piece of hay in his eye.

I had the feeling Mother would dismiss the poor before dessert if they confessed to skinny-dipping or missing their periods or other forms of dirty sneaking, but if the poor had that in mind they managed to keep it to themselves.

I had another problem with Christmas. The year before my father died, he read *The Little Match Girl* to me. I couldn't listen to the end. Like Esmé. I was dissolved. What with Esmé and the wan kid in the snow and the lanolin-smelling poor, I gradually got the idea that Dickens and Bob Cratchit gavotted around on another planet. Most years, it was all I could do to get through Christmas.

Hayes and I would have anything but austere Christmases. We'd celebrate in a riotously pagan way, making love under the Christmas tree, knocking ornaments off and short-circuiting the lights. He'd carve crooked little figures to hang on the tree.

That year, Mother said I was being an adolescent. She meant a pregnant adolescent. And she didn't say she was lonely. But the antiques were dusted within an inch of their lives.

> *Dear Bitsy,*
>
> *So I'm a Renaissance Man? How nice! I've spent a full fifteen minutes wondering why you're the only person who's ever called me that. It fosters a certain ecstasy, bordering on the physiological, to read those paragraphs. I think I'll frame them.*
>
> *Have you noticed your handwriting has changed? Are they bending you out of shape? You've got a few ornamental capitals and effete dots over your i's these days. But never mind that. I*

have the positive conviction that behind your Ionic calligraphy lurks a coal of sensuality, awaiting ignition. Allow me to apply my torch at the earliest opportunity.

Me? Not want you to read Pygmalion? *I want you to read everything. I'm glad you found it cultured and stimulating and in harmony with your aesthetic lusts. You're probably right; we should have discussed it at length. We'll do it in the summer. For now, put your perspicacious head to work trying to see the difference.*

My lusts are not exclusively aesthetic, but you may twist them that way if you choose. They run more to matters like making warm and violent love on tops of mountains. Or on rafts. Or almost any damn place you can name.

Freak is having hard philosophic thoughts about our foul world right now. I'm going to get him drunk and solve it all.

How is your little totemic religion doing in your free-thinker-baiting school? Are you catching the

Hayes sent partial letters. The next section arrived a day or two later. Just to see if I was paying attention.

prelates up on their antedeluvian theories and axiomatic moral-ity? Grabbing them by the sleeves and telling them they're a pack of pious frauds?
Who is M3?

Do you know you're the cleanest girl I've had anything to do with since I was twelve?
Love,
H

We were on our best rhetorical behavior in those letters. Never belched or scratched, never left a sentence unfinished. And we paid unremitting attention.

I finally got my period. I called my mother and told her. She was relieved.

Peter Abelard was the most cogent heretic I ever ran into. *Eros* and *logos*. He lacked the dark, tortured impatience of the Gnostics, but he made staggering sense. Knowledge had to precede faith, and he was relentless about it. He tossed established pronouncements into the air, went to the very edge of credibility, waged an assault on the cornball church leaders that threw them on their ears. And he had that wild love affair with Heloise. She never recovered. In that respect he was a dirty bastard. Every time she wrote him a letter from the nunnery he got snotty and preachy. Still, he had a striking head for argument. He seduced me out of my second round of marginal H's in church history class.

Father Payre was glad I'd "graduated from metaphysical dualism to piercing dialectic." I told him it wasn't altogether impossible to like them both at once. He rolled his eyes and jet-propelled himself off to play the organ.

Beth got her own copy of the *Nine Stories*. When things got too terrible, we got flashlights from Mrs. Martin and read to each other under the covers after lights out. Mrs. Martin never told anybody. Beth said we were like the early Christians underground. We had a purple headmistress named Miss Kenyon; actually, she was heliotrope—her clothes, her office, the upholstery in her car. She wouldn't have liked our reading Salinger under the covers any more than she'd have liked the smoking or the drunken *Ave Maria*. Mrs. Martin was discreet.

I didn't know I had *Catcher in the Rye* memorized. One morning it just started coming out. While I found some clean underwear I started with the beginning of the nuns' section in Grand Central Station, and by the time I got my blazer on and my hair combed (what there was to comb), I'd finished the chapter. Beth was sitting on the bed in her pajamas.

"Bitsy," she said, sun on her red hair, "that's a very strange thing you've just done."

"I guess so."

"Why did you go and memorize it?"

"Beth, I didn't try. Maybe it came to me in my sleep."

"Do you know any more of it?"

"I don't know. Put your clothes on. We'll be late, there won't be any bacon left."

"Can I wear your red Lollipop pants?"

"Sure." I fished them out. Charge-a-plate pants. Colorful underwear made the uniform a little less dyspeptic. And without meaning to, I slipped into the part where Holden hangs Sunny's dress on a hanger.

"You know, for somebody who can't even remember a decent mouthful of French, memorizing something like that is just more than a little weird."

"Get dressed, Beth."

She was right, of course. *Tu ne fixe pas* usually came out "tuna fish pie" and I couldn't master Beth's dry-mouthed, discursive *merde* when we had Spanish rice for dinner. But every now and then Holden's pellucid confessions just popped out. Beth began to depend on my coming over to her in study hall and whispering to her about Ackley kid.

I didn't let Beth talk me into getting my ears pierced, but I went along with her while she had hers done. She couldn't figure out why I thought only scarlet women had pierced ears, whereas she thought it would add to her poise. On the way back, after stopping in a drugstore to get alcohol and cotton and junk to keep her from getting infected, I told her about Hayes and the rusty earring in the back seat. I hadn't meant to tell her about it; I just wanted her to be careful about ear infections.

She thought it was either genuinely malicious or genuinely dumb. "Some guy who loves you that much doesn't even clean out his ashtray, and leaves the remains of his—Bitsy, I don't think that's a Renaissance Man, I think that's a bastard."

"Oh, come on, Beth, I asked for it, really. I asked for that kind of treatment when I—"

"I just never knew anybody like that."

"Well, smart people have their quirks, I guess," I said.

"What makes you think he's so damn smart?"

"You sound like my friend Judy. She said she thought he and Fred were 'educated beyond the level of their intelligence.' Now how in the world can you be that?"

"It's easy."

"No, really. How can you learn something if you're not smart enough to learn it?"

"Bitsy, it's like this: if I learned every bit of Latin there is to know—"

"The thought makes me barf."

"Every bit. I'd be the best Latin scholar around. Then maybe the U.S.A. would suddenly decide to revert to the Roman senate system—and because I knew the most Latin, they'd make me a big lawmaker. See what I'm saying? I could learn all the Latin, but I wouldn't know what to do with it."

"Then I bet there're a lot of people who're educated beyond the level of their intelligence."

"Probably."

"Boy, I don't want to be. You know what that'd make you, Beth? It'd make you dangerous."

"I still think you ought to get your ears pierced, Bitsy."

"Beth, do you know there's *one person* in the world who understands me and he's three God thousand damn miles *away*?"

She grabbed my arm. "Bitsy, you just can't go around saying things like that. Not at the top of your lungs."

"Why the hell not?"

"For one thing, about four people in cars turned around and looked at us. For another thing, it's not nice to do when you're wearing a uniform."

"Beth, if I didn't like you so much, I'd wish you'd get an ear infection."

From time to time I faked cramps or a sore throat to get out of class, and went to the dorm and played my violin. Mrs. Martin was always either out or didn't mind. One morning she asked if she could listen. I was in the second movement of Handel's third sonata in F, the part right after the first repeat. I was supposed to be in chemistry. Even the begonia bowing made more sense than the valence chart.

"Bitsy, you love music, don't you?" She pretended she didn't smell stale cigarette butts in the room.

"Sure, Mrs. Martin, don't you?" She listened to opera on the radio on Saturday mornings.

"Yes, I do. Sometimes when it seems the world's gone slightly mad, music helps. Yes, I do love music."

I loosened my bow. "I don't think the world's really mad, Mrs. Martin, do you?"

"Well, the contradictions we live with, there's disorder in the world. Why did you choose Handel today?"

I suddenly remembered Beth's gin bottle under the bed she was sitting on. I hoped she'd sit still so she wouldn't have to cope with the mad disorder of a gin bottle rolling, and come all unglued.

"My mother gave me the Handel sonatas for my birthday. I like this one . . ."

"What a lovely gift, Bitsy. It must have been a very pleasant birthday. Would you like to play some more for me?"

I did. The birthday hadn't been exactly what I would call pleasant, but it had had a certain color to it, I had to admit.

Dear Bitsy,

Your boy has been immutably drafted. Not to be confused with beer of the same variety. Or maybe so. Freak, too. Except he's not going to go. It seems he's headed for jail. His recalcitrant pacifism, combined with his mellifluously dreamy nature, has brought him to this pass. My syntax isn't all it might be, since we've been up all night debating the age-old ethics-versus-survival issue. Somehow I came out in favor of survival.

I think I'm bound for some fetid boot camp. But first, this very morning, we're going to

    1. the draftboard

    2. a hot lawyer's office

to see what can be done for your friend and mine the old guitar player.

In addition to other visionary remarks, Freak put his fist through a closet door at about three A.M. *and hollered, "They're gonna cut my hair off and my balls, too!" I quote you this ruthlessly Anglo-Saxon declaration because I feel you'll sense the poetry and cadence in it, and more or less understand what he means.*

I have one thought that directly involves your winsome self. (Read between lines, if you please, which means put on your glasses. Do you wear them all the time? Do you know I (1) don't know how you look in glasses, and (2) don't know how you look in a crew cut.) The thought runs more or less like this:

On my way to boot camp, let's have that reunion. Meet me in Chicago. That's about midway. Don't hitchhike. Fly. Spread those spiritual little wings of yours and hie yourself eastward. Tell your mother that travel is an intensely wholesome thing. Tell her I've become a priest. Or an oboe player. Tell her I'm not going to rape you. Tell her you'll stay at the YWCA. Which you probably will. Tell her we're talking about a period of a couple of days, which we are, and that you'll be back in time to exercise that horse with the Leroy Anderson name, and to weed the garden.

I don't have dates yet. Get permission first.

Oh yes. I got the summa cum laude. *As we say in the gambling casino, big deal.*

Freak has just thrown my shoes across the room at me and asked me to please prepare myself to fight the noble fight for peace. And to give further thought to screwing the army myself. I frankly don't think I have the guts.

Now, before I make any more disillusioning confessions,
get hold of your mother and tell her Chicago's a wonderful
town.

Love and confusion,

H

P.S. I'm going to seduce you. With vigor and blurred patriotism.

"Blurred patriotism! You've gotta admit, that says something
for the Army."

I turned around. "Beth, I don't read your letters. Over your
shoulder without asking you first. I haven't looked up 'fetid,' I
haven't had time to decide what I think of this whole thing—you're
a hell of a friend."

"Well, are you gonna go along with the seducing?"

"I don't know. I don't know whether God gives a damn or even
exists. I don't know whether I like M3. I don't know if I'm any
good at the violin; I don't even know whether my mother loves me.
How the hell do you expect me to answer a question like that?"

"You're gonna wait 'til you figure all those out before you get
seduced? Bitsy, You're gonna be ninety years old or something
before all that gets clear."

"Just let me think awhile." I thought I should go to jail with
Freak. My *summa cum laude* marching around carrying a stinking
gun. My laughing thrower of beer cans crawling through rusty
barbed wire. What the hell kind of God would let that stuff go on,
anyway?

Beth said I was crazy, I should get myself to Chicago, get
seduced with vigor and come back and tell her all about it. I told her
that was a horse's ass kind of request to make: I wasn't going to tell
anybody. She said it wasn't quite fair, but she saw what I meant.

I didn't. How did you do that stuff, anyway? That end-of-the-
stars-and-back thing? With your mother and the *Reader's Digest*
and the YWCA and everything? Maybe, like a cocker spaniel,
you'd know what you were doing when the time came. Maybe.
And if I did some very fast, very smart thinking on the plane, just
maybe I'd figure out what love is when you fall into it by the time I
got to Chicago. And if I didn't get it figured out, would I stand there
in the airport biting my lip and say no again? And hope he'd
understand? How much could you expect somebody bound for a
fetid boot camp to understand, anyway?

Mother, however, threw a bit of a hitch into that part of my education. She thought that midway Chicago, while it might be a very fine town indeed, was a rotten idea for me.

"Beatrice, I've missed you. Do you know that?"

I tried not believing her, at the dining room table.

"I'm not saying I forgive you for your dreadful tricks last summer. I'm saying you are my daughter and I love you."

Hayes loved me, too. Moreover, he hadn't shown it by kicking me out and then sending clippings in the mail.

"I will not let you go. I love you, I want you here—"

"And the garden needs weeding, right, Mother?"

"Beatrice, you are ungrateful. If you try to sneak off to Chicago . . ."

"I won't." I couldn't. The mechanics of it. "I'll weed the garden, I'll thin apples. But I love Hayes, and . . ."

"You're very young, I'm being patient with you . . ."

She was.

"Okay. You're being patient. I love you, too. It's just very difficult to see how love keeps you from—okay. But when it comes time for me to go to Stanford you will let me do that?"

"If you get into Stanford, if we have the money by next year. We can't predict those things, the weather, the—"

I went out to weed the garden.

Hayes went to a fetid boot camp, Fred went to jail, along with his guitar. I thinned apples with Judy and packed cherries from a conveyor belt into boxes in a packing house where they kept the temperature at about fifty degrees, in the middle of the summer.

We didn't climb any mountains. We did swim across the Columbia, with a boat and two summer forest rangers going along. No Sibelius in the middle, just huffing and pretending we weren't tired. We skipped the Fourth of July with its 7-Up booth to learn to water-ski. Same boat, same forest rangers. Judy had decided she was going to be a doctor.

Mr. Seligmann's wife was really sick. She looked terrible. We closed the door when I had my lessons. Mr. Seligmann thought my bowing was in rotten shape; I couldn't tell him it was because of the begonia teacher. Not when it was because of Mr. Seligmann that I was playing in the first orchestra of my life. Not when his wife looked so disastrous. But I think he knew anyway.

My brother taught me to drive the car and the tractor. He even offered to take me up Mount Adams, but my heart wasn't in it.

Judy and I visited the Parkers one day, and had a chat with Waltzing Matilda and took Penny water-skiing. Casey allowed as how I was getting a little fancy with my boarding school talk. I kept trying to remember not to sound like a St. Maggie. It was hard.

Dear Bitsy,

Fort Sonofabitch, the A-hole of the world, my new home.

There's an understated racism here that arouses an understated rage. I should have gone with Freak. But here we are. Evil-smelling, antihumanist, very khaki landscape. By the time I get out of here and back north again, half (psychologically speaking) my career in uncle sam's Legion of Goodness will be over.

Our house will have seventeen rooms. Including your practice one. Glass walls, a scattering of pines about its edges, and hand-hewn beams, hewn by mine own hand. You may have a bust of Beethoven here and there if you wish. We shall have small, intimate dinner gatherings with Walt Kelly, Aldous Huxley, and J. D. Salinger, to mention a few. And your small, intimate self can roam lithely about, preferably stark naked, warmed by the light of my strenuous lust, picking flowers from god's (note lower case) colorful garden.

Don't tell your mother, but I don't think much of her views on travel.

I think we should explore the beauties of the Amazon, now that you can water-ski. How are the coyotes in your back yard?

Work hard, keep your head out of spiritual crap, remember you're going to throw that uniform away in a short while.

Love,
H

Mr. Seligmann's wife died. I went to her funeral, the first since my father's. Music, flowers, no chocolate pudding, a very accepting Mr. Seligmann.

"She vas a good vohman, Beatrice. She gafe me two daughters. And she nefer complained when I practiced all night long."

My father died of a heart attack near Christmas because the hired man got drafted and left the harvest to be done by my father alone. Mr. Seligmann's wife died of cancer in the freest country in the world after surviving flight from Germany and the loss of two daughters. Mr. Seligmann now had his violin and his one-eyed cat. I was understanding less and less about life.

I was seventeen years old, wore a crew cut and glasses and a watch, knew some Latin and no Greek and more big words than I'd ever thought I'd know, and Hayes was carrying a gun around for some reason I kept trying to figure out. Something about making the world safe.

six

Hayes, Fred, Judy and I were all in uniform. Hayes marched in khaki, I trudged in and out of chapel in maroon, Judy whooped and jumped reluctantly in cheerleading green and white, and Fred played his guitar wearing a number. It was as if they'd put us all in barrels, miles apart, to see how much of the laughing mountain-climber they could take out of us. I didn't like thinking about it that way, so I put the barrel-picture in the very back of my mind and counted the days until I'd get the hell out of St. Maggie's.

I don't know why I got Tommy before Beth did. Except that I was nearer the curb when the Cadillac pulled up in front of the library and asked us in some polite variation on English whether we were too busy to go for a ride. The variation turned out to be Greek. I found that out about three blocks later, looking up at a profile that had to come out of a museum. Hayes said to get a classical education—there it was.

Tommy had one unmatched virtue. He was simply the hand-somest boy I'd ever seen. I'd like to be able to say there was a great deal more that held us together for several months, but facts are facts. Aside from eyes you could go swimming in, cheekbones you wanted to put on your desk to relieve the tedium of Latin and history, and the kind of mouth every girl dreams of having nuzzle her prom formal, Tommy was like most other boys.

Except that he took me for politely bilingual rides in that car, was very sweet about attending the crumby dances that St. Maggie's staged every few weeks (and leaving my classmates panting damply in crepe-paper corners of the gym in total disbelief that God ever made anybody so good-looking while he nuzzled my very own charge-a-plate formal) and gave me a stuffed dog. I don't remember why.

I took the dog to English. Everybody passed it around, petting it instead of paying attention to Hamlet as a Renaissance Man. M3 stopped in the middle of "One supposes, then, that the dilatory Hamlet—Bitseh, beware of Greeks bearing gifts... this little affair..."

And she told us about the Trojan Horse. As if she didn't want us to know about it first, so she could tell us then and there in her lengthy and patronizing way, Tommy's poor little dog taking the brunt.

Gorgeous Tommy. I never learned how to pronounce his last name. Truthfully, I wasn't particularly interested. Hayes was, of course, my true love but Tommy lived in Portland. You had to go to dances with somebody, or else the social chairman would get you a blind date with her cousin or something; and all the St. Maggie's cousins I ever saw either had boils on their necks, or else they told you how brilliant they were and how sure they were that they were going to be accepted at Yale.

M3 was in charge of getting us applied to colleges. They all said they had expansive liberal arts programs, whatever those were; they all said they had terrific campuses, they all said you went in one door a floundering, cretinous searcher and went out the other door ready to change the world. You had to start reading the brochures' fine print. The more I looked at them, the more I got interested in the hard ones. The ones that wanted you to take four different College Boards. I tried to figure out which ones Hayes would like. What it finally came down to was Stanford and three other fancy places. We wrote the essays (in which I tried to sound like an Eleanor Roosevelt who was actually Heifetz' stepsister) and took the College Boards. The Boards were proctored by soldiery people who walked up and down the rows while I tried to make some sense out of Latin poetry I'd never seen and history I didn't think I remembered.

We gave all our college application stuff to M3 and tried to forget about it for a while. It was a very funny thing, wondering where you'd be unpacking your suitcase in the fall. Beth and I assumed it would be Stanford. The odds were against us—being girls, being from Oregon, and being so hot for it. We assumed it nonetheless.

St. Maggie's was equipped with bad days, like any school. A bad day ran predictably enough. Wake up with a hangover, find no clean underwear but three new pimples insulting your chin, go to a pukey breakfast and an even pukier chapel, with a sermon about diligence versus sloth. A French test you'd forgotten to study for. No letter from Hayes, and that made three months without one; but the letter from your mother told at piteous length about the two Douglas firs she'd had to sell to keep you in that expensive school, how the virgin timber was little by little disappearing under the slashing meanness of your sins. You'd get your period in the middle of gym and drip all over the volleyball court before someone shouted that you were messing up the game. M3 would come up with "E. E. Cummings thinks he can break *every* rule, you know, this little affair..." Somebody'd say something so violently stupid in history that Hayes would be on the floor laughing, only he wasn't. You couldn't do a self-respecting Mozart trill for the twenty-eighth time that week. Spanish rice for dinner. (*Merde.*) By ten-thirty P.M. you'd find yourself out the window with Beth and a gin bottle, working on *adolesco, adolescere, adolevi, adultus.*

I suppose there were scores of those days. I didn't count. I wasn't one for score-keeping.

When enough people were having bad days at once, the St. Maggies had ideas about livening things up. Contraband food from the kitchen, Hate Night, Terrible Letter Night (everyone wrote a letter to someone else's parents telling them the worst things they could think of about their daughter), Award Night. You never knew when they'd happen.

"Bitsy, come in here, I need algebra help." They might start that way.

"I'm no help, I barely passed."

"Come on, don't be an asshole."

I wrapped my bathrobe tighter around me and went down the hall. Everybody was in pajamas all over the floor.

"Hey, you said you—"

"Award Night!" Beth was standing in the middle of the room, holding a square necklace-size box.

"Okay." I started to sit down. Usually the awards were a tube of Clearasil or a jar of deodorant. I wondered if the army was any more diverting.

"No, Bitsy, you get the award tonight. It's the first annual B. C. Award, and you're the recipient."

I was game. They had weird senses of humor. I stood up.

"This award is presented for diligence in the search for Basic Cuteness. Naturally, Tommy is the most Basically Cute of them all . . . we want you to have this token—" She shoved the box at me while laughs went around the room like spilling bobby pins.

I couldn't figure it out. A brownish-gold miniature frisbee kind of thing, the texture of a rubber glove, with a sort of hard rim and a printed number on the edge. I took it out of the box. The whole room laughed.

"What the hell—I don't get it."

"Yes, you do, it's yours."

I held it up to the light. The pajamas wouldn't stop laughing. "Thank you," I said limply. And went back to our room. Beth showed up eventually and explained. She was there within five minutes.

"Close the door, will you?" I asked from my desk. I was trying to finish a cultured and stimulating letter to Hayes all about the Trojan Horse and *Hamlet* and going to Stanford.

"Sure. You like your trophy?"

"Beth, I think I'm supposed to know what this is, but I don't. Please don't tell anybody—"

"Wow. You don't know. Okay," she laughed and sat down on her bed. "Here's your sex education. It's called a diaphragm, and it's for birth control."

"What do you do with it?"

"You stick it up inside you."

"Beth, it's *huge!*"

"Oh, it folds or something, I don't know, I got it out of Daddy's office. It's so you don't get pregnant."

I picked it up off the head of Tommy's stuffed dog. She was right. You could fold it. I put it back. "I understand that part, but why—it's such a yukky—why doesn't the man do something instead?"

"Well, some of them do, but I think they don't want to very much. You know, rubbers and stuff, but my brother says it's like taking a shower in a raincoat, I don't think guys like them."

"Well, what the hell do they think it is for the girl to shove a folding frisbee up her? Fun? Can't the girl just say she doesn't want to, and then he has to do the birth control?"

"I don't know, Bitsy, they're . . . well, if you're underneath, it's just hard to insist on things like that."

"Beth, is the girl always underneath?"

"I don't know. But this is what I think. If she's always on the bottom, wouldn't every married woman be flat-chested? I guess you could avoid it by marrying some skinny little guy—"

"I bet there are a lot of different ways to do it."

"Probably. You gonna let Tommy show you?"

"I just bet there are."

Beth asked her father about different ways. He said yes, there was an exhaustive variety of positions, but you had to be limber to take full advantage of them. Beth and I would do an exhaustive variety of limbering exercises in the fifteen minutes before we leaned out the window to conjugate and smoke. Usually with Dave Brubeck on the record player. Hayes wrote me to go out and get the Disney album, and I'd done it the same afternoon. We agreed with Hayes that the Alice in Wonderland was consummately sexy. We were all for being limber and consummately sexy, and taking full advantage.

I had a feeling Hayes was going to be a fair-play, exhaustive-variety person. He'd say, "Okay, Bits, if you in your whimsical interpretation of women's suffrage have mulled it over in your conscience and think you've got an inalienable little right to the top once in awhile (or the side, or the chandelier, or the faucet end of the bathtub full of iridescent bubbles), it's fine with me." And I'd swing around the edge of the chandelier, one eye on the scattering of pines outside the glass wall and say, "Guess what, smarty! I don't have to look up *any* of those words!"

Then somebody decided to teach me a little more about the euphoric lad named Yorick. Oddly enough, credit for that cursory anatomy lesson went not to Greek Tommy but, unofficially and with a minimum of fanfare, to a Reed sophomore (first oboe), who thrust my hand quite coolly onto the front of his squeaky corduroys one night at a drive-in, while I was intent on the next twirk of Marlon Brando's mouth. I thanked him ungraciously enough for the cool thrusting by calling him a definitive horse's ass and hitchhiking back to St. Maggie's to look in the dictionary, more carefully this time. I had one regret about the evening, and that was not seeing the end of the movie. When I jumped out of the car, Marlon Brando was swooping into the night on his motorcycle with his mouth doing the most outrageously sensuous things. That regret remained, even after the first oboe called me a Goddamn professional virgin.

Apparently a first oboe couldn't understand that someone who hadn't straightened out matters with the Gnostics, Peter Abelard, Latin verbs, her mother, martinis, charge-a-plates, folding frisbees, cocker spaniels, blurred patriotism, fetid boot camps, Stanford University, and M3 just wasn't ready for cool thrusting.

I tried to write Hayes and say, "Hey, you guys *don't* carry Clark Bars around in your pockets! But Corinthian? You're kidding!" But you couldn't just send that in the mail to somebody in a uniform. Especially not if M3 was hanging around to peek at letters.

I had a strange dream after the oboe player. In the dream, Marlon Brando rode his motorcycle right into my bedroom at home, in black and white, and Heifetz and Mozart didn't like the noise one bit. He parked the motorcycle beside my bed and postured around my room in the sexiest way possible, all swinging shoulders and insinuating mouth. "What are you doing here, Marlon?" I asked, with maybe an eighth of an idea of what he was doing there. Then he started changing into Hayes. He said, "Seducing (or raping, if necessary) you." I got scared to death, partly because of the raping suggestion and partly because I wanted to know who was doing it, if anybody was. He was Marlon one second, and Hayes the next; he kept changing back and forth. It was very confusing. I woke up before I found out what happened. I was still a virgin.

I told Beth that Marlon Brando talked in parentheses. She said nobody talked in parentheses; but I was sure Marlon did, and made a point of remembering to ask him about it if we ever met. I supposed that if you had a mouth like that you might get special privileges.

Our sex curiosity continued. Some of it focused on M3. Beth thought she was doing it with Father Payre. Some of the girls thought she was a lesbian with the social studies teacher. I had the feeling that if she was doing it with anybody she wouldn't walk around thudding like that. Still, I wasn't doing it with anybody, and I didn't thud. Maybe it was more a question of the kind of shoes you wore. Hers were more than necessarily strappy.

I didn't care much what her sex life was. I was having other problems with her.

We were reading Thoreau. I thought he was beguiling if a little overeager. Some of the girls didn't like him at all.

"Now, girls," M3 began one morning, "he was what one calls a nature nut, a . . . this little affair . . ." It drove her batty when we didn't laugh at her dumb efforts to be contemporary. "He had a fondness for inconvenient spots like swamps and such, things we find distasteful . . ." Her rhinestones fastened on me. "Bitseh, your home is in one of our most bucolic areas. Do you think you could share with us some understanding of Thoreau's feeling for life *au naturel*, life in the out-of-doors?" When she tried to twinkle she was grotesque.

I'd like to have told her how you could have mopped up the floor with me when I read "My love must be as free/As is the eagle's wing." Instead, I said, "Well, Miss Montgomery, I think it's kind of different, it depends on whether you go there for a change of scene, to get away from crowds, like Thoreau, or whether you're diogenous to it from the beginning. You might *feel* the same, but—"

"Bitseh, I believe you have a malapropism there." She'd caught me in several before, and I'd always thanked her for straightening me out. "I must correct you. I think you mean 'indigenous.' Diogenes was the famous *Greek*, Bitseh, who went searching with his lantern for an honest man. I don't think that word quite fits our discussion. Now girls," her mouth got more snaky than usual, "for those of you who aren't aware, Mrs. Malaprop is a figure in literature who, like our Bitseh here, gets tangled among large numbers of syllables and suffixes, rather like a hare in a snare . . .''

Goddamn, how she could go on! Nobody laughed. She kept smiling a sinister lopsided mouthful of menacing nicotine stains.

" . . . what our Bitseh has, however, is a sense of humor, we'll let her off easily today . . ." She chuckled like bones rattling.

I wanted to throw my book down her throat, but she would have said, "Ah, Thoreauing your Thoreau, eh, Bitseh?"

She forgot all about Thoreau in her fox-and-hare game. " . . . and, Sandra, I believe you're paying more attention to those letters in your lap from a certain *fraternity* than you are to our . . ." Poor old Sandra, a hundred and forty-eight pounds with pores the size of gopher holes. Those letters were, I think, the closest she ever got to ecstasy.

Of course Hayes laughed at me. Of course. But he didn't hunt people down and try to humiliate them. I waited for M3 after class. I didn't mind being late for history, I'd be late for my own wedding if I had to, she was the biggest horse's ass I'd ever seen.

I stood by her desk staring at the SMH on my blazer pocket until everyone had gone. She crossed her strappy ankles and turned sideways to face me, rhinestones trying like mad to look like stars. I didn't quite like what I was going to do, but Hayes had said to lead with my guts. Okay, Hayes, here we go.

"Yes, Bitseh? Is it something about our bucolic Mr. Thoreau?"

I held my books in front of me, thanking God for good strong arms. "Miss Montgomery, I think you're a disgusting human being. I don't care if you personally get me kicked out of here. I think you hurt everybody you can get your hands on. You're one person at this unctuous place I was gonna like. Even the humiliating way you treat every one of us. Even your absolutely stinking fetid comment about the Renaissance woman. And about the unpolished gem. I was gonna go right ahead and like you. But you know what? Maybe I did mean Diogenes or whoever he was, looking for an honest man out there in the wilderness. Maybe I did. I bet you don't even *like* Thoreau. I don't know what gives you the right to be so patronizing, unless it's your—"

She squinted her eyes very hard and stuck her nicotine-y teeth out over her lower lip. If I said maybe she'd better switch from the chaplain to the social studies teacher, or vice versa, I'd be kicked out by dinnertime with no place to go. I came out in favor of survival.

"Unless it's my what, Bitseh?" Like the guillotine blade rising on the pulley rope.

"Never mind. I thought I'd like you. I hope God's gonna forgive me, but I don't."

She breathed in and out with that heavy chest for a while. Then she picked up her fountain pen and turned it around in her hand. "Bitseh, I'm not going to say anything about your zealous impropriety to . . ."

"I don't care if you do or not." I must have had a temperature of a hundred and six by the time I got out the door.

Dear Bitsy,

Someday, when the insanity is over, you and I must come back here and do this place up right. We shall drink gallons of glorious beer, slog around the countryside, and stare at cathedral windows until we're walleyed. Only one consolation in your Mr. Seligmann's being driven out of this beautiful land: he gave you something to do with those nice arms until I came along.

It's great comfort to this boy in absurd government costume to know you're doing no more ass-kissing than is absolutely necessary. It's greater comfort yet to anticipate your getting excommunicated from that place. You have a more than cordial invitation to move in here. I weary of these hairy-chested types very quickly.

You may go right ahead and like Thoreau. Please do. We'll do lots of it. Tell M3 she can forget about being a bridesmaid.

Freak writes that when he's sprung from jail he's going to buy some land in Minnesota and be a recluse. Minnesota, for christ's sake! Not that it's not beautiful there, but I think he's going to hang his guitar and his life on a nail and desert us all. We may still get him to the wedding, though. He'll be the only saint there.

We shall have three children, all named Rance, regardless of gender but distinguished from each other by Roman numerals.

Yes, your French is, as you so aptly put it, lousy. I shall interpret for you.

How are Seligmann and your mother making out?

Love,
H

Making out was fairly close. The uncanny Hayes had hit it. Mr. Seligmann and my mother were actually getting together. I had a hard time believing she was the same person who'd thundered me out of the bosom. Every time I went home she was full of new lore, about what Chopin did when he was twelve, who Charles Ives really was, what Isaac Stern said when he broke a G-string in the middle of the Beethoven. She was beginning to laugh, and I finally began to figure out some reasons why my father had married her.

I told Mother about M3. What got her was something I hadn't thought of.

"Beatrice, I think she's a little afraid of you."

"Afraid of me? What on earth for?"

"Well, because she doesn't have a man to love her."

"A *what*? What in the world are you talking about?"

"Beatrice, don't raise your voice. She sees certain things in you that she once had, only she's overdone them. Like being pretty and smart—"

"Come on, Mother, I'm not—"

"Those are things that men respond to. But not if they're overdone. She was probably once quite pretty, and maybe feminine, too. But she has become so very aggressive, and I think she regrets it. Men don't marry women like that. You know, marriage and children are our noblest office, and aggressiveness gets in the way. It obtrudes; men want us to be submissive. I think she wishes she had another chance. Men are simply afraid of women who are too smart."

"Why in the world should they be that? Afraid?"

"I don't know, Beatrice, but they are. They just don't want us to go to extremes."

There was something there that made my teeth itch, but Mother was sitting on the piano bench holding my hand, as if she'd never tossed me out, and I wasn't going to blow it by going to the extreme of arguing.

I didn't know how to argue it anyway. Aggressive, submissive, smart but not too smart, feminine, our noblest office—I didn't have any of that in mind when I sounded off at M3. I just wanted her to stop being a cruel fascist.

The person to ask, of course, was Hayes. But I couldn't put it all in a letter. Besides, he wasn't exactly the kind of neuter answerer I needed. As he kept reminding me.

M3 was busy pretending it'd never happened. And we still didn't know whether she was doing it, or with whom.

Beth wasn't neuter, either, but I settled for her anyway. We leaned out the window, damp from limbering exercises. We were on *descendo*.

"*Descendo, descendere, descensi, descensus*. Jesus, what a crumby verb. Bitsy, do the part where Holden gets on the —"

"No, Beth, I've got questions for you."

"I feel like descendoing right out this window." Beth was having boyfriend troubles for a change. Some basketball star had decided to take training seriously and go to bed early every night.

"Beth, do you think guys want us to be submissive?"

"Sure. Aren't they the ones who always do everything first? They make the decisions. They make the wars and things."

"Well, then, do you think they want us to be smart?"

"Of course they do. Smart enough, anyway. That Hayes guy, that one with the funny hair and the rusty earring, he does, doesn't he? Isn't that why you applied to those fancy colleges?"

"Yes, I think that's the thing he most wants me to be. I think. What do you think femininity is?"

She dragged on the cigarette cupped in her hand in deference to curious neighbors and passed it to me. "Bitsy, that's a terrible question to ask somebody who's just been dumped."

"I can't go around timing my questions. Mr. Seligmann says my timing is pretty terrible sometimes, anyway. Did you ever try to explain femininity?"

"No. Let me think. I think it's making the guy think he's super, and laughing at his jokes. You know, being terribly soprano. Staying one step ahead of him."

"Beth, that's being aggressive."

"No, that's being feminine."

I rolled the butt and flicked it. Poor Mrs. Martin. She'd come apart if she knew we were still smoking. "I just want to be even, I think. Not ahead or behind."

"Who? Tommy?"

"No, dopey, Hayes, of course. Hey, you want Tommy?"

"Sure, why not? I'm not doing anything else."

"Good. I'll tell him."

"What do you mean?"

"Oh, I've sort of had it with Basic Cuteness. And I think he's had it with my always asking him fourteen times what he's saying. I'll even give you the frisbee back. You think you'll use it?''

"I don't know.''

"You know what I want, Beth? I want to make sense out of something for a change. I just want something to make Goddamn sense.''

"Let me know if it happens, Bitsy. And explain it to me.''

When I slipped the diaphragm into Beth's blazer pocket while we were down on our knees in chapel I didn't know she was going to go all out and get hysterical. In the front row. The domino theory went flawlessly into action, and by the end of the prayer the whole school was a mass of whispered, hiccuping giggles. On its knees.

Father Payre looked out over us stumbling into the pews, leaned his head back, the sun coming into his mouth like a dentist's light. Everybody tried to stop shaking. Poor Father Payre. For a holy man, he was a hell of a nice guy, and I made a mental note to improve my timing.

"This morning,'' he said in his forbearing voice, "I am going to discard my prepared sermon and talk about something a little different. We have here in evidence today one of God's greatest gifts to us. The gift of laughter.''

Sonofabitch. He wasn't going to have a fit.

"The cosmos, with its myriad mysteries, gives birth to—''

He stopped and waited until the second wave of fisted laughter rumbled and coughed away.

"We are sometimes awash in a mass of confusion. We dream false dreams, build false idols, the way seems not at all clear. We must remember then that it is not heretical to laugh. To rejoice in living, whatever the cost, whatever the enigma. We must not be afraid of the mystery, we must accept, merriment is part of our acceptance. It keeps us from folding under pressure . . . ''

Beth and I were the only ones coughing into our laps, but he waited for us.

"A sense of humor is one of our magnificent blessings. It is when we can no longer laugh at the human condition in all its apparent absurdity, no longer smile at our own follies, that we as a race are lost. Let us pray.''

There it was. Goddamn sense dropped right in my lap. I got

down on my knees and closed my eyes. I felt Beth slip the frisbee into my hand on the prayer rail.

On the way out of chapel, Father Payre stopped me with a wagging index finger. I began to wonder if I should make a career of getting stopped on the way out of chapel. I got out of line, held the dumb diaphragm inside my pocket and stood in front of his white lace robe. He whispered, "You're incorrigible, Bitsy." And patted my shoulder. I got back into line and went to Latin.

We still didn't know whether he was doing it with M3. I bet Beth my new blue cashmere sweater they weren't.

Beth had a vivid preoccupation with mirrors. Beginning, I think, when she got her ears pierced. I've never met anybody who wasn't subliminally preoccupied with them, but Beth was different. We'd pass a full-length one together, she'd grab my arm and jerk me to a stop. Two people in barfy uniforms looking not much like *New Yorker* ads for poised sportswear. She'd whisper, "I hope you like these people, because you're sleeping with both of them." It gave me considerable pause.

She carried a little hand mirror around in her pocket. She'd put it down on top of the book you were studying, with a note. It would say something like

> Does this person really love Latin?

or

> You are cordially invited to grow old with this person. How does that grab you?

When she put that one down in front of Sandra, with a P.S. that said

> And she'd be fabulous-looking if she'd go on a diet and Beth is willing to help her if she'll try.

Sandra was so affected that she managed to lose five pounds the first week.

Beth always knew when the mail arrived, and she could raise my temperature a degree and a half in study hall with the mirror on my history book (Woodrow Wilson and the League of Nations made me cry, which I never could explain to the teacher's satisfaction) with a note that said

This person has a scrawly letter from Germany in her mail cubby which she can read immediately if she'll develop a quick coughing fit and have to leave the room. And tell me the big words he writes this time.

Once she stuck the mirror on top of church history with this note:

How many hours do you think this person has spent in church in her life?

The thought was intriguing. We calculated that by the time we graduated, with the six hundred eighty chapels at half an hour each, plus the hours we'd put in at Sunday school and church, the total for each of us would be roughly one thousand three hundred fifty-two. 1,352. Even if we lopped off twenty hours or so for chicken pox, bloody noses and fake cramps, the figures were shocking. It wasn't like spending a third of your life sleeping, and those other fractions people were always handing out. You had to allot those. Somebody had come up with the ingenious ruse of keeping us in headlong confrontation with our sins for 1,352 hours out of our lives. And we couldn't even figure out what our sins were.

We drank a quarter of a bottle of gin that night to get over it. Sloshing around on the floor doing unsteady limbering exercises and telling each other we might never get over it.

Three girls, including Beth, got rejections from Stanford. I didn't get anything. I asked the headmistress what she thought was up. She wasn't quite sure, she said, but she'd check. I got called out of French to go to her purple office. Heliotrope office.

"Sit down, Bitsy. How are you this fine spring day?"

"I'm fine, Miss Kenyon. How are you?" I'd seen her two hours before.

"Very well, thank you. Is your violin getting its share of attention these days?" She wore about seven rings.

"Miss Kenyon, yes, my violin is. I have to know about Stanford. I have to. Did you find out?"

"Well, Bitsy, yes, I did. It seems there was a little mix-up—"

"You mean I got *in*?" I got up out of the purple chair and started for the window, sunshine like crazy all over the maple trees. I felt like Katherine Hepburn.

And then I didn't.

"Uh, no, Bitsy. It's not that Stanford rejected you . . . "

I turned around. "I'm on the waiting list, then?"

"Bitsy, the mix-up was here at St. Margaret's. I know this is a disappointment . . . " There was a purple iris on her desk.

She didn't want to tell me. I didn't want to hear. I felt like FDR's legs.

"Your application, my dear, somehow got misplaced."

I tried looking at the portrait of the founder behind her. "How?" came out like Helen Keller.

"It's one of those very unfortunate things, Bitsy, Miss Montgomery's briefcase, her file folder . . . she found it this afternoon . . . "

"Goddamn! God holy damn!"

"Beatrice! I know you're disappointed—"

"Miss Kenyon, you don't know the half of it—"

I never spoke to M3 again. What Father Payre said was very fine and noble and theoretical, but it did not apply to my relationship with M3. We went through the last eight weeks of school without exchanging a word.

She even tried congratulating me the next day when the other three fancy colleges accepted me. What I did instead of letting her get within six feet of my envelopes was go to Miss Kenyon's office and apologize.

She still had the purple iris on the purple blotter on her desk. I knew I was a rotten kid to swear in her office.

"Miss Kenyon, I'm sorry I blew up yesterday . . . "

"Bitsy, we're all very happy for you. Which college do you think you'll choose?"

"I don't know yet, Miss Kenyon. I have to think about yesterday. I want you to know I'm sorry about—"

"I understand, Bitsy. I've been an educator for twenty-nine years." Whenever you had a problem she told you how long she'd been an educator. "I know these disappointments . . . you don't think Miss Montgomery purposely misplaced your—"

"No, I don't think that." I lied. I don't know why.

"Certainly nothing of the kind could happen at St. Margaret's. Miss Montgomery is one of the finest, most sincere . . . a little disorganized at times . . . "

"Miss Kenyon, do you think I'd have gotten in?"

"Bitsy, that's something we'll never know."

Not even if I got reincarnated and tried again?

"You will let me know, won't you, Bitsy, the minute you decide?"

"Sure, Miss Kenyon, I will."

She even showed me my College Board scores, which she said she wasn't supposed to do. They were pretty good. I had a feeling she'd done a lot of that in twenty-nine years. A little consolation gift. I've noticed that people who are pretty good at their jobs hand out consolation gifts from time to time. Whether the rules say they're supposed to or not.

Each of the three colleges wanted fifty dollars if I was going to go. The very next thing to do was get a letter off to Germany. I faked a headache and cut two classes to write it.

Dear Bitsy,

    Girl Wonder does it again. Get your fifty skins off to Smith. And congratulations.

    Now that the feculent M3 is out of the way, when you're at Smith and I'm at Harvard Law School, we'll go roast weenies somewhere in the hills. It will do you a grand lot of good to get out from under the salvation merchants.

    You don't have to go to Stanford to get to San Francisco. We'll stop in there someday. I'll ravish you in the lobby of the goddamn Mark Hopkins if you like.

    I enjoyed your kaleidoscopic references to the battles waged between confusion and sense. Someday you must sit your little self down and tell me what you mean.

    I can't think of a good reason why I'm here. Want to go to the Yucatan?

    I love you. Do you know you've never misspelled a word in all your correspondence with me? Since I'm the best speller in this useless and misplaced artillery corps, that makes a great big impression.

    Get hold of the communion wine.

             Love,
               H

Smith it was.

And that's why I didn't get kicked out two days before commencement when the algebra teacher eloped with a guy who worked in the kitchen and we got hold of the communion wine to celebrate. The very same lithe algebra teacher who'd once walked into class and written on the blackboard:

$$\text{And God said } (y^4 + z^8)m$$
$$\text{And there was light}$$

The celebration was a nice way of saluting St. Maggie's, the whole class agreed. Someone caught Mrs. Martin trying to clean up the mess. Beth complicated things somewhat by accidentally setting fire to the back seat of one of the school station wagons when Miss Kenyon walked into the garage and caught sight of her cigarette. They almost didn't let Beth march in the graduation line.

Nobody'd gone from St. Maggie's to Smith in years. And if I hadn't gone to St. Maggie's and started studying via Hayes, I wouldn't be going there. Now someone could run right over to the printer's and add it to the brochure they were always rewriting. It had pictures of concretely devout girls bending over the Latin ablative absolute, no macaroni and cheese on their blazers.

Instead of kicking us all out, they fired Mrs. Martin for covering for us. I think they decided to start fresh.

We had a falsely gay party for her. Her sitting room was bluer than ever. Everybody knew why she'd been axed, but nobody talked about it. She'd covered for every one of us at one time or another, and she'd covered the communion wine for the whole class. When we tried to tell her we appreciated it, in feet-crossing, arm-scratching kinds of ways, she laughed and said she was going to visit her sister in Omaha. She wasn't making any more sense than the rest of us.

Our room was too littered with junk and memorabilia to allow for limbering exercises. Beth stood in the middle of it, holding her Latin book. The half-finished gin bottle was on the floor of the closet, door closed.

"Bitsy, you know what this is? It's absolute, no-shit truth time. We graduate tomorrow, nobody lies tonight. Do you think I got poise here?"

Her fantastic hair hung down over flaming orange underwear. She knew more Latin than I ever would, she'd carefully avoided falling in love with Tommy, she could play Rhapsody in Blue (not well, as she'd be the first to admit in a screaming frenzy of foot-stamping and hair-swinging), she'd taken up a collection to buy Mrs. Martin new Omaha luggage, she'd lived with my Handel until she could sing every sonata, she'd provided me with lessons in how to get clerks in stores to pay attention to us, she'd gotten Sandra to go on a diet and stick to it. And burned a station wagon seat. Poise?

"Beth, I don't know what poise is."

"It's knowing what you're going to do in the split second before you do it, dummy."

"Then I think you've got some. And that hair—"

"Do you think you got poise?"

"That's not what I came here to get, Beth. I think—I don't know if I'm effete or bent out of shape."

We leaned out the window with our cigarette. "Isn't it funny," she said, her hair hanging on my shoulders, "we're both getting out of here virgins?"

"I don't know if it's funny or not. I don't think I'm ready to get besmirched yet."

"It's not getting besmirched, Bitsy."

"Why can't I send my graduation picture to Hayes? Why can't I just put it in an envelope and send it?"

"I think maybe it's your short hair."

"Beth, this probably sounds perverted, but I'm not gonna grow it out until he and I get together." I shut my eyes. "If you're laughing at that, do it without making any noise, okay? I don't want to know how dumb and perverted it is." I didn't hear anything.

"I think the real reason I can't send it to him—it's not the six pounds I've put on since he saw me, I don't know if he cares about pretty, even. If you're gonna get really old with somebody, I don't think it matters so much. It's a thing about mouths. You send somebody a picture of your mouth in one position; like an apple that gets candied. You might be thinking some half-assed thought like there's a piece of lint on the lens, or about how you have to go to the bathroom, your mouth gets sent off to somebody you love so terribly much, all stuck in a position of petrified banality. If all they've got of you is a banal thing like there's a piece of lint on the lens, what the hell kind of gift is that to give somebody? In Germany?"

"Bitsy, that's very peculiar. I can't decide whether it's profound or nonsense."

"Look, Beth, I don't know, either, but here's something else about mouths. Now, I think I'm kind of a half-assed expert, because the very first thing I noticed about Hayes was his mouth, and it knocked me out. I didn't know he was gonna have those José Ferrer *s*'s I told you about. And no, I'm not gonna try to imitate them for you again, I can't do it. You know, that's the one thing I'm gonna remember about him long after he divorces me on grounds of dumbness—"

"Hey, do you mean that?"

"No, it just slipped out. I don't think I mean it. Anyway, it's this thing about mouths. Do you think we're drunk?"

"Damned right I do. You haven't made any notable sense for the last five minutes."

"Well, keep listening, you never know when I'm gonna. If your mouth is—well, your mouth tells what kind of person you are. Take Father Payre. He's got this open, rhetorical mouth, you know, open to possibilities. Like he's willing to take the world in, its myriad mysteries, that stuff he talks about, the laughing and the rest of it. He let me go on and on about the Gnostics, they've been dead for centuries. Like he's willing to taste. People call it open-minded, but I don't think that's it. I mean, nobody can look into your mind and see anything. You look at people's mouths. Now, take M3. She's got a tight, perverted mouth—and a lopsided, sadistic smile. That's how I knew she and Father Payre never did it together in bed. Or anyplace. Their mouths wouldn't fit."

"Bitsy, do you know where M3 was a WAVE?"

"No, and I don't care."

"At Smith College."

"She was where?"

"She was. She wore a uniform, she marched. At the same time college was going on, they were training WAVES. She told me. She'd tell you if you were speaking to her."

"Good God. She's gonna haunt me there."

"No, she's not. You know what's gonna happen? Father Payre is gonna get himself into a really good school; he deserves it. And M3 is gonna stay right here 'til she dies, poisoning people. That's the way life is."

"Beth, why is it that everybody I start to like is such a damn skeptic?"

"I don't know. Why did I have to burn up the back seat of the station wagon?"

"And why am I always saying good-bye to people?"

"I don't know. Life's myriad mysteries."

"Beth, what I'd really like to do is have a huge party. Everybody I love, all together. Here's who'd be there: my mother, my brother, Hayes, Judy, Freak, you, Fritz Seligmann, Father Payre, this guy named Casey Parker and his family, I'd just like to get all of you there at the same time. I ever tell you about Hayes and the universal thump?"

"No, you never did. Anyway, life's not like that. You don't get everybody together at the same time."

"What a damn skeptic you are."

"Can I come to your dogwood and strawberry wedding anyway?"

"Sure. You'll be poised as hell. Hayes'll knock you out. You'll hear him say those *s*'s. Hey, that'll be my big party, all the people I love and all the people Hayes loves, the big drunken universal thump. Fritz'll play some mad romantic scherzo on the lawn, it'll be hysterical."

Every time I turned around I was saying good-bye to somebody.

Father Payre didn't say anything about life's myriad mysteries at graduation, but he hinted that they hadn't all been solved yet. We liked that, somebody who wasn't telling us we could go out and make sense of it all right then and there.

Dear Bitsy,

So your mother and Fritz had sherry at the wedding. Sounds so very carnal and merry. Give them my best wishes.

Before the wicked and questionably sober atmosphere of college life settles around you, drink in a lot of that wholesome mountain air. Vivace, please. See how very musical I'm getting?

I'm going to try to stay an arm's length away from the specifically libidinous in this letter, as a gesture to your having given two years of your life to the nunnery. I have in my memory a young lady who was going to hate it, and wept copiously at being ripped untimely from the womb. You seem to have weathered it well.

I wish I could say the same for this. We have a little sport around here called bivouac. Originally it's German, but we'll leave the derivation aside for the moment, recalling your ineptitude with languages.

B *belly-crawling, blighted by the illusion that it has some inherent purpose*

I *inhuman, a symbol of invincible self-importance*

V *vile, vicious, vividly pointless*

O *onerous opportunity for people to pretend they're accomplishing something*

U *uncomfortable as hell*

A *antipathetic to all that's good and true in all of us*

C *crudely cenozoic with regard to the civilizing process*

In a few months I'm going to burn these contemptible costumes, call a rifle a gun and a field piece a cannon, tell the general he's an immature adolescent and a quaking, duplistic excuse for a human being, and come and get you.
That wasn't so very libidinous, was it?
Read Nietzsche.
I love you, light of my frazzled and disjointed life.

H

Mother and Fritz had indeed had sherry—and pheasant from our own woods, brought down by my brother for the occasion. The dining-room table expanded to include about fourteen people, violets and marigolds sat in teacups at everybody's places, my brother and I lifted glasses with the rest of them, the whole scene was merry as hell.

Mother leaned across Fritz to me, holding a petit four in her hand. "Beatrice dear," she said, her little finger on my wrist, "love has many different arms, like a tree. Young arms, very green and enthusiastic, eager to bear fruit. And old arms. Wrinkled and weathered. They've been through the storms. It's the old arms that know what serenity is, Beatrice, and they prize it above all else. God lets each of us find that out in our own way. Do you know what I'm saying, dear?"

Serenity. The old wrinkled arms and the hobbling down to the lake in Switzerland or maybe China at sunset. "I think maybe I do, Mother."

The one-eyed cat twisted around my leg under the table, Mother whispered in Fritz's ear, he passed on to me the message that it was time to give the guests the Léclair Sonata in D for violin, viola and piano. He'd been polishing the viola part for weeks.

Most of the women cried during the second movement.

If I'd told anybody that the woman in a lavendar dress smiling and radiating an orchestrated sort of commitment to serenity was the same humorless virago who'd deported me to St. Maggie's for being "bad" and daring to fall in love, they wouldn't have believed me.

My brother and I camped out in the woods on their wedding night and talked a lot about Thoreau. He said Thoreau should have come out west where there were real mountains; I said I thought he did all right where he was. My brother also didn't think it was such a hot idea that I was going so far away to college. I didn't tell him about Harvard Law School and the specifically libidinous. Our family just never talked about that stuff.

I continued to wish Hayes had gone to jail. I spent the summer as the lone waitress in a diner, carrying six plates of French fries and banana splits up my strong arms. And trying to read Nietzsche. Nietzsche gave me bad dreams. I thought it was only a mildly morbid coincidence that he'd died on my birthday, but I preferred not to celebrate my birthday anyway. Mother said she couldn't understand why.

The first time I heard of brainwashing, I thought it was what Mary Martin did in *South Pacific*. Courtesy of a full-page ad in *Life* magazine showing her lathered and glistening, confident that laundering her brain several times a week would solve everything. But between the onerous, vividly pointless bivouac and my Nietzsche dreams, I began to think there might be more to it. I was happy as hell to be going off to college where they'd teach me about that and everything else. I'd wipe out my provincialism, get a gigantic and sweeping view of the world, and finally know what on earth Hayes was talking about. I wasn't particularly poised, but I was going to learn to tell my ass from my elbow, get the truth in my brain, and sail off elegantly stimulated to Switzerland or maybe

China, making endless sense. So strode my thoughts among the French fries.

The night before I left for college, Judy picked me up at the diner and we went to the Columbia with a six-pack of beer to celebrate something. We weren't sure what.

We sat a few feet east of the spot where Fred had sung his song. It was a gray night, no good for swimming.

"Judy, this is an endless round of good-byes," I said on my third beer. "I should be handing out Hallmark cards to everybody."

"It's your choice. You could be going to the University with me. I'm gonna major in biology—"

"You'll probably be homecoming queen or something, too."

"I doubt it. I'm just not interested in that stuff anymore. Do you think you could explain clearly this time why you're going so far away?"

"It's the same thing I've told you before. That's where Hayes says I should go, he's gonna go to Harvard Law School, they're really close together—and they gave me that squinchy little scholarship. I don't know, maybe I'm trying to prove something."

"What?"

"I don't know. Prove to Hayes that I'm smart enough for him, or prove to my mother that I'm not terrible—"

"Everybody's gonna say it's a stupidly swanky thing to do, Bitsy."

They already were. Betting I'd come back smoking filtertips, talking in tongues. But after Hayes had wedged himself between me and a local drunk I hadn't any choice. I didn't mind the Pygmalion part. I wouldn't be the first one of those, either. And then there was the matter of Rance I, II, and III. I had to learn a lot before I could give birth to those glorious creatures with flying locks of hair.

"Judy, you're just gonna have to live with it. You gonna do that cheerleading thing in college?"

"Are you kidding? Somebody who got me to reading Thomas Mann when I was fifteen is sitting in jail, and I'm gonna be cheerleading? What kind of hollow thing do you think I am?"

"Jesus, I'm gonna miss you. You know I'm getting to the point where I don't even like anybody who isn't a noble skeptic? I bet when you and Freak see each other at our wedding, you'll get all excited and—"

"And have an affair under the dogwood tree? I don't think so. How do you have an affair with somebody in a prison uniform? But I did keep track of the times he pulled me out of the river. Thirteen. I'm willing to bet that's the cleanest thing we'll ever do, that summer."

"I don't think so. I'm gonna do my best to keep our wedding clean, even though Hayes is gonna bring his raunchy, sotted friends and vulgarize it."

"And I know you really want it vulgarized, or you wouldn't be going into it with him. There's something about you that's drawn to the honestly vulgar. Do you think it has something to do with music?"

"Judy, you're gonna do just fine with that vocabulary in college. And I don't know if it has anything to do with music or not. Sometimes it feels that way."

"Also, and here's something you may not know—" She started laughing. "I did some research. Of all the kids around here, you and I are the only ones who climbed the mountain and helped save somebody's life and didn't lose their virginity all in the same summer!"

Cottonwood branches blew around, water lapped grayly about twelve feet away. I could hear the slosh of the backwash against the cliffs. I sifted a handful of sand through my fingers.

"Judy, do you realize that was two whole years ago?"

She looked across the river at the blinking lights of the sawmill. "And you still love the same guy. That strange guy. Three thousand miles' worth."

"I really still do." He'd think it was such a dumb conversation.

She uncuffed her jeans, letting sand fall out. "I think you're slightly crazy. There's some kind of sideways ethic at work in the world. I just wish I knew what it was. Is."

Judy came from a dust bowl family. I got sprung out of a Victorian bunch. Together we pieced out a view of the sideways ethic that carried us through puberty.

Portland Airport became PDX. Bradley Field, Connecticut, the airport for Northampton, became BDL. The first links of a labyrinthine charm bracelet that wound its way across the top of my suitcase over the next several years. My little cardboard travelogue.

I had to take all Hayes's letters with me to college, in case Mother began to poke around looking for me to get pregnant via air mail.

I watched Mount Hood go by past the window. I'd never seen it from the air, I'd never thought before about just how much of a damn it didn't give about the logging business. I'd never even been on an airplane before.

seven

I'm sure I wasn't the first or the last person to hit Northampton and regard with some slight surprise the preponderance of Muffy's, Puffy's, Katsy's, and Toto's. "Bitsy" was no encumbrance at all. In fact, it was something of a plus, since I didn't have a blond pageboy and couldn't say "Haahry, Baahry, and Laahry" yet. I was still saying "Herry, Berry, and Lerry." Not that it's terribly important, but it was one of the things that underwent a hypnopedic change. I woke up one morning and could say them all. Along with "ahnvelope" and "hahrible" instead of the "ehnvelope" and "hohrible" of my orchard-trotting childhood.

They had peculiar totems on their bodies, these Katsy's. One was a round gold pin at the blouse collar, called, aptly enough, a circle pin. The other was a bracelet made of simulated petrified dung beetles. Simulated and petrified. I never did figure it out.

I'd never seen so many bikes in my life. Every time you turned around someone wanted to sell you one. I paid four dollars for mine.

A contrapuntal jargon swelled out of the windows and doors. Comfortable, in a hurried, ballpoint-pen-jabbing way, and easier than Latin. Weekends were Blue Cards, easy courses were guts. To be chic was to be shoo, infatuated was snowed, stood up or passed out on was flushed or shot down, flunking was taking gas, going off with some date not your own was birddogging. House duties carried the liturgical titles of Watch and Wait. There seemed to be a rule that you couldn't call certain selected things by their right names.

My roommate was very tall.

"Bitsy? I never heard of anybody called that. It's kind of a wifty name."

I thought Muffy, Puffy, Katsy and Toto were wifty in their way, too.

"My name's Gayle. I'm from Chicaago." I wondered if she'd found blurred patriotism there. "You know, your hair is shorter than the mean around here. If you've noticed the mean."

"Yeah, I have," I laughed. She was more than generously pretty, with a mouth that sloped just this side of marked fervor. She wasn't wearing dung beetles. "I'm from Oregon."

"Auragon? What're you doing here?"

"It's Oregon. You say the *e* like an *e*."

"Did you look in your box? There's a letter for you. Who's *H* that sends letters in green ink? Is it a fag?"

"God only knows by now. No, I don't think so. *H* is the reason I'm here. I think."

"You mean it's a benefactor?" She had dark brown wavy hair.

"No. I mean I'm going to marry him, I'm getting an education first. He's in Germany."

"Being Goethe?"

"No, he's being a big strong soldier boy. I don't know why they have soldiers in peacetime. I don't know why they have them in the first place."

"They have them so we can go to our fat little colleges and get tidy little educations and marry into slobby, divorce-ridden, capitalistic families. It's all related." She had huge, unhesitating brown eyes. I took a long look at her.

"You know, Gayle, sometimes I'm wrong about these things, but I think I'm going to like you. How tall are you, anyway?"

"Five eight. Not to be confused with Phi Bet. You going to let your hair grow out?"

"Not for a little while." I put my violin down on one of the beds. "I think I'll run down and get that letter. Are you sure it's green?"

"I bet he's a fag. Wait, I'll go with you. Let's tour this place. I haven't seen it since my interview."

"You had an interview here?"

"Sure, didn't you?"

"No, I had mine at school." M3 had showed me into the chandeliered greeeting room, dragging her cigarette holder behind her like a sword. She probably wanted to get me as far away as she could. Or else wanted me to be a WAVE and get in the next war. Maybe that's why she told the interviewing woman I was "one of the outstanding girls, with a real interest in serious study." That was before I stopped speaking to her.

The unfaggy Hayes said there'd be lots of forces lying around college waiting to mold me, that our house would have a balcony looking out over the lake so we could keep an eye on the kids when they leaned out of the canoe to catch newts, and that as soon as he figured out what resemblance his army shit bore to life he'd let me know. I made a mental note to watch out for molding forces, stuffed the envelope in my jeans pocket and went biking with tall Gayle.

New England didn't have any mountains. And not many evergreen trees. But there were deciduous ones everywhere; leaves squeaking against windows, huge trunks for sitting under. Gayle and I biked around the campus, which bore a strong resemblance to the one in the catalogue. Gayle said the architecture was hysterically eclectic, running from Classic Brick Shithouse to Dithered Gingerbread Whimsy; plans for a couple of new buildings suggested they would look like giant terrariums. I took her word for it. There were an awful lot of different kinds. I thought the variety was a nice way of telling us we'd get a lot of different kinds of knowledge. We biked among the trees, she showed me where the music building, Sage Hall, was. It had nice Ionic columns. Next to it was a terrific pond, Paradise Pond, with an island in the middle where you could beach a canoe.

When we crested the hill past the pond, the chapel stared us in the face. I'd had enough of chapels, but it had more nice Ionic columns. We dodged about forty other bikes and let the September breeze take the conversation on the way back to the Quad. Gayle came from a slobby, divorce-ridden, capitalistic family. She was also valedictorian of her class.

"You were valedictorian of your class. Look at the girl on your left. And on your right. They were, too."

So began our orientation by a stentorian dean, whose fondness for regional and categorical percentages took us into half an hour of just how many of each kind of us had come stampeding on Northampton from all corners of the world. A handsome attempt to demonstrate that we weren't a monolith. I wasn't even a valedictorian.

Gayle and I decorated our room in what she called Early Alimony.

Having left the Bible Belt behind me, I began to learn something about the other belts out there.

For one thing, I dated quite a lot of Jewish boys. You knew they had a religion somewhere, but they didn't tend to flail you with it. One of them told me I was a WASP. I didn't know there was a name for me. When he explained it I told him he could leave off the P, but he said that made me a WAS, and it was a little early to put a whole life in the past tense.

I didn't exactly avoid Catholic guys. I was sure they had more problems with their religion than I did, and a certain compassion was due them. And I felt some sense of commiseration with Protestants, so I didn't exactly avoid them, either.

I also got interested in Martin Buber. The two-ness of him, I think.

For still another thing, some Zen was floating around the religion department and made its incandescent way into my mind. In a vigorous and windy excitement, I took archery at eight A.M., deciding I'd try to go the whole way, and that maybe one hand clapping was a little like the shining silence of standing still watching Hayes standing still beside the East Fork when I'd just screamed out the most heaving part of my soul to him.

The archery instructor didn't seem to attach any spiritual transcendency to the art of picking up arrows from the ground at eight-forty, but I plugged away at it until the frost hit and I couldn't make any tactile sense out of Telemann at nine.

I had to hurry and learn how to take notes, something they'd left out of my training at St. Maggie's. I decided it wasn't a part of M3's plan to get me flunked out of somewhere.

(pst,fut) pres c'est pourquoi, G's, stud hist

Past and future are contained in the present. This is why, girls, we study the lessons of history.

MD=vst BM

If I let it go for a few weeks before looking it over, *Moby Dick* appeared to be a vast bowel movement. After I gave it my careful attention, it turned out to be a vast Biblical metaphor instead. What a relief.

Smith was full of girls who knitted sweaters and socks while they took notes. They must have been taking notes for years, knowing reflexively when something was important enough to stop knitting and write. I knew no such thing.

Exams were a mixed bag of novelty and adrenalin-churn. St. Maggie's assumed we had no honor at all, and tested us accordingly, teachers tapping orthopedic shoes near a rear window. Likewise the College Boards, with marching thrown in. Smith took the position that we had honor coming out our ears and named the system after it. As far as I ever found out, Smith was right.

Just beginning my romance with the exam Bluebook, I knew why Hayes had been doing all those years. Squeezing his chin between thumb and index finger, flattening a hand across his nose and mouth with pen sticking out like a newly lit cigarette, scrutinizing each cagey question with knuckles against upper lip as if to anchor the hand and mouth would clarify the question, in the explicitly legato ballet of test-taking. He'd be a hand-to-mouth tester, a blower of flies off Bluebooks. A right-hand paper-flattener, he'd scrawl page after yellow page of wisdom in that lanky script. Among the cuticle-biters, foot-swingers and ballpoint-clickers, he'd forge pinnacles of thought, microcosms of enlightenment. If anybody else had said that about some guy, I'd have puked.

I became an upper-lip-knuckler, a ballpoint-clicker, a wrist-blower. Acing tests wasn't easy at Smith.

I also learned something about writing papers. You got extra points for humility. You still sneezed up your ideas in the voice of "one," but you could balance that invitation to monumentalize your thoughts by tacking on two specific, humble words at the very beginning. Whatever your topic was, you called it "Notes on" or "Notes toward." "Notes toward a further study of Shakespeare's Sexual Metaphors." The unassuming lower case was very im-

portant. These techniques could make the difference between a C
and a B. At best, they could send you shooting toward an A-plus.

I wasn't exactly sure what kind of good they were going to do me
("one") swimming nude a few yards from the incredible
seventeen-room house in Switzerland or maybe China, but if that's
what Hayes wanted, that's what he'd get.

As a matter of fact, he'd enjoy a further study of Shakespeare's
sexual metaphors. Whenever you ran across orchards, tillage, ears
of corn, husbandry, ploughs—in fact, any time you saw anything
remotely connected with farming—Shakespeare meant it to be
sexy. Unweeded gardens were political, but orchards were sexy.
I'd lived in an orchard all my life and had never known how sexy it
was. Hayes and I would go canoeing on that lake and I'd tell him all
about it, if he didn't already know.

The Bluebook nominative case stretched to the dining room and
the bike rack. People were always saying, "One finds it so very
nebulous, you know," when they meant they couldn't make sense
of their history notes. I was collecting regionalisms like mad.

Dear Bitsy,

 *The world is full of surprises and small ironies. I've met
two people I have to tell you about. One has long red hair and
knows a lot of Latin, comes to the University straight out of a
burning station wagon. One is a humongously fascinating
person named Howard who wants to make me his wife. Don't
say I've flipped anything. He's a senior, phys ed major, comes
from Seattle, and the very most important thing is that I love
him. Do I have to tell you how that kind of thing takes you by
surprise? One morning we were drinking coffee from a thermos
after he'd run around the track I don't know how many times,
and I looked at him and knew I loved him.*

 *He's very logical, and doesn't know how to be crazy.
We're going to have a Christmasy wedding. Please be a
bridesmaid.*

 *Rumor has it that your brother is headed for Phi Beta
Kappa.*

 *Beth is on a campaign to get a date with at least five
members of each fraternity by spring vacation. She asked me to
imitate Hayes's s's for her, but of course I couldn't. She also
asked me if he really existed. I said I was close to certain that he
did. She says hello. And "Facio you." What does that mean?*

     Matrimonially,
      Judy

Naturally I thought Judy, the premed biology major, was nuts. But she had a point. It happens, thermos or no thermos. The sweating runner could at least have had the consideration not to be a senior already.

If Hayes thought I was inept with languages, he knew me for a moron in history. James I, Charles I, Charles II, James II, I repeated them to myself to get the order right during orchestra rehearsals. All I knew was that they had something to do with an imaginary "divine right" and enjoyed a flagrant tendency to push their toadies (pardon me) around. The four names fit nicely with the Jupiter Symphony, first movement.

I took art history. And learned chiaroscuro. That was the word for the black and white Columbia at night, one near-dead body being resuscitated while the river flowed historically on.

Coincidentally, about the time I discovered chiaroscuro I had little or no use for it. The grayness of life was settling around me. With two qualifying factors: one, I knew it would—life wasn't supposed to be a very clear matter—and two, I didn't recognize it right away. Like gray fog in the morning—you put on jeans and a sweater, and by the time you look again, the fog has sort of lifted. You kind of forget about it, you wonder if it was there at all. What you do is get used to the gray fog coming and going, you get on your bike and ride through it. It usually doesn't last long.

I began to drip with heady adjectives, like a tree whose apples, fed and sprayed and thinned and measured, brag with weight and proud insolent juice as they speed through the shortening days toward harvest. I knew I wasn't ready for harvesting yet, but by the time Hayes hit Harvard Law School I'd be ready. It was a matter of hurrying, gray fog or not. Since he had all those years on me, not to mention all that mileage, there was simply a hell of a lot of classical education to get.

A ripening apple sitting atop a four-dollar bike, slavishly slogging in the direction of a history lecture. Hayes would have laughed his head off.

Dear Bitsy,
    I wondered when you'd run across old Emily Dickinson. Of course I know where she lived! And spent her entire fifty-plus years in sententious prodigality of metaphorical extravagance—if I may be permitted a redundancy.
    I prefer other forms of extravagance.

And you, my girl, listen hard to this: you must not lose your agile grasp of the vernacular. Do I know "her incredibly translucent sense of the eloquence of death?" I'll reply in the style of Bitsy the mountain-climber:

Holy shit. What kind of dumb question is that?

I gather from four elegiac paragraphs devoted to Sibelius that you want to go to Finland. We'll do it.

Love,
H

P.S. Each scruffy German-speaking buddy of mine, all two of them, sends lust. That was meant to be kindest regards.

Men. They could be such enigmatic clods. How was I supposed to get the classical education and hang onto an agile grasp at the same time? If it had been anyone else I'd have told him to jump in the lake. Considering that it was Hayes, I applied myself with marked fervor to the task of classical education *cum* agile grasp. It wasn't easy.

Smith had open stacks and was openly boastful about them. You could get any book, almost any time, without anybody having to unlock anything. That's where I got MD, Shakespeare and Emily Dickinson. I didn't even know open stacks were unusual until I began to venture away on Blue Cards.

The Ivy League mesh crawled with guys of various descriptions. Birddogging guys who veered brassily across deciduous campuses on ebullient football afternoons, spilling giant paper cups of beer, failed to match the appeal of Hayes and Fred laughing up the riverbank, lifting cans in a toast to mountains or Huxley or little green apples. Likewise, somebody leaning sideways out of a tweed jacket to remind me to save my filtertips because they made Tampax for Pygmies out of them paled before the glimpse of Hayes in a sweatshirt pointing out a flying squirrel darting twenty feet over my head.

The guys were mostly okay, and it seemed only mildly unjust that they had the exclusive right of pursuit. You couldn't walk up to a really great-looking guy and say, "Can I take you out for a beer and put my hand on your chest?" If they were the ones who had to go and get drafted, you could accord them that muscled prerogative. And I wondered if "muscled prerogative" was the sort of thing Casey Parker had in mind when he said I was talkin' funny. I supposed it was.

Blue Cards took me to seven or eight different campuses, all with closed stacks. Virginal? You bet your ass I was. Every time I got in a supine position I'd see the Big Three—Father, Son, and Holy Ghost—wailing at me like some frowning atonal Kingston Trio in the sky. Hovering just out of punching range, taking care of me, whether I was snowed for the moment or not. Their attention-getting devices included chastizing threnodic moanings of

> All hail the power of Jesus' name
> Let angels' prostate fall

and a few others too reminiscent of M3's tedious puns to bear repeating. But they got me up off the couch. I wasn't sure whether it was their jarring atonality, or their lean and leering message, or the fact that I'd stopped going to church.

Every important thing I ever went into, I had to audition for. I don't think the Kingston trio had to audition at all. I had a feeling they'd signed some kind of contract with my mother, though.

Now, as committed as Presbytarians were to truth, Mother had impressed me with the importance of one particular lie. She said to me one August day over the ironing, shortly before my uncelebrated eighteenth birthday, "Beatrice, you mustn't let boys think you *like* that sort of thing." I knew very well which sort of thing she was talking about, and didn't waste time with a lot of what-do-you-mean's. By then she'd had ample experience with my deceptions and she knew I was pretty good at them, but she must not have thought I could carry that one off. So she sent the Trinity along to make sure.

Hayes, of course, was safely removed from my virginity in Germany for a while. By the time he got to law school, he'd plough through that particular form of blarney in seconds flat.

> First-year law student breaks own record, 19:24 seconds, accepts trophy, gives press conference . . .
> *The Harvard Crimson*

So the Trio went along with my Blue Cards. There wasn't much I could do about it, and I didn't know whether I even wanted to. I still didn't know whether or not I was effete. Or if they were.

With all the kinds of classical education at hand, I hardly had time for the violin, except for the symphony and chamber ensembles. But I didn't tell Mother and Fritz that.

Gayle didn't think it was so weird that I came out with Salinger once in awhile, although she said all his characters were victims of lifetime premenstrual depressions. She came out with some odd things herself. Like calling me the girl in the Freudian slip. I asked her what that made her, and she said it made her the girl in the Jungian trenchcoat. All I noticed about her trenchcoat was that it was full of holes and the bottom of it had greasy stains from her bike chain.

Suddenly that Christmas (BDL to PDX) my brother asked me to get the Christmas tree with him. He'd put his Phi Beta Kappa key in a drawer and didn't mention it to me. We were a regular family of non-mentioners.

"What? You mean it?" My hot chocolate spilled.

"For God's sake, Beatrice, get your stuff."

Ski underwear, jeans, boots tangled themselves around my room. I made what sense I could of them and clumped down the stairs. He stood at the front door, with its body-length window. "Dad sure had the right idea, didn't he, Beatrice? Putting us way up here. You know, most people in the world can't see one mountain from their front door. We've got three. It's almost not fair."

"You know what else? There's a bunch of people, in Africa somewhere—the women collect firewood all day for their whole lives, and the men sit around and smoke something that gets them high. What do you think of that?"

"Beatrice, you're getting an astounding fund of questionable information at that school. What're you going to do with it all?"

I looked at the snowy spot where Hayes and I'd said not-good-bye. "I think I'm gonna go around the world . . ."

"Let's get a tree." He took the folding saw off a needlepoint chair and we scraped through the snow into the woods.

"Do you remember, when you were a little kid, you ran clear to the end of the lawn and back in your pajamas and bare feet, in the snow?" I bent low under a loaded cedar branch.

"No, I never did that." He walked like Paul Bunyan.

"I remember perfectly. You had red and white pajamas—"

He shook a cedar branch down my neck on purpose. I was so surprised I almost couldn't grab him in time and throw him and his folding saw in the snow. He hadn't washed my face in a snowbank since I was nine years old.

It was the first time in twelve years we'd chosen a Christmas tree together. A lovely tree. And I stopped minding about Mickey Spillane and the flashlight making their sudden departure from the hayloft. Just possibly, Currier and Ives might have lived.

The next day I obliged my mother by going skiing with the spiritually fraudulent minister's son. She wouldn't have been so thrilled if she'd found out, as I did, that he'd graduated from hubcaps and blouses to syphoning gas and trying to impregnate parishioners' daughters in ski-lodge kitchens. Mother beamed at him in church the next morning, while I lifted my middle finger at him behind the hymnal.

The only thing that blighted the Dickensian gaiety of Judy's wedding a couple of days later was that Mr. Benson had accidentally backed the coupe over Jimmy Lee's leg that morning while Jimmy Lee was doing something under their snowplow. He refused to go to the hospital. The doctor had to make a thirty-mile drive to set his leg.

Everyone but the Bensons turned out for the ceremony. Casey and his family in new Christmas clothes; the minister's excuse for a son with his face washed, and with who knew what going on in his Hieronymous Bosch mind; Judy's parents laughing and proud; the whole town in wedding garb and boots.

Judy was somewhere under a balloon of white net; I wore yuletide green. I had a hard time keeping a straight face during the vows. I kept seeing Judy falling in the river and Fred pulling her out, and I kept telling myself to grow up. Howard was to all appearances a very sincere fellow, with football shoulders that invited a leaning trust. They were going to live in Seattle (the home of Fred's ostensible uncle), where Howard would be coaching football and track.

At the reception in the church basement I had a talk with Casey, Penny, and Mildred, trying to keep to a minimum the eclectic mess my conversation was becoming.

"Beatrice, you hear about Matilda?" Penny's face was a Sunday school glimmer.

"No, Penny, how is she?"

"She died." She picked at a thread on her red dress.

"Oh, my God. What happened?"

"We bred her, she was doin' fine," Mildred said. "Then she got into the wet alfalfa. Just bloated up and keeled over."

Pure Guernsey. Letting Hayes milk her in the dark. Just keeled over.

"That's hahrible—hohrible—"

"Yep, she was the best cow we ever had. Got a new one. Holstein." Casey put his arm around Mildred's plump velvet shoulders.

"Couldn't even get the calf out," Penny said, to make sure we all knew it was the end of the line.

"That's all she wrote . . ."

I left Casey in mid-sentence and walked away. Only old people cry at weddings. I could feel the aging all over me. The mountain had more snow than ever. The dogwood tree was huge and bare. The diner was closed for winter. My violin had a cold-weather malaise. Hayes was having Christmas and his birthday in Germany. Judy was off to Seattle in a glow of sudden and chicken-frying adulthood. Matilda dead.

I felt scratchy net around my ankles and Judy's veil on the back of my neck. The laugh I'd slept with and sledded with and got drunk with shook itself onto my yuletide green. She smelled like cedar.

"Don't look now, but you're standing on a historic spot," she whispered.

I turned around, trying not to drip on her dress. Hayes giving the minister's son his first spirited piano lesson.

"Hey, don't cry. I'm the bride, I'm supposed to do it if anybody does. Will you stop it?"

"I'm trying. It's just very hard to sort it all out."

"Bitsy, I can't even tell Howard this, but I stood there and watched my whole childhood just slip away, right in front of the paunchy minister. And you know what I decided?"

"What?" I sniffled too close to her veil.

"I decided maybe when I'm eighty I'll come to terms with it."

"Judy, stop that dumb crying yourself. You gonna take the Flexible Flyer to Seattle?"

"No. Jesus, there's not enough room in the Porsche for my whole childhood!"

"Don't tell anybody, but a white bride and a green bridesmaid dripping all over each other is too pukey for—"

"Bitsy, you know what I'm gonna wear to your debauched wedding?"

"What?" Hayes would make damn sure nobody cried under the dogwood tree. He might make some long, specifically libidinous speech and cause the Presbyterians to faint, but nobody was going to cry.

She leaned into my ear. "Absolutely nothing!"

We kissed too quickly for anything but best friends, and she was off like Disney on Parade.

Old Judy.

PDX to BDL. To classes, wrapped tight in a striped six-footer some Harvard guy had given me, the part over my mouth hanging with half-inch icicles. One thing you could say for New England, they sure knew how to have a cold winter. The snow wasn't six feet deep like Oregon's, but the air had an insistent way of getting frigid and staying that way. I pictured myself trying to zip the Rances' parkas with immobilized fingers.

I tried to stop biting my fingernails. I couldn't even remember when I'd started, but I thought it was maybe at St. Maggie's. Along about the time M3 pointed out the stark puerility of my letter to Hayes. I mentally thanked her; I'd never sent him one since that had that sloshy stuff in it.

Sometimes I felt surrounded by skiers. Especially at Williams and Dartmouth. I wasn't such a hot skier, and it wasn't like Mount Hood, and I was studying pretty intensely, but every once in a while I took off on a Blue Card and did it.

I remember one weekend at Dartmouth, watching a couple of Smith girls trying to learn the very most basic stuff. They could hardly snowplow, they fell down on the ropetow, hanging on and laughing with pageboys flipping under their tassled fastcaps. I thought of myself trying to figure out Shakespeare's sexual metaphors, and Episcopalian kneeling. My date and I were behind them on the tow, and we had to scoot out around them when we got off. They didn't start down right away, they stood around laughing and trying to plot out their path, staring off at the pink hills in the late afternoon sun.

My date told them to hurry and go on down, that they'd figure out which ways to turn on the way. He was a nice guy, one who didn't keep putting his hands all over my chest all the time but who'd infuriated the housemother one Sunday night by shouting as I came down the front stairs, "*There's* my warm body!" in front of about four parents saying goodbye to their daughters. It was just reminiscent enough of Hayes to be in delightfully bad taste. His name was Moose or Rat or something.

Eventually the girls took off, terrifically unsure, into the satiny air, my date quite nicely hollering encouragement as they started down. He was right. They did figure out which ways to turn as they went.

I think he was the one with the speech about the violin. After putting in about four hours on the slopes, he put on a Segovia record and a dripping candle within arm's length. A couch, of course, and candled shadows rolling around the walls. Apparently I hadn't told him I was a musician.

"The body is like a—" puff, puff, "—a *violin*, Bitsy, you have to learn to—" puff, puff, "*play* it, to make it *respond*—" puff, puff, "—to respond to your *touch*, let me *teach* you—" puff, puff. He had no idea why I was laughing in total disregard of the great Segovia's finesse. It wasn't nice to laugh, not nice at all. But I was doubled up with hysterics. Hayes would think it was the funniest thing that had happened in weeks. It probably was.

The Kingston Trio sang something about teaching little fingers to play, but I was off the couch anyway. Wondering why the Segovia-playing, candle-lighting hopeful violin teacher didn't want me to rub his back which he'd said was sore from carting two pairs of skis around.

The next day on the slopes, bright with winter sun and snow-flakes melting on my cheeks but not on my glasses, I noticed that both Smith girls had figured out their own version of a stem Christie.

Dear Bitsy,

How can I say the horseshit that this is?

Bavaria and environs: beautiful, lyrical, charming to a fault. Smutted with the spectre of the u.s. army marching club. Germany is rebuilt. Yes indeed.

The cold war. The day-to-day war. Take your pick. They're playing a convoluted game with the country that produced Goethe, Wagner, Hitler, some mighty fine beer and months of blatantly meaningless war games for yours truly. One of our u.s. soldierboys on highly significant guard duty shot an old woman who was picking through the garbage. For the cause of peace, Bitsy. Don't look for it in the papers.

Macht nichts. That's what they say around here when they tell you it don't mean shit.

Freak is rotting in jail with his conscience intact.

Study your little head off, Bitsy. Don't worry about being First Lady. I ain't gonna bother. Or maybe I will. If I do, you can be the first one to parade around the White House in Recessive Jeans.

Read lots of T. S. Eliot. Do right and do good. Sit your sweet little self down and write me a nice letter. I'm gonna go out and lift up the front end of a jeep.

Love,

H

I managed to couple T. S. Eliot with James Joyce in three weeks.

TSE and JJ spoke to me of quite concrete forms of horseshit afoot in the world, and with more than translucent eloquence. But neither of them explained why a u.s. soldierboy shot a woman picking through garbage. Nor did the newspapers.

I was still looking for God, but God didn't seem to have a hell of a huge desire to explain it either. So I went on with Shakespeare and T. S. Eliot and James Joyce and art history. In the most convoluted of ways I felt my classical education beginning to take hold.

But I was tired of the triangular categorizing of guys. They were three places. In Germany playing blatantly meaningless war games and lifting jeeps, on the other side of lecterns with reflecting bifocals between them and their notes, or trying to get you to lie down on some fraternity couch with them. It looked like monstrously poor planning on someone's part.

When I asked Gayle what she thought about it, she said I was too young to try to be a philosopher or a sociologist, that my hair was nasty, brutish and short—and that I hadn't played my violin in a month.

"A month, Gayle? How did that happen?"

"Jesus, you've been at the books like you had some chronic reading disease. If you don't watch out, you're gonna end up a Phi Bet or something. Have you always been like this?"

I flicked a thumbnail over the ends of my fingers. She was right; the calluses weren't their usual selves. "No, not always. Before I met Hayes I hadn't read a—"

"Hot damn, Bitsy, do me three favors. Stop talking about that creep in Germany. Start playing your violin a little more, I like to hear you. And be willing to put your damned books away before two A.M. for a few nights. I want to get some sleep."

I took both Nietzsche and James Joyce to bed with me with a flashlight.

That was about the time I caught myself picking up another regionalism. It amounted to taking off my glasses and holding one earpiece in my teeth, little finger stuck out in the antepenultimate moment before gulping out the pithy cerebrations of "one" regarding the changing faces of the contemporary philosophical experience, the divine right of kings, the ulterior if relative conflict between reason and unreason in *Moby Dick*. It looked funniest of all when I applied it to the unprompted recitations of Salinger, which I was doing less often, anyway. Parts of it I couldn't even remember anymore.

Alumnae seemed to drift into a polysyllabic plexus of names. They became people like Mrs. W. Hinkley Whiteside Hoynes (Muffy Hoynes) or Mrs. Benjamin A. Mandelbaum (Toto Mandelbaum). They made generous and menopausal gifts to the museum and library. Or they became Lavinia Chong Rhomstadter, Ph.D., translator of Chinese, who declined honorary degrees. I couldn't tell if they'd figured out life's myriad mysteries or not. I hoped so.

Hayes wrote that we wouldn't have paintings of mallards and fox hunts in the dining room. I thought there might be a slight connection there, but I couldn't figure out what it was. I wasn't against mallards any more than I was against menopausal gifts or Chinese translation, if they helped in the figuring out. I decided it was kind of like the Gnostics and T. S. Eliot. It would all fit together eventually. And I didn't know whether that decision made me more effete or less effete, and more or less effete than what. I wished to hell Hayes would get himself back from Germany and explain it.

We went for months without writing each other. Actually, Hayes started it, I just copied him in a mindless sort of way. And his letters were getting more scrawly all the time.

> *Dear Bitsy,*
> *They've gotten me. The ludicrousness of it confounds even my raw sense of humor. To wit: one of our finest in green, whose crystalline judgment and alertness aren't winning any awards, while cleaning his shiny weapon of peace, blew off the end of my goddamn finger. My writing hand. Prepare yourself for someone who can't even make a guileless, graceful gesture of contempt with decent aplomb. My middle finger, Bitsy. The absurdity grows, multiplies, creeps around us.*
>
> *I have a wrily ominous sense that something's wrong. Shot my chances of ever being an oboe player all to hell.*
> *But I'm getting out of here in a while. Save me a place in bed.*
> *My goddamn hand hurts.*
> *Love,*
> *H*

"One" hardly knew what to say. But she tried. The pain. The ludicrousness. The changing faces of the contemporary philosophical experience. The ulterior conflict. "One" applied most of what she could get on paper of TSE, JJ, and bits of Nietzsche and MD to the impossible task of making up for the absurd carelessness of one of Uncle Sam's finest in green, adding in agile grasp that it could be worse. It could be a real war. "One" even typed the letter, to show how grown up she was.

Hayes was one of the few guys I knew whom I'd never seen make that gesture, anyway.

I checked my bank account and the travel agency, but I didn't have enough money to go to Germany, or a passport. Besides, I had a history test coming up.

I began to think we ought to live in Sweden, which my history professor called "that nahsty little neutral country."

Gayle decided one night after we'd been out drinking beer that we should make a list of the guys we really liked. And that we had to do it at our own desks and not sneak a look until we finished. We had to write reasons.

My list:

one virtuoso swimmer from Amherst: because he's the only boy who knows about the mole on my breast and is keeping quiet about it. And because he wrote me a postcard at four A.M. once to tell me how excited he was about JJ (James Joyce).

one Phi Beta Kappa premed: because he said in a drunken and lugubrious moment that I was the only person who understood him and because he saves his sleekest raunchy jokes for me.

one carillon player: because he risked getting his key impounded just so I could play the carillons in the middle of the night, and because I like his airedale.

my Shakespeare professor: because he cried when he read "Let us sit down upon the ground and tell the stories of the deaths of kings" in class, and because he drinks beer with me.

the guy who works at the coffee shop: because he doesn't mind that I can never remember how much anything costs.

one clarinet player: because he taught me who Sydney Bechet was, and writes sexy if artificial poems to me and gave me a book of Rilke.

my brother: because he has strength of character.

one jailed blond guitar-player: because he was smart enough to stay out of the Army.

Fritz: because he's ecumenical as hell and taught me my favorite hobby.

my new violin teacher: because he hasn't tried to push a third kind of bowing on me, even though he plays in the Boston Symphony.

Hayes: because he made me what I am today, whatever that is, and because I wish he were here instead of lifting jeeps in Germany with a short hand.

Gayle finished her list before I did.

Her list:

> My math professor inasmuch as he agrees with my extremely analytical position that history is a pile of caribou crap
>
> My Shakespeare professor inasmuch as he didn't object to my view of Lady Macbeth as a manic-depressive
>
> My father inasmuch as he survived alcoholism and our family for awhile
>
> My brother inasmuch as he lives with my father and keeps him off the bottle
>
> Eugene, who's been accepted into graduate school and inasmuch as he's the only moral idealist I can stand to be around I'm going to marry him this June

"Gayle, you're kidding." I sat down on the floor.

"No, I'm not. I just sort of didn't know how to tell you."

Why couldn't people just say those things, without being parabolic and writing them on a chilly, margined sheet of paper? What were they, afraid of their own voices?

"You're going to—"

"Listen, Bitsy, don't talk to me about throwing my education away, or blowing my chances to be a philosopher or something—"

"I'm not, Gayle. It's our highest office—"

"Stop being sarcastic, Bitsy. There ain't no highest office. But when the world is an enormous mix of love and striving and zebra manure, I'm just gonna get that first third while I can. Can you understand that?"

"I understand. But it's oversimplifying—"

She stood up and opened the window. "Bitsy, I am *so tired* of sitting around writing papers on how everybody oversimplifies— and going into big, empty paragraphs trying to make something complicated out of a word with three different translations—just so somebody can follow my twisted logic and decide whether it's A-minus or B-plus twisted logic—I could simply scream with it all. Aren't you?"

"No, Gayle, I'm really not. And I don't think that's what it's about, anyway . . ."

"Well, you've got that smutted Bavarian bivouac person to get

your education for. With a fragment of his moral idealism shot off.
We're really talking about the same thing."

I pulled at the fringe of the Alimony rug. "Gayle, maybe it's
because you were valedictorian or something, but I don't understand you all the time."

"Will you forget the valedictorian part? I think that's something
they hang on people to make them feel guilty when they don't come
up with A-pluses in everything from bike-riding to history to
love-making. It's a plot, just like everything else."

"Jesus, Gayle. One finds it so very nebulous, you know . . ." I
had the earpiece of my glasses in my mouth.

She threw her dictionary at me.

So Gayle, whether she admitted it or not, was headed for an
A-plus in love-making. She didn't stop studying altogether, but she
spent a lot of time putting scrolly E's up and down the margin of her
history book. Shades of my pre-Gnostic days with Father Payre.
And I felt as if I were standing on the gangplank of the Ark,
watching everybody rush in, two by horny two. Everybody was in
such a damn hurry.

I was having a horrible (hahrible) time finding God. I blamed it
on the Gnostics. If they hadn't come out with their accursed why's
and how's and whether's, I'd have stayed with Hayes's interpretation. On the other hand, if he hadn't come along, I might have stuck
with the crayoned coats of many colors and the Baby Jesus jazz.
Maybe the 1,352 hours in church had something to do with the
elusiveness of God.

Some glorious truth. Exploding in my face like a huge bouquet
of quintessentially radiant flowers. The old landscape architect. I'd
frankly gotten nowhere. I had the feeling someone was playing a
bleak and cunning cosmic joke. Just how bleak, and just how
cunning, I was to find out within a few months.

There were two other things I didn't know anything about:
money and sex. I never knew how much was in my bank account,
whether I'd have enough for a round-trip ticket to New Haven. I'd
sit in the smoky coffee shop that always smelled as if someone had
forgotten a dozen cheese sandwiches on the grill, not knowing
whether I'd be able to pay for the sandwich I'd just ordered.

The sex discussions I'd had with Judy and Beth had undergone
an undergraduate (u/g) change, and now took place among five or

six girls in curlers and nail polish, with copies of *McCall's* open on the bed and JJ, James MacGregor Burns, and I. A. Richards closed on the floor. I think it was the symposium quality that caused me to limit my appearances to fetching or returning a set of notes.

"Hey, can I come in?" I'd ask at the edge of the stacked spiral notebooks.

"Sure, Bitsy. Anyway, he said he just wanted to put his hand there, not anything else—"

"I just want the history notes, okay? I missed the Reign of Terror."

"Yeah, you can take them when you leave."

"So, did you let him?" asked the curlers.

"Well, we were double-dating with Katsy, but I—"

"Seriously, I just want the history—is this it?" Fumbling through the spirals, catching a wiry end on my sweater.

"Stick around, we're getting to the good part. Don't you want to hear?" The room smelled like Ban roll-on.

"Well, I'd already let Jeff and I'd let Harvey, so—"

"I'll just take the notebook, you can have it in the morning." And I'd get the hell out. Hayes would think I'd gone down the tube with a thud if I listened to stories about how a horse's ass named Harvey put or didn't put his hand on something round and private that belonged specifically to the vulnerable and letting Muffy.

So I settled for D. H. Lawrence. I was probably the only person who read *Women in Love* without knowing they were actually doing it. I had to read it twice to find out. Then a copy of *Lady Chatterley's Lover* fell into my hands. Courtesy, I think, of the premed who saved his jokes for me. I read a lot of talk and considerable sex, deciding I was doing two valuable things at once: getting literate and getting sexy.

Hayes's next letter, written with the bandages off, sounded off on nine different philosophical points, none of which made much sense to me except to indicate that he was now a socialist, and to imply that I'd better do a hell of a lot of studying if I was going to keep up. He wanted to know what the hell I'd gone and memorized the entire *Wasteland* for.

I'd gone and done it because I thought that was the sort of thing he wanted me to do. Men certainly had weird quirks. Still, I wasn't in a peacetime war with a lost part of a finger.

I didn't know why Gayle carried a paper bag into the history final. Until we sat down with our Yellowbooks. I started looking over the questions, knuckles to upper lip, and she picked up the paper bag and did an outrageous thing. Into a copped bowl she crumbled about ten graham crackers and poured a carton of milk over them, took out a copped spoon and ate the whole thing, using the Yellowbook as a placemat. Then she picked herself up and walked out.

I tried to get the whole tangled saga of western civilization (second semester) into one and two-thirds Yellowbooks.

> Discuss the historical governmental processes of evolution versus revolution, with specific reference to . . .

When I finished my climactic sentence—"If France had had fewer kings and more queens, one can't help positing less bloodshed in the tangled saga of French history . . ."—I biked back to the House and found Gayle up to her elbows in Woolite, washing socks in the shampoo-smelling bathroom.

"Gayle, you might just tell me what that was all about." I started to wash my face.

"The snack? My small way of telling them what I think of the exam system. A crazy, ill-conceived witticism."

"You can't just do that." I turned on the hot water. "That's just not the sort of thing you do with your—"

"You think exams are an education? Think again, country hick. Do you think exams make any difference?"

"Not really. But how do you expect—"

"What I expect has nothing to do with some insane bunch of centuries in a Yellowbook. What I expect is—in the way of sense-making—I expect that in a few weeks I'll be married and doing some real living for a change."

I stood up, suds on my face. She had suds up her arms. "Gayle, I don't think that's very sane of you."

"You think exams are sane? You're crazy. Was it hard?"

"It was evolution versus revolution."

She hipped the sink and sloshed suds onto her jeans. "That again. I think I'd have aced it."

"Gayle, why didn't you try?"

"I told you. It doesn't make any difference. When you and that mountain-climber get together, you're gonna know I'm right."

My history professor thought my logic was a bit twisted, but my grades were good enough to keep the scholarship. Gayle got hold of her files and tore them up. I thought you had to have a hell of a lot of nerve to do that, whether it made sense or not in your whimsical interpretation of the academic system. It wasn't quite like burning a diary after you'd just pruned off all your hair and gotten glasses and been tossed out of the family bosom. Gayle's was more of a grandiloquent gesture, the kind Hayes couldn't make with any kind of satisfaction with his left hand anymore.

And so, one precocious, recalcitrant, determined daughter of a Chicago alcoholic made a temporary exit from the scene. What I didn't know about Gayle was that something more puissant than the canoeing, biking, and coffee-drinking arguments was going to render her, within a relatively short time, a figure that would make Jesus Christ look like a crunching and virulent misanthrope.

eight

BDL to PDX. I was getting used to seeing Mount Hood through airplane windows, and I wondered if anybody else on board had ever been on top of it.

I spent the summer being a camp counselor in Oregon and getting ready for Hayes to hit Harvard Law School in the fall. It was great being in the woods again. You could see Mount Hood in the most deliciously super-postcard panorama right over the dead-white-tree-rimmed lake, and at the right time of day the water reflection provided two mountains, one upside down.

My violin didn't go with me to camp. Mostly because I couldn't stand how badly I played. I just hiked around, swam, picked huckleberries with my little girls, sang sloshy songs around the campfire, and watched squirrels and raccoons. I read *Point Counter Point* and started to let my hair grow out.

September. Harvard Law School. My virginity and the Kingston Trio would be laid to rest. Very nice, with one strangling exception: was I going to be ready, smart enough, urbane enough, polysyllabic enough, all that?

Dear Bitsy,

    It looks as if Harvard wants me. When you meet me at exactly two P.M. at the information booth at Grand Central Station on Sept. 11, I'll bring you up to date on the goings-on of our blessed boys in green around here. While we're driving or training (not sure which) to Boston later in the day I'll fill you in on some of the more xenogamous workings of my fuddled mind. During the orgy we're going to have in Cambridge at the home of a friend of mine I'll talk your head off about the world, the cold war, the warm war. Which brings your little form to mind.

    Will I recognize you? Is your hair still short? Will you recognize me in my quasi-deranged state? Just look for the telltale left hand.

    Plan to spend several licentious days in Cambridge before I put your exhausted, spent little self on a train for the beginning of your classes. Hypnotized by the awesome strength of my ardors. We shall send out for pizza once a day. We shall break, at the very least, forty-seven and a half cultural barriers. You may even find time to recite passages from The Wasteland.

    Freak is due to get sprung soon. He's been a good boy. Someone at Stanford is willing to take a risk and has sneaked him a teaching fellowship. He says he'll give it a year and then take to the hills of Minnesota.

    Two P.M. Sept. 11. Sharp.

                   Eager to get out of here,

                       H

According to the date, the letter had taken forty-two days to get to Oregon. It arrived September 9. I hadn't planned to leave for a week. Fritz and I were to play for someone's wedding reception, but both he and Mother understood, especially when I left out the parts about licentious and hynotized. I wasn't too sure about those parts myself. What if the Kingston Trio had something super-powerful up their sleeves? I threw my doubts and my clothes in a suitcase, got the first plane reservation I could, and hopped aboard at PDX, aimed for IDL.

Mechanical difficulties, the favorite euphemism of the airlines, downed us in Minneapolis. They found another plane for us, I tried not looking at my watch, we got to IDL at 1:38 P.M.

Every fingernail on my right hand disappeared on the limousine ride. I tore into Grand Central near heart attack at 2:26. He'd be leaning on the information counter saying, "Bits, my own true better-late-than-never love, what the hell took you so long?"

But he wasn't. I circled it three times, violin case bashing into people. The guys behind the counter said there wasn't any message. He could have thought of something.

He had. A page from the *New York Times* was Scotch-taped to the side of the information booth, rib level. My ribs. Crayoned on it, between two torn-off ends, was

TS I COULDN'T WA

Bits I couldn't wait. TS I COULDN'T WA. No phone number for the friend in Cambridge. I sat on my suitcase, looked up into the imitation heavens with their gold-leaf imitation stars, and swore. Methodically I picked them off, one Zodiac sign after the other, cursing every one. I spewed an effluvium of profanity at Capricorn, at Virgo, at Libra and the others, going round and round the dome, and didn't stop until I'd castigated kindly old Ursa Major with some vile scatological fragments I'd picked up from D. H. Lawrence and in front of fraternity fireplaces.

Drooping on a suitcase, both arms hugging a violin, torn *Times* in one fingernail-bitten hand sat someone almost old enough to vote, her head crammed with literature, history, and ontological scribblings, three thousand miles from home, staring straight up in the alleged direction of an alleged God, stalling for time and measuring out the dirtiest words she could think of in a low, tired voice.

Her accent was part Pacific Northwest residual dust bowl, part New England Ivy League seminar room. And if you'd asked her where she belonged, she wouldn't have been able to tell you.

I got to Northampton much too soon. Nothing was happening except that a friend of mine at Amherst was back early, working on a huge chemistry experiment that he was trying to win an award with. We went out and got quietly drunk, he took me back to the House and I played my violin late into the night. I'd never heard anybody play so badly. Nobody was around but the housemother. The whole House smelled like mothballs.

I switched out of a psychology course into Bach and Handel. I had to do some fancy talking because sophomores weren't supposed to take it, but they decided, with a warning that I'd be in too deep, to let me go ahead. I knew what I was doing. I could figure out Bach and Handel much better than I could figure out psychology.

Dear Bitsy,

I hope you got my message.

As you may notice from the postmark, we have an unexpected little turn of events. Briefly, the facts are these. I ran afoul of some high-ranking folk who deemed it consummately whimsical to shit all over the Harvard Law School papers, not to mention holding them up eight lousy weeks and then seeing to it that they got sent by boat. Harvard found fault not primarily with the shitting but with the delay.

Ergo, I'm at the U. of Michigan Law School. Heart of America. I couldn't wait in New York because I had to get my ass out here to be sure they'd take me. I'm now chiefly occupied with going to class and alienating everyone within earshot with my candid observations on the pile of capitalistic hogshit that builds daily, threatening to seep in and drown us all. But perhaps I've mentioned this to you before.

We've been breeding dogs and cattle for years, as you well know. Why can't we do a little selective breeding with goddamn people? And while we're on the subject, let's consider how American youth would present fewer problems if they had compulsory drill periods in elementary school and got slapped on the sides of their heads a little more often.

Maybe I'll try South America. Want to come along?

Where are you? What are you doing? Quo vadis? I note a letter from you dated several months ago, in which you report loving Vivaldi and Sibelius, being lousy in history, being confused by Nietzsche, falling apart over Ulysses, etc. By now you should have categorized your academic interests. But be careful about trying to impress me with endeavors that don't interest me.

You also report, with not uncharming embroidery, having found Lady Chatterley somewhat too sleepy, and her ardent gamekeeper rather lacking in "the right kind" of conversational expertise. I hope you've finished the book by now. Men are men, Bitsy.

Set some of your own conversational expertise on paper. Send it to me. When are you going to send a picture?

Would you care to hear my definitive statement on the condition of the world? It sucks.

What has the Kingston Trio got to do with anything?

Let me know how you're doing in your snotty girly place. Read Proust.

Angry as all hell,
H

So. The shitheads had probably got my delayed letter on a boat, too. Part of me was a little relieved that he didn't have to find me unfinished yet.

But there was another part of me that went to the phone probably twenty times in the next week, only to trek up the stairs again, my jeans jangling with unspent change. How in the world was I going to talk to that person?

Look here, Hayes, what the hell has happened to you?

Do I want to go to South America with you? You bet your sweet ass I do. That's why I'm here, you creep, getting all studied and clever, just so I can keep you elegantly stimulated company on those voyages. Do I want to go to South America with you? I'll go swimming in the Amazon and get eaten by a piranha with you. I'll lie naked in the sun and get bitten by the tsetse flies with you. You've got to be kidding when you ask if I want to.

But there are a couple of things we'd better clear up. Drill periods? Slaps on the side of the head? Wait just a holy God-damn minute! Those kids I'm going to be bearing you? At the rate of nine months apiece? Those beauties of fresh air and sunlit innocence with flying locks of hair? The ones who're never gonna have to lie? Not those kids, buster. You slap those kids, those Rances, on the sides of their heads and you'll have yourself a large problem with their mother. I've been slapped, and thrown out of my home, and drilled in and out of chapel, and I'm not so very lyrically much the better for it. Do you really think you're better off because somebody's shot your finger? After you slap the kids on the sides of their heads, you want to go on and shoot them in the fingers?

Those kids we're gonna have, the ones I'm gonna carry around inside me and push screaming and bleeding out of me for your inspection, your adoration, your smile? Not those kids. You slap those kids and I swear I'll—

You're quite acidly critical of what I write to you, aren't you? I should have categorized my academic interests? I'm trying, I'm trying. There's a lot coming in my eyes and ears, stuff I've never had before, I'm trying to categorize. Okay, I'll read Proust. Is that gonna teach me to categorize?

Which of my endeavors don't interest you? Which of my curiosities don't you like? Maybe you'd better elaborate. I've got lots more you might not like, either. Shall I tell you how I cry when I lie in the grass and think about e.e. cummings? How he says

i carry your heart (i carry it in my heart)

Shall I tell you about that? Or won't that interest you either?

You want to deflower me? Send me shooting to the end of the stars and back? Say the word, and I'll hop a plane. But are you gonna laugh at me for bringing my violin? Should I arrive with Nietzsche? I'll be in Ann Arbor in a few hours—even if I haven't figured out what love is when you fall into it. Should I arrive with my hands ready to slap the first kid I see? Should I be a walking categorization of my academic interests? I'm nineteen years old, Hayes, give me a few minutes—

I've been scooting out from under guys on couches for quite a while now. *That's* what the Kingston Trio has to do with.

Yes, I'll go to South America with you, with the piranhas and tsetse flies, I'll be deflowered by you, but are you gonna treat me like—

And you want to know what else I think, Hayes? I think it doesn't matter too much whether you live socialist or capitalist or what, just so long as you live with somebody you love and tell the truth all the time and have babies you love and sing songs together and laugh a lot. That's what I think. You want to tell me how puerile that is? Maybe we'd better talk about that, too. It seems I used to know a mountain-climber who would understand precisely what I'm talking about. But I could be wrong—

You frankly scare me a little. I don't know if you'll scare me in person. How can I love somebody desperately who's gonna—

And that's why I kept trekking up the stairs again, away from the phone. Instead, I wrote "It's okay about New York" on a piece of paper and left it on my desk. I couldn't think of any expertise to follow. Three weeks later I found it and reminded myself to do something about it. When I'd figured out what. To do about it.

I'm reasonably sure Hayes made similar abortive trips to and from the phone. But it's one of several things I didn't ask him about.

Gayle was in her tiny graduate-school apartment in Princeton, and I did my note-taking alone, proceeding to learn how to talk in parabolic paragraphs. As a matter of fact, I was getting close.

Dear Hayes,
  It's okay about New York.
  The veritable phenomenon of existence, when one examines it by supra-rational or sub-rational process, reveals itself solely and uniquely as a consummately authentic act of

Into the wastebasket. He wanted that stuff and he didn't. What the hell did he want?

It was a grey quandary I was in. I wandered around with thick books under my strong arms, reading feverishly for the revelation. In the gray light. To categorize my academic interests. To make some sense. Through a very tiny window at the top of my gray quandary, an uninvited Frenchman named Albert Camus made a sideways appearance, but I barely noticed him. Looking back on his sideways entry, it's abundantly clear that I should have paid more attention.

Maybe that kid-slapping was a phase Hayes was going through, like Debbie Reynolds, the Gnostics and a lot else. To the phone again.

  Look here, Hayes, I don't know what to write to you, I don't know how to categorize my academic interests—is that a test I have to pass or something? You must have been going through a phase, all that about kid-slapping . . .
  I have this feeling you don't approve of me, and besides, my words get all twisted, in the antepenultimate moment before I say something I forget what it is, or . . .
  Do you not want me to play the violin?
  I'd love to be deflowered by you, but not until you sort of approve of me a little more, you know, not until—that kind of thing is important to a girl, it really is, Hayes, and besides, I'm still working on what love is when you fall into it, and . . .
  You use to approve of me—didn't you? Didn't you?
  Are you enjoying law school? What do you mean, I don't sound like myself?

  i carry your heart (i carry it in my heart)

Back up the stairs, away from the phone, nickels and dimes and quarters jeering against each other in the pocket of my jeans.

Friend Beatrice,
  I'm getting hot shit grades.

What in god's (note lower case) screwed-up universe is up with you? Broke both your arms? Gone to sleep under an acrid gamekeeper? Read Magic Mountain. *I'm reading Walt Kelly. Write me a paragraph or two. Let's not reduce this thing to christmas cards.*

I still like people in the abstract.

Love,
H

Nothing was up with me. Aside from Bach and Handel, everything was gray. Like my quandary.

Dear Hayes,
    It's okay about New York.
    The changing face of the contemporary philosophical experience, the harsh empirical maxims with which it becomes overweaningly necessary for the human soul to comfort itself, render

Oh my God. Categorizing my academic interests? Every time I picked up a pen that crazy stuff came out. Every time I opened my mouth. A strenuously flatulent compendium of false, tormented, obscene, humiliating, inverted Faustian wheeze.

I couldn't even order a grilled cheese sandwich in my native tongue anymore.

Dear Hayes,
    It's okay about New York.
    No, I haven't broken both my arms. I'm trying to categorize and theorize and memorize and itemize and legitimize and rationalize and focus my eyes and dot my i's and hold onto the agile grasp, too. And I still idolize you. Sometimes you seem like a creep, but there it is, I adore you.
    I've never even met a gamekeeper.
    It's kind of gray around here. You know I haven't had a real laugh in months?

I thought I wrote that one, but I must have dreamed it. When I wasn't having nightmares.

BDL to PDX. Mother and Fritz thought that one postcard since September was somewhat inadequate. I tried to explain the subrational process of examining the authentic act of living, and Fritz suggested some duets. I played as if I'd traded left hands with

Hayes, but Fritz didn't mention it. Tree-hunting with my brother. I let him choose it, while I stared into the gray sky. Christmas dinner with the poor. I didn't notice what they smelled like.

A Christmas card from Hayes. I hadn't thought he was the kind. I opened it at the historic dining room table, where Mother had thrown me out, around which the cocker spaniels had scooted in their search for the life process, where Mother and I'd discussed Chicago, where we'd had sherry and pheasant to celebrate the wedding.

A leering Santa, riding a donkey, toting a sideways evergreen tree. Scribbled inside:

Where are you? I don't know whether to go east or west to see you.

Love,
H

Quite fancy existential question. He did have a way of driving to the heart of things.

PDX to BDL. My quandary was gray as all cold hell.

I don't even remember January, February, and March.

Spring made her stirrings known in an exhaustive variety of ways, some elegantly Chaucerian. Among them, a giddy breeze that blew fragrantly right up my shirtsleeves one morning as I walked down the hill past Paradise Pond to Sage Hall to practice some Vivaldi. I couldn't remember having smelled anything for months.

Wow, Yes, There it is! By surprise! What love is when you fall into it! It was something about all your five senses knocking you out with their reach, their embrace, their hunger and their song, their golden sunshiny quintessence, the whole firmament right there in a blinding flash, taking you in and screaming at you with a harmony you only hear once in your life, a melting beauty of all the colors in the universe boiling over you in a roseate flare—that was what love was when you fell into it! I was being so profound I couldn't stand myself. Except that I could. Wow, could I stand myself! That was hardly the word for it!

I grabbed hold of my body, turned it a hundred eighty degrees, humming the sweetest of Vivaldi springs, passing two or three frisbee games on the way back to the Quad. I put the violin under the bed, grabbed a yellow legal pad and a pen and sat under a maple tree. Roots digging into my blissful rear end, I tried to write in agile grasp, but I know a little Chaucer, TSE and Vivaldi slipped in. Not to mention snippets of Proust and the rest. What the hell, I said, at this point in our lives, what with Hayes's markedly fervent scowling cynicism and my gray quandary, the motive is what counts. And my motive was one he had to applaud. My motive was, in a word, lust. Complicated by an inordinate amount of Wow, Yes, There it is.

I was cagey, though. I wrote the sexiest letter I knew how to write without actually saying the words. The hypnotizing, rampantly florid, exhaustive, pizza-ridden sex would be my delightful little surprise. I wrote eight and a half pages of love and green growing things and rebirth.

I couldn't remember how long it'd been since I'd written him. Months, I supposed. I didn't mention the gray quandary—he certainly wouldn't want to hear that stuff from his sunshiny love. His sunshiny love who'd finally figured out what love is when you fall into it. I thanked God (whoever God was) that old Hayes had been so patient with me.

I'm coming to Ann Arbor. After exams. Hang onto your flying lock of hair, old Hayes. I'm going west! And have I got a delightful little surprise for you once I get there!

I put a snapshot in (finally), rushed to the nearest mailbox, threw the whole huge envelope down the chute with a trilling flourish, and headed for Green Street.

To buy sneaky underwear. They had it on Green Street; you just had to say it was a shower gift for somebody exactly your size.

I wrote two electrifying papers to make up for what I assumed was a winter of sloth.

> "Notes on the Final Comedy of Camus's *L'Étranger*"
> (A-plus. Original.)

> "Introductory notes on a view of Proust's room"
> (C-plus. Suggest you take a further view.)

I wondered whether the esoterica of necking I'd picked up since Hayes and I'd said not-good-bye would stand me in good stead for this affair. I had only Lady Chatterley to go on. Well, Hayes loved me, he wouldn't mind if I did some things backwards. And the Kingston Trio would be so intimidated by the Wow, Yes, There it is, they'd shake their heads in wonderment and shut up forever. My own little contribution to musical history.

And I'd explain, when I got to Ann Arbor, that when you finally figured out what love is when you fall into it, you'd never in your life even think about slapping kids around, and Hayes would laugh and say, "Sure, Bits, you're right. I was going through a phase. You're terrific, Bits, you really are!"

I had to walk everywhere, since my bike had been stolen, but I didn't mind. It was good to feel something under my feet, and besides, the grass was the kind of spring green that makes you want to roll around and make crazy, naked love with grass stains on you from head to toe. Not that I knew how. But I'd learn before the grass faded out of its loud newness into plain, dusty summer green.

I felt like jolly old reborn Scrooge on Christmas morning. A little unseasonal, but I couldn't remember Christmas anyway.

After about three days I started checking my little green mailbox almost hourly, in case he'd become delirious with joy and in its feverish excesses had decided to write special delivery.

When the *H* finally stuck laterally out of my little box, I tore it open right at the Watch desk. For somebody who'd part company with her virginity in a matter of weeks, privacy wasn't a huge priority where letters were concerned. I was going to be the most gloriously scarlet woman alive.

A small, neatly-cut clipping fell out onto my right sock. Law Review or something. I picked it up first. No, a picture of his sister . . . golly, how nice. No . . .

An impish smile peeked out from under bobbed hair. Mr. and Mrs. M.P. Something announce the engagement of their lovely daughter Nancy to Mr. Hayes . . . the lovely Nancy is a graduate of . . .

> *Dear Bitsy,*
>
> *I hate to push irony too far, but the enclosed took place two days before I got your letter. From my point of view I thought that thirteen months of silence from your end portended something like a lack of interest.*
>
> *I hope you will let me keep the picture of you since it is a reminder of many fine sentimental and romantic moments. I am just a little bitter that that's all it amounted to, though in fairness to Nancy I think we have a very good plan going.*
>
> *Not suggesting anything like being "good friends." I hope*

*this doesn't mean we can't hear from you or keep track of each
other. I wouldn't dream of coming within five hundred miles of
your orchard and not coming over for a little recapitulation,
and I hope you will feel free to drop in on us if you ever get over
this way. We're not the kind that feels any undue embarrassment
over this kind of relationship.*

Freak is coming to visit me in a few days.
Hope to see you sometime.

Love,
Hayes

It was happening to someone else. What a relief. But I was
getting to the disquieting point where I couldn't trust my rich and
dexterous imagination anymore. Coming up with scary junk like
that was wearing me out. I felt like JJ in Nighttown.

Except that when I woke up in the Infirmary and found my
clothes on a chair, the letter was still in the pocket of my jeans. I put
on the jeans. Some divagated sense of humor old Hayes had these
days. Playing a nutty joke like that on his adoring better-late-than-
never love. If he didn't watch out, I'd show up in Ann Arbor
wearing nothing but the sneaky underwear, and even the libidinous
Hayes would be embarrassed to claim me at the airport. I put on my
sneakers.

Except that the newspaper clipping was still in the envelope.
Prodigious waggery he'd come up with in the visceral heart of
America. I checked it for the frisky punchline I must have missed.

Hayes wasn't kidding.

I checked out of the Infirmary via the window and fire escape.

nine

It takes under two minutes to run from the Infirmary to the Quad on a leafy spring day with both sneakers untied, gritting a hahrible ahnvelope between your teeth and holding up your unfastened jeans. In the brisk ninety-second run, certain ineluctible realities made themselves brilliantly clear. I hoped this photogenic graduate would have nine stillborn children, grow fat and carbuncular, and drink herself to a slow, putrid death. With thoughts of taking her up some Himalayan peak and removing her rope and crampons, I wrote Hayes a letter that was little short of operatic.

* * * * *

"Bitsy, you have the distinction of sending me the nastiest letter I ever got," said the forty-nudging Hayes. I could see the lights of Fresno out the window.

"Good." I laughed and straightened my sleeves.

"But you don't answer a letter like that. Somebody tells you they hope you drown in kerosene while your wife is delivering a baby, what do you say?"

I bet he had to look up the one about "rotten Neapolitan bone-

161

ache.'' I'd got it straight out of *Shakespeare's Bawdy* and hoped the redundant splendor of syphilis-double-syphilis wasn't wasted on him.

"I don't know. What *do* you say?"

"You also said you hoped I'd get leprosy and my eyeballs would fall out on the dinner table—"

What a terrific memory the old fellow had. "Oh, Hayes, they didn't, did they?" I said in C-sharp.

"I ought to throw you off this plane, Bitsy."

"Don't. You'll go to jail, lose your job—"

"No, really." He pointed confidentially past me, left-handed, one partial finger short. "See those little screws up there on the window? You just take a nail file and you—"

"Cut it out. If you don't, I'm gonna tell them—" I raised my voice just the smallest bit, "—about the bomb you've planted in—"

He put his hand over my mouth. I bit it. He pulled it away.

"You know, you have another distinction."

"And what's that?"

"You're one of the very few women I ever knew who played absolutely, totally, no-shit fair."

I wound my watch, still on New York time.

"And that explains why I went on a six-hour drunk with Freak after reading your masterpiece of vitriol, and—"

"I hope you had the hangover of your life."

"I did, thank you very much." He grinned. "Bits, don't put any heavy meaning into this, but what was I supposed to do when you didn't write for thirteen months? Just what was I supposed to do?"

I didn't know it was thirteen months. I didn't know he'd gone through that Capricorn birthday and come out twenty-four years old. I was trying to categorize and memorize and theorize and itemize and uneffetely dot my i's and I didn't know he—

"Well, Hayes, when in doubt, trill."

"Straight, Bitsy. I don't play the violin."

My yellow wool lap had ketchup on it. Airplane rides insist on leaving their mark on you. "If you want the shitty, anachronistic truth, Hayes, you were supposed to understand. God understands."

"You're a moron."

"Wrong, Hayes. Was a moron."

"You was a moron. Did I tell you I quit law school?"

"No."

"Well, its charms began to pall fairly quickly . . ."

If he mentioned the charms of that woman, the one in the newspaper smile, I was going to need the nausea bag. Damned pedestrian name.

" . . . and I switched to political science—"

"—joining the horses' asses and pricks—"

"Bitsy, if you don't watch your language I'm gonna pull out Huxley and read, you'll miss hearing—"

"Go ahead then. The drollery of political science—"

"Bitsy, will you let me finish a sentence?"

"Sure. Tell me."

"So. I hung around taking tests and busily qualifying my ingenuous self for the foreign service . . ."

"Why didn't you hang around and work on getting yourself elected President?" Oh, yes, that's right. We had another gleaming young man with a flying lock of hair who took us into a blurred Camelot and then—

"Will you be serious for a minute? Anyway, they took me, I started my round-the-world thing—what did you do, Bits?"

"Me? Then? I didn't feel so hot for a few days, then I turned into a music major."

"That's logical."

"I thought so. As a matter of fact, I thought it rang with the most sonorous logic in the world."

* * * * * *

I made a number of errors in dealing with Hayes's dazzlingly agile dismissal of the symbiotic strawberries-and-dogwood scheme. As they used to say with a gritty semblance of credibility, the boy just pushes it in and pulls it out, but the girl gets *involved*. It becomes so *untidy* for her. She tends to *think* about it a lot.

At first I thought it was men. They shaped you, changed you, took the bits and pieces of you that looked good, layered them over with their own philosophical misdemeanors and xenogamous muddle. They gave you orders. Take Latin. Read this, read that. Hold onto your agile grasp while you're reaching out with both your pretty little arms for the classical education I'm sending you three thousand miles to get. Play your violin if you've a mind to, I'll just put egg cartons all over the place.

They created a system into which you moved with a Debbie Reynolds wiggle. They'd work away at your head, but only if you wiggled first. Read Nietzsche. Don't read Emily Dickinson. Let me know what you're thinking. Now that you've let me know what you're thinking I'll tell you what you're thinking is full of shit. Bear me three children, all named Rance, so I can slap them around from time to time. Keep plugging away. I'll have my way with some rusty earlobes whose names I don't remember, but you can take your deflowering (along with your discovery of what love is when you fall into it) and bug off.

They called you "little" all the time. Your little self. Your little form. Every time they talked to you you got shorter. It was a wonder I was still more than two feet tall.

How had we got so dependent on them in the first place? What was so splendid about a deep voice and facial hair? And that thing, whatever it was, between their legs that came equipped with its own lavish delusions of Doric, Ionic and Corinthian grandeur? Was it simply that they were the first ones up in the morning, ready to spear the local mastodon, leaving us in a feculent cave, mucking around with an agilely grasped blunt stone? And that they'd gone around thumping their chests ever since? While we admired their prodigious cleverness and sonority?

Well, of *course* hell hath no fury like one of us. Because when they scorn us they do it so Wagnerianly. Down to our liver. With marked fervor, that's how they do it. It's not like the mountain that never gave a damn about the logging business in the first place. They gave a tender, gentle, arm-sticking-out damn.

They had some divine right to push you around. James I, Charles I, Charles II, James II. We cooed at them and watched while they made themselves into little gods.

They hated to push irony too far, but did so with amazing aplomb. They up and told you one day to take a flying leap. The only thing they didn't tell you was how to execute the flying leap.

Wait a minute, I said one day in the middle of this churning rant and reason. Go back two or three of those paragraphs you've learned to think in. No, not the mastodons, go to the Jameses. Lying around one spring afternoon with nothing to do, I said, wait a holy Goddamn minute! I began to get it: the Cosmic Joke.

The Cosmic Joke

Nobody who isn't being god (note lower case) causes a mountain to laugh. Or sends light from magic fingers down its glaciers to the children of darkness. Or promises to lead a lost nation, reducing its false gods to impotence. Or has such a lot of information whose source he never discloses. Or awaits annunciations. Or preaches in an alluring new dialect. Or turns the tables in church. Or breathes life into somebody who's already dead. Or pours purifying creeping jesuses down you. Or is bafflingly tender and gentle amid gouging pain. Or feeds voraciously on your freckled trust. Or has such astonishing skill in the water. Or gets you to hearing voices. In the middle of a river. Well, why didn't He gather His Radiance up and *walk* across?

No wonder at all that the Kingston Trio in the sky wouldn't let me do it with anybody. In the most obscenely paradoxical way I was saving myself for one of them.

He could take his preposterously serene glass house with many mansions in Switzerland or maybe China and shove it rectally skyward. I hoped every wall would shatter mercilessly on the way up.

Jesus H. Christ.

I couldn't stop laughing. For days. Old Father Payre. I was clearly insane. Somebody suggested a sedative. What I needed was a mental enema.

The very strange thing about a joke like that—there is no joke like that—is that if you keep old Father Payre quite close to the top of your mind you eventually stop being insane. If you lie quite still and think about it long enough you can hear the laughter changing, way down in your liver, and you simply aren't insane anymore.

And that was how, several days later, I managed to locate and throw away twenty-seven consummately mortal letters, the good-behavior, non-belching, complete-sentence relics of my innocence. If my brother could run barefoot across fifty yards of snow, I could make that simple fleeting gesture toward strength of character.

That left only the Pogo book, the carved mountain with its inaccurate glacier, and the *Nine Stories*. We'd never been gift-givers. I'd never given him any, except the one I'd planned to offer wetly in Ann Arbor. I sent Uncle Pogo to Penny Parker. I gathered up my Salinger—all my Salinger—and hiked down the hill to a church that was having a rummage sale. I laid them down on the book table like an unwanted baby and got out before any of the smell attached itself to me. The pine mountain was sitting in Oregon in my room, along with Heifetz and Mozart.

The definitively mortal Hayes never even knew for sure that he'd have had total, absolute claim to my virginity in the Ann Arbor springtime, cherry trees blooming, or whatever blooms in Ann Arbor. I gave away the sneaky underwear, too.

Along with my mutilated innocence.

The real villain took a while to disclose itself, as real villains are so very inclined to do.

A round, graceful, whirling world that got created in a gloriously mysterious display of accidental fireworks. A world that could become so murderously muddled with anger and greed that it would turn a radiant shouter-off-mountaintops into a toter of a stinking gun. A shining thrower of beer cans into a cynical, sneering crawler under rusty barbed wire fences who hunted down a simulated enemy in peacetime. An eager, *summa cum laude* lifesaver into a scowling short-handed scribbler of *macht nichts*. A world that left its expensive little women at home with their Proust and their Nietzsche, that severed their hearts from their brains and paralyzed their writing hands, letting them wonder feverishly what the hell was going on.

It's of considerably more than academic interest to trace the history of our disenchantment through the accidental trek of Levi Strauss from Bavaria to San Francisco. A chancy capitalist who decided, part joke and part cunning vision, to give us copper-riveted pockets and indigo denim. More than a hundred years before Hayes and I privately patented, on a raft in the middle of a secluded lake, the design for Recessive Jeans. It's my own personal theory, buttressed by extensive field research, that for every one of the more than two hundred million pairs of pants that Levi has thrust on our eager, limber legs there's an emotional torn ligament, a water-on-the-knee romance with survival.

The jeans worn by the club-footed shoe salesman in Greenwich Village who fits twenty pairs of sneakers a day. The ones worn by a twelve-year-old violin student who crosses her legs whenever she has to do anything even slightly chromatic. The ones Hayes and I wore when we shouted raging, laughing love at each other and spilled beer down the denim in the sunshine.

There's innocence sewn into those orange seams. Underneath is a mutilator or mutilatee, or both.

And inside every pair of those jeans is someone who will go to war, refuse to go to war, watch someone go to war, cheer or accept or revile war, write letters to or from a wartime or peacetime war, sit at home and ponder the untidiness of war, or feel the zing of bullets and the dull muddy ooze of an abdomen seeping out onto the ground and sob, *macht nichts.*

We've been wrapped and zipped into a denim brotherhood that we can't escape. Even if we wanted to.

And that was how I managed to pull out of the incinerator twenty-seven partly seared letters—non-belching, good-behavior reminders of an innocence I'd thought was something else.

Letters like that were called Dear John's. I found that out later. It wasn't a regionalism. In the years I spent with the Muffy's, almost all of us either got one or sent one.

Like a draft notice, a dear john offered a choice of replies. Sniveling, desolate, tear-stained ones were popular among the conspicuously woeful. But they accomplished nothing beyond making you feel like a horse's ass for years, knowing that some guy had your desolate snivels and tears in a shoebox at his parents' house and that when he went home for a family funeral or something, he could skim over the tears and snivels and imagine just how Katsy looked when she splayed them out: uncombed, with mucus-y pain streaming out her nose, witless, artless, pathetically candid, bereft.

You could pretend you hadn't gotten the dear john and write one of your own, as if the U.S. mails had fallen down on their job. I knew people who did that, and who derived a hollow and temporary joy from it.

A few of the Puffy's returned the dear john with spelling and punctuation corrected. That wasn't one of my options, even if I'd thought of it. Old Hayes and I were the champion spellers and punctuators. He and I could have gone out as a syntax team. A little grease paint, a little soft shoe . . .

If Hayes had really been on his toes, he'd have been thoughtful enough to send me a singing telegram.

        I   hate to push i-ro- ny too   far

But I suppose everybody has days when they're not on their toes. Besides, that way he wouldn't have been able to send me the newspaper clipping.

I never wrote a dear john. I told a couple of guys in person, in my freckled and lip-biting way. Guys who nodded their heads, said they understood when they didn't, guys who got angry and then apologized for getting angry, guys whom I told it was okay if they got angry, guys who took their ski poles in one arm and their hurt feelings and steering wheel in the other and went off in a muscled cloud of dust. They wouldn't have understood if I'd said I knew how they felt.

But write a dear john? No. Somehow I could never come to terms with the fleet and searing eloquence of the postal flying leap.

Now, the thing I found out about the Muffy's, beetled or not, was this: there was a ruddy vigor—combined with a slender, pageboy-flipping, upper-lip-knuckling serious concern for the nebulous—that rendered the coming of age in Northampton a lifting kind of experience. Sometimes, like a primitive ski tow, it took you by ropy surprise and you went along with your ass in the snow for a while, poles and femurs akimbo, but eventually you righted yourself and held on with both arms a little shaky, and went humming right to the crest. Whereupon you disengaged yourself from the entanglements that had carried you up, set yourself in a decent if windblown position, and sailed off, bent forward, letting the gale hit your goggles and the snowflakes melt on your cheeks, scared to death and pretending you weren't, right through the trees, criss-crossing the tracks of the ones who'd gone before, and what you got was a brisk and faltering hell of a ride.

The Muffy's were good at that. Resilient, determined, even brave. They, we, jabbed ballpoint pens in every direction, took off our glasses every now and then in the antepenultimate moment, bent over our books and our canoe paddles, hunting out—yes, damn it—hunting out the quintessential. Every place we could. It wasn't our fault that, clutching Bluebooks and JJ and Nietzsche and the rest, we couldn't see our way to an ingenuous lift of the rear end, cocker spaniel style, in the living room. We were too busy trying to figure out the rest of it first.

The dean of our class made a grim and throbbing error in her greeting to us as freshmen. To wit:

> Time will tell who is who.
> Meanwhile, welcome to an even start.

The singeing transparency of her error escaped us for awhile. One by one I think we discovered it:

We were Who. Blundering through the proud open stacks, under an avalanche of creeping and quivering literacy and Yellowbooked water-on-the-knee, greasy from our bike chains, shampooed and cuticle-biting, groping after the damn primordial questions, we came out in the windy, cloudy air as bloody Who as we could bloody Be. We didn't understand all of it, but we said thank you very much and sailed off, elliptically Who.

As a somewhat wilted music major, I delayed the actual non-symbolic deflowering (N-S D) several years, until I connected with a barely malloclusive French horn player who was so stoned most of the time he couldn't find his chest, let alone thump it. I never figured out how he could play such crafty horn in that condition.

By that time the Kingston Trio had traded in their grins and their record contract in the best interests of a music-loving public.

I was a Peace Corps reject. Not so much the language problem as the fact that I couldn't pass the physical.

I eased out of "Bitsy" as smoothly as I could, and never gave a moment's serious thought to blessing Hayes with a sudden surprise career as a counter-tenor.

By the time I got to New York I wasn't buying any Brooklyn Bridges. What I was buying was a violin. Thanks to a small inheritance my father had thought to include with the johnny jump-ups by the porch steps. In a series of lucky and sensible maneuvers, I got hold of a Giusseppi Rocca some time before everybody else wanted one, making myself the envy of squadrons of violinists at orchestra auditions.

What with putting in some time at Julliard and at Marlboro, throwing uncheated fermatas and wadded paper napkins around with the musical greats in the mountains (well, not quite mountains) of Vermont, I had a hell of a lyrical ride. Eventually I gravitated to Suzuki—learning, teaching.

New York turned out to be quite full of those fellows who fancied themselves so radiantly Doric. In college they classified us in hoarse and unrhapsodic ways. They'd consider it only fair that we eventually came up with a listing of some of them.

> guys who carped if you wore a bra
> guys who carped if you didn't
> guys who insisted the fourth measure be flagrantly *attaca*
> guys who didn't care whether it was or not
> guys who lost their tempers repeatedly
> guys who never lost their tempers at all
> guys who thought Auragon was a town in Nevada
> guys who stashed their speeding tickets in the glove compartments of their Porsches and eventually made decks of playing cards out of them
> guys who were married and misunderstood
> guys who were married and all too well understood
> guys who voiced a strenuous commitment to the Third World
> guys who were rather fond of the first two
> guys with quiet integrity
> guys whom quiet integrity bored to tears
> guys with sexual problems

I'm sure I'm not the only person into whose bedroom Marlon Brando never rode a motorcycle. I can't say honestly that I wish he had. But then again, you never know. I was sure that would be the only way I'd ever find out if he talked in parentheses.

Now, old Hayes left some fascinating stuff in the wake of his swift and sleek departure, toting his volume of pelvic politics. For one thing, he caused me to take stock of my timing.

I did several things a little early in life. Having my father die at five was visibly precocious of me. Starting to play the violin at six was a bit of early ripening. Falling in love at fifteen wasn't what you'd call dragging my feet, getting kicked out of my home at sixteen indicated a tendency not to sit around, and getting on the receiving end of a dear john at nineteen, when I didn't even know what a dear john was, seemed a clear case of overeagerness.

On the other hand, I did some things late. Like begin to read books. Like figure out what things meant. Charge-a-plates and so on. Like rid myself of an unbecoming freckled trust. Anyone who's ever tried to get rid of freckles knows it doesn't happen overnight.

I admire timing. It's rare. Who's got it? Isaac Stern, Heifetz, Willie Mays, who else? Hayes? I was never quite sure.

One summer I learned how to make a drowning rescue. It's not so hard. All it takes is quick thinking and a lot of wind.

It came to me during a tenor aria in the Bach B Minor Mass in Pittsburgh, while I fingered the hem of my first-violin basic black: if Hayes had wanted a beauty, would I have spent four years under mud packs? Basketball—four years dribbling? Hockey—pucking? You had to give him credit for a little sense there. What he thrust me into so coolly turned out to be something I enjoyed, what with the brave, snowflake-melting, stem-Christying Katsy's.

People have all kinds of reverberations hanging around them. Mine was that of all the music I ever attached myself to—like tendrily, mindless moss on the north side of a pine tree—I couldn't go near the Sibelius Violin Concerto. Four months to the day after Hayes zestily pushed irony too far, Jean Sibelius died of a cerebral hemorrhage in Järvenpää. I wrote a bleakly brief note, but I don't know whether they bothered to translate it.

I had some difficulty with Brahms's First Symphony too, but that wasn't Hayes's fault. That one was my own inconclusive little project.

My brother married a lucid beauty who'd spent her youth in the fleshpots of Berkeley. Rather, on its tennis courts. She gave up something of an irresolute doubles career to live in a house they built together, across the hay field from my father's log monument.

One day she and I were rummaging through drawers in my room looking for a sweater I was sure would fit their middle child, who was banging a pair of skis around in the woodshed looking for some wax. Hot mugs of tea in our hands, we flipped through piles of old check stubs, concert programs, luggage tags and exam Bluebooks.

"Bea," she asked, her long fingers running down the thumb-length Chimney of the pine carving, "did you do this in your quixotic youth?"

"No, somebody gave it to me. Somebody who hardly sculpted at all. It's kind of an albatross thing. I don't know—I just keep it here." If it hadn't been for Sam Coleridge, people wouldn't go around talking about a squawking seabird all the time. I think it would serve us right if everybody who said they had an albatross actually had one. Around our necks.

"Somebody who didn't get the glacier right." The real glacier had moved several inches by that time, anyway.

"I know it. I told him. Anyway, he didn't live around here. We climbed Mount Hood once. He had funny s's. He started shouting on top—some metaphorical nonsense, I can't remember what . . ." I lied about that part. I remembered every word.

"He sounds like a vibrant sort."

"Yes, Tania, he was possibly the most vibrant sort I ever knew."

"What else did he do? Besides hardly sculpt?"

She sat on my lumpy bed and laughed her italicized laugh, even about the sneaky underwear. "Bea, those aren't the people you marry. Those are the people you celebrate, in a non-marrying way. I knew someone like that—or sort of like that. He came breezing through Berkeley on a Honda one day, I had a wild romance with him for about three weeks. Then he went on to Mexico, I went back to classes. You don't marry those people." The Honda fellow didn't sound quite like Hayes, but I let it go.

"And you know why you don't marry them? Either because they turn around and get like everybody else, or because they stay so unlike everybody else that you end up a one-woman banana factory from trying to live with it."

"That doesn't make any sense, Tahsh."

"I know it doesn't. But every time I hear a story like that I feel obligated to say it. Even though it's not true. Besides, that story is so wholesome it reeks."

"Tahsh, what was so hypnotic about my brother, when he came along?" The story of their meeting involved an Irish Setter, a volume of Keynesian economics, a satchel containing a small grainy packet of hashish, three milkshakes and a tennis racket, on the steps of Hoover Library. I never did get it straight.

"Hypnotic? Bea, it's so simple I have trouble making anything special out of it. He made sense. I told him I played tennis, and he said, 'Tania, I'm from the earth. Concrete hurts my feet.' And it made the most loud, echoing sense I'd heard in a long time. That's what it was about him.''

I could hear my brother saying it. Orchard boots trumping through dirt, crampons mountain-goating it up and down dead volcanoes. But shoes on city streets—they wouldn't go down right for very long. That was pretty wholesome itself.

I'd left out one part of the story.

I'd love to go home in the ebullient blue and green mountain summertime and water-ski with Tahsh on the Columbia. She can slalom, I hear. But for one reason or another I've never made it.

My brother never got drafted. Courtesy of a very unhorse's-ass law that said if you were married with kids before you were twenty-five you didn't have to go. When I think about it, it becomes a question of hating to push irony too far.

Jimmy Lee Benson lost his life when a logging truck somersaulted over a guardrail. He'd bought the truck from Casey Parker and was still paying for it. His father packed up everything and moved to California. Not quite everything. Hank Benson stayed on the mountainside, continuing to grow those incredible strawberries and romancing Penny Parker. Penny decided one day she might as well marry him. I played at their wedding, in the wintertime. She carried a bouquet of Oregon grape and red roses; she was lovely.

I had a surprise reunion after a concert in Minneapolis once. I was backstage cleaning rosin off the fingerboard of my Rocca when a pair of coveralls stood in the doorway saying "Bitsy?"

"Yeah," I said, eyes on the fingerboard. "That used to be my name." People from college tended to show up in the oddest places. "Do I know you?"

The coveralls angled sideways and said, "The mountain don't give a damn about—"

"Jesus! Freak!" Reunions like that are crazy things. One of you's balding, one of you's got two gray hairs.

"I just thought I'd come around and say hi . . ."

"Wow! Just let me get this thing put away . . ."

We sat in the green room until they closed it up, then walked around outside in the autumn evening. It had just rained and the mud puddles were oily under the streetlights.

"How's it going, Fred? I mean, what are you up to?"

"The very funny thing is, Bitsy, it's a good life."

"Sure it is, Fred. I know that. What do you do, anyway?"

"I raise chickens, I write songs, I play the guitar . . ."

"It's not hung up on a nail? Your buddy Pygmalion said it would be."

"Not anything like that. It's good, waking up in the morning, haze lying over the landscape—" Terrific pun, but I didn't mention it. "Anyway, I've got these chickens, you'd be surprised how early they get me up . . ."

"Not me, Fred. So you really have—hey, you know that e.e. cummings poem, about the uncle that had a series of farms and eventually started—"

"Yeah, I know that poem. Started a worm farm. From underneath. That's okay, too, isn't it?"

"Yes, I guess it is."

"You want to hear about Hayes?" He leaned on a red pickup, apparently his red pickup. It had one fender wired together.

"I don't know. Sure. Yeah. You ever see him?"

"They came up here once, in the winter, they've got kids galore. He's some sort of globe-trotting spectre of—he travels a lot. Foreign Service."

"Oh. That's nice, that's really nice. Say hi to him if you—no, don't, I guess."

"You want me to or not?"

"No. Hey, wait. There is one thing. I want to know if they slap the kids, Fred. I want to know that."

"God, Bitsy, I don't—no, I didn't see them do that . . ."

"Oh. Thanks, Fred."

I wasn't going to ask about the carbuncular condition of the scrutable Nancy. And Fred, bless him, didn't volunteer. "Hey, Fred, you and your chickens, and your songs, it's not that simple, is it? I mean, is it?"

"Hell no. But at least I can get around to asking some of the right questions. Like, is it guts or stupidity that separates you from a system? And like, what's justice? Things Hayes works on, too. We just do it at opposite ends of the world. Hey, you want some music?"

He reached into the cab of the pickup and got a guitar out. Of course I wanted music. Hayes tried to get at those things? Good heavens. The lord of hosts seeking justice.

Fred was strumming, tuning up, strumming again. Then he started

> Mountain strong,
> Mountain grim,
> Mountain don't care if the moon goes dim.
>
> Mountain blue,
> Mountain light—

"Fred, that's not it. Mountain *white*." I put my case on the pickup bed and opened it.

"Sorry."

> Mountain white,
> Aurora borealis in the middle of the night.
>
> Mountain cold,
> Mountain high,
> Mountain's gonna watch me when I die.

I had my violin out in time for the last verse.

> Mountain sits,
> Mountain—

"No, Bitsy, it's an E major. Listen." He did it again. I should have remembered. I did something else, on the G-string. "Hey, that's okay, Bitsy. Now, what I decided was, a bridge between— just listen to it, come in when you're ready."

I did. He'd gotten very good. We did the whole thing twice, I went in and out around the melody while he sang. "And then you need a last verse, one for the here and now," he laughed.

> Mountain is,
> Mountain are,
> Like to climb a mountain but it's too damn—

"Far!" We both hollered into the wet night.

"The definitive lyric. Revisited. You want to come and see my chickens?"

"I'd love to, Fred. But I've got a plane to catch. A rain check, okay?" I put my Rocca back in the case.

"Sure. Take it easy, will you?"

"Yeah. I will."

He put the guitar back in the pickup, got in and drove off, one fender wired together, Minnesota license plate fading away, splashed with muddy water. I took my violin into a taxi and went to the airport.

Old Freak. More brave than me, more blond than you.

What Judy did with herself made everyone on the mountainside proud, up to a point. She got tired of watching Howard coach track one day and hauled herself back to college, pregnant and all. Then with one in nursery school and one at the breast, she went to medical school. Howard abetted her effort by developing a winning track squad and getting a big salary. She took her internship between crayoned horses and spoonfuls of strained squash. Eventually she and Howard went to Canada, with a hockey player and a violin student eating ravenous lunches that they prepared themselves. Judy performed medical services for the amnesty bunch in Montreal. (That was the point.) Howard turned to the bruising business of being a hockey referee. I visited them once and played duets with their daughter, who had three pairs of wet jeans hanging on the clothesline.

A Christmas card from Beth said she almost hated to admit it, but she'd become a hotshot teacher of Latin and Greek. Her last name is a highly unpronounceable Hellenistic item. When I think about it, I've got an astonishingly consistent bunch of friends.

The last time I heard of the minister's son, he had full and desperate hold on a small pastorate in Idaho, and was working on updating certain of the Songs of Solomon with a women's committee from his congregation.

And Father Payre? God knows. St. Maggie's gracefully accepted his resignation one June day, and he made off toward the Orient. Or so said the stapled alumnae communiques, which I asked them to stop sending, and which continue to arrive, the concretely devout and unmacaroni'd girls intent on the Clearasil'd pursuit of *veritas* and whatnot. Those girls in the fund-raising blazers don't look as wary of being besmirched as we were. But appearances are as deceptive as anything else; they may be getting their thrills from hooking the communion wine. It's hard to tell from the brochures.

I eventually figured out why I smoked, beginning with Lucky Strikes in the orchard. Because that was the only thing I could do defy my mother that wouldn't get me pregnant. Or so it must have seemed in the myopia of puberty. And so, having figured it out, I stopped.

The smoking was just another terrific example of my ability to behave badly.

My brother and I sat up late one Christmas Eve with lights blinking on the tree and everyone else asleep. Snow heaped around the dogwood tree, and we talked of householding and the wicked world.

"You know, there's something I never figured out," I said, putting a log on the fire in the fieldstone fireplace that he and Tahsh had built. "That terrible summer, the—"

"The year you got excommunicated."

"Yes. You know what unglued me? Mother said I was bad. She really did. That's a rotten thing to tell a kid. Even if I asked for it, it's still—"

"Listen, Beatrice, she was a lonely, misplaced and terribly horny woman who worked too hard and held her religion by the throat and—are you seriously still bothered by that?"

I told him I was, just a little.

"Then I think you're crazy. Just think of the desperate lengths a horny person will go to dispel the anger—"

He was right. We kissed good night and he climbed into bed with Tahsh. I put on my boots and slogged across the snowy hay field.

Other folks were around, of course, even if Hayes wasn't. And with the propinquity of these other folks, the *frisson* of perineal and erolalial esoterica made a slow but not unremarkable entry into my life. Encounters with the sensual aren't always predictable or linear, and by the time I discovered some thematic variations on the subject of erogeneity, I was acquainted with several people who enthusiastically regarded foreplay as a twenty-four-second-to-shoot operation.

And between the mellifluous if hungry Shantih's of some Hindu investigation that related obliquely to the art of raga, I found that musicians, Presbyterian or not, just are very sexy people, whose lives take them to water and melody with a relentless urge to center themselves in harmony and bliss. If old Hayes had played his cards right, he could have deflowered me in the University of Michigan swimming pool (humming snatches of *La Mer*), put my relentlessly dithered and spent self on a plane and gotten back to Nancy within the next hour.

Hayes was twenty when he was ready to ravish me. I was

nineteen when I was ready to ravish him. More than. If you thought
about it, I beat him by a year.

And I never did figure out whose lipstick-stained filtertips
warmed the Chevy's ashtray that summer. Fortunately. If I had, I'd
have committed vigorous homicide. Even though I was a full-
fledged pacifist.

My mother had a stock nuptial response. It amounted to, "I hope
those two young people will be very happy." It allowed inflec-
tional variation, depending on whether one of the two young people
was pregnant, or had just finished painting the honeymoon kitchen
or receiving a degree in music or biology or home economics.
Eventually, Mother got around to asking what had happened to that
cultured and stimulating young man who'd crossed our paths in my
troublesome youth. I explained that he'd taken off connubially for
parts unknown, and Mother said she hoped those two young people
would be very happy. I'm personally very glad that this small event
took place. Because it was a lesson I'll never forget. I listened to
my mother say that and knew in a blinding flash that deep in my
heart I was no longer a Presbyterian.

And as to whether or not I was effete, more or less effete, and
more or less effete than what, I finally decided it was like trying to
get a rear view of yourself without a mirror. I don't know anybody
who knows just exactly how effete they are, although people seem
to be working on it, in that they seem to know pretty much how
effete everyone else is. You have to give people credit for trying.

I gave up trying to figure out how in the world I could have been
so dumb, when I was surrounded by valedictorians who tore up
their files and Phi Beta Kappas who hid their keys. Maybe Hayes
picked me out of the Fourth of July crowd. Maybe he said to
himself, there's the dumbest person I've ever seen.

So. Hayes had taken himself into the arena of bold thrusts,
pioneer breakthroughs, viable steps forward in restructuring
priorities and feasible microencapsulations. Good for him. If there
was anybody who'd be able to figure out what all those meant, it
just might be Hayes.

As Fred said, they traveled a lot. And Nancy doubtless spent
ample time in foreign maternity wards. As long as I never met the
fecund bride, I wouldn't tear her tweetish eyes out.

It came to me one morning in the final bars of an astounding tour de force by an unknown composer, still unknown, flourishing my battered way to the end in five fortissimo sharps: Hayes. He was out of Terry and the Pirates or something. Yecchh. And me. Norman Rockwell painted me in a hurry one day when his coffee was lukewarm and he was coming down with the flu. Double yecchh. Hayes and I were cartoons of ourselves. We barely missed being cartoons of each other, in a perverted Sunday school book.

What never occurred to me, in the busy reaches of a secular and peripatetic adulthood, fraught as those reaches were with assassinations, global hysteria and real war, was that the sprawling nebula that we call home might provide anything like—remotely like—a nudging-forty, single-reservation, air-pocketed, one-way, Huxley-toting second coming.

ten

Every airplane I've ever been on has landed like a disgruntled mountain-climber: shrugging, settling reluctantly for the unreality of the ground. I got the violin in one hand, Hayes reached under the seat and took out an attaché case that looked too bold-thrust for words.

The accordion-pleated chute gulped us in. Convoluted, whorled affection and seething distilled rage danced a fierce tarantella between my sternum and my skull as we walked side by side toward baggage claim.

(Princes, Nancy? Sometimes they bear a strong resemblance to digitally-sawed-off, cynical law students with newly-grown-out flying locks of hair who—shall I tell you about the universal thump?

Melville, of course. Thump me now, Hayes.

And Nietzsche?

God is dead. Let's get going, Hayes.

Proust?

I'll be your madeleine. Yummy Yummy Yummy!

T. S. Eliot?
April is the cruellest month. Off with your clothes!
Thomas Mann?
Climb me, Hayes! You've got it, I want it—Whooeee!
How many languages do you speak?
All of them, Hayes!
Do you like to travel?
My suitcase is packed!
Marry me, Nancy?
Ja Wohl! Do you always talk so much?)

Their wedding invitation, oddly enough, hadn't read like a UNICEF card. I know, because Hayes in his puckish exuberance had seen to it that I got on the guest list. It was in a Unitarian church. As it happened, I didn't attend for three reasons. One, I was quite busy with some mild-mannered Boccherini. Two, I couldn't decide what to wear. Three, I didn't want to see him decked out like a rented penguin.

The lanky necktied and cufflinked microencapsulator was making getting-off-plane jokes while I watched for my suitcase to come round. I picked it up and turned to shake his hand.

(Have you categorized your academic interests, Nancy?
Long ago. The trivium, the quadrivium, the . . .
Good for you, Nancy!)

"Have a good trip to Tokyo—"

"Hang on, that's my bag coming up." Why don't people say Please?

The row of taxis looked like a gas-rationing queue. He set my bag down. "Listen, Bits, concluding remarks are in order." He laughed. "I just don't know what they are."

"It's all right. I don't either. You really didn't have to carry—"

He leaned down to give me a forehead kiss. I've watched people do that in airports for years. The taxi door stood open, I got in.

"See you in another twenty years or so, Bitsy? And take care of the violin that ate Brooklyn—" He closed the door and walked away. I could imagine him walking out of feasibility meetings without saying good-bye to people. I wondered if he knew the word. A full ten seconds went by before the door opened in mid-takeoff. My Rocca lurched.

"Lady, will you share your taxi with—"

"All right, Hayes, get in then. You could break your neck—" I moved over. My new yellow skirt was looking older all the time.

"Thanks a lot, lady. Actually I've got some time before I leave for Tokyo. Where're you going?"

"Some friends. Some Suzuki friends. Tell me about Tokyo. Oh, I just thought of the concluding remarks. Thanks for the education. I'd be in a Texaco station right now if it weren't for you—"

But he had my right hand in both of his. Fourteen and two-thirds fingers. Quite warm. Warmer than I'd have thought.

"I loved you, Bits. I did."

I didn't like the lazy-eight the taxi was doing. What was I going to do with that hand of mine?

I cleared my throat, for openers. "I know that." He let the hand go. I sat back.

There's a kind of foreboding I sometimes get. The kind of taste when you'd been eating thimbleberries too close to the orchard; you'd suddenly get the feeling they might have more than their share of malathion spray. You knew it was fifty-fifty whether you'd be taken by green, gagging surprise in another half-minute.

"Listen, Bitsy, are those people really expecting you? Could you go over a little later?"

Fifty-fifty. I weighed the matter of the long sleeves against going over a little later. The scales tipped back and forth, ticking metronomically at a hundred forty. The woman holding them was, as usual, blindfolded, and no help at all.

In the seconds it took to say no, I couldn't go over a little later, I grasped, quite agilely, a stunning truth. I was doing Nancy a favor. Deferring to the sensibilities of someone I'd never met, someone who had had the unspeakably obscene gall to be alive and available in Ann Arbor one spring. I sat there and said no.

I think it was the armies of Presbyterians applauding in the California sunset who caused me to change my mind.

"Yes. I mean yes. I mean yes, I can go over a little later." I tried to sound undereager. Without the smallest amount of success. Molly Bloom.

Gayle had assured me (years after we'd left college, in a conversation that embraced—quite prejudicially—assorted modish and colorful genres of chauvinism) that while the old devil might enjoy a perfectly reputable relationship with *logos*, he'd be exponentially lousy where *eros* was concerned. That I was well rid of someone who'd no doubt plant a hand somewhere and hang on as if to a lurching subway strap. That Nancy was stuck for life with a roommate who'd rut and grunt like a suspicious boy scout; who'd grope frenetically like a spastic pinsetter; and who'd treat the archetypal act as a fiendish and gargling opportunity to see who could finish first. I thought it wasn't altogether kind of Gayle to make that sort of assumption, and told her so. She said kindness came in an exhaustive variety of forms, and that sometimes I didn't recognize a good thing when I saw it.

Of the myriad ways that we as a race have found to stop laughing, the way I stopped laughing in the taxi was to focus on the singularly sobering thought: I was going to lie to Hayes.

The Mark Hopkins Hotel, with its opera-house facade. I could have walked right out while he was bent over the counter. But you don't just do that to somebody whose family is waiting in Tokyo with a bowl of raw fish.

Waiting for the elevator, Brahms's First Symphony swam around my head. Crazy and ominous. If I looked up and said something nice and polite just before I turned around and ran out the door, everything would be all right. I didn't move.

Something must have happened awfully fast; I was in the elevator, out of the elevator, walking down a corridor looking at room numbers. The bellhop turned a key in a lock. *Huit Clos*.

Putting my violin on a chair, I walked straight to a window, with only the most theoretical thoughts of jumping out. San Francisco in the evening, from high on the hill: an outstretched sparkling drama, hundreds of thousands of lights, an arabesque of votive candles, one lit for every human error taking place in that ponderous instant. Many of them were mine.

The master of microencapsulated pioneer breakthroughs walked across the room behind me and took my hands in both his. Fitting the words together statue-fashion he said, "Listen, Bitsy. I'm going to make a short, two-part speech. One, you feel funny and I feel funny. It's a funny world. And two, you cried all over my arm one day about a book. And nobody else ever did that in my whole life."

I stopped cataloguing zippers and light switches when Mickey Spillane left the hayloft. Much, much later, I became an afficionada of the choreography of tongues, the orchestration of fingers, the singing excitement of the warm and dark impatience that Hayes so aptly named in the opulent sunshine of my piny youth. It was only fair that the old shouter-off-mountaintops avail himself of the swelling opportunity to reap the rewards of his first subtle, breezy and laughing lessons in the art of making loud and violent love.

And I'm reasonably sure the Department of State would stop mucking around in their nerve-jangling plexus of furtive, duplistic huff and enjoy a reverent, honest moment of silence if they knew the Sibelius Violin Concerto was sailing voluptuously around a hotel room in San Francisco. The second *largamente,* where it resolves sweepingly into double-stops in five flats, the part where you're a flower in the middle of the river, watching the hills not cave in on either side.

If the State Department is too busy to notice, it serves them right. Gayle was mistaken.

"Hey, did you *hear* that?" I couldn't help asking. It was too oddly coincidental, even in a life that's been so fraught with coincidence as to appear untrustworthy.

The old mountaintop-shouter removed his tongue from my ear, where it'd been searching languidly, like a drowsy Winnie-the-Pooh, for the last trickles of a youthful memory. "Hear what?"

"You didn't hear any music, Hayes?" It was mildly surprising that he didn't smell like woodsmoke.

"No. What're those marks on your arms?"

"You're sure you didn't hear anything? Any music?"

"I'm sure. Tell me about those." He ran a finger up the inside of my left elbow. One thing I'd forgotten about him was that he had the most nearly perfect hands of anybody I'd ever seen.

"Tell me about Tokyo, please . . . ''

"I still like your arms, but those marks aren't too gorgeous.''

"No, they're not too gorgeous. Listen, Hayes, let me tell you about the music, it's very strange, I've never—''

"They're awfully unusual marks, Bits.'' He was sitting up. I'd also forgotten what a terrific chest he had. Not an imperious chest, not the kind that roars at you, but the kind you like to sit and look at quietly for awhile.

In the taxi I'd been so sure I'd be able to lie. But in the taxi I hadn't looked him straight in the face. "You know, I used to ask you lots of innocuous questions and get answers I wasn't ready to handle. Like, can I come and visit you in Ann Arbor. This is sort of like that.''

Suddenly there were four people in the room. They were present as surely as the music was. Two fumbled toward integrity, maturity, autonomy, college diplomas, and truth. Two were long past voting age—practitioners of compromise, disciples of pragmatism, purveyors of ersatz wisdom. These looked at the younger ones with a mixture of nostalgia and embarrassment. The young cocked their heads quizzically sideways, almost sanctimoniously pleased at how the others had botched the job. According to the rules of the tribe, each of the four sat in judgment of the other three—without sympathy, without tenderness, as if irony were the only thing that mattered. I didn't want to be scrutinized, but I had no choice.

"What're you talking about? You can skip the introduction, Bitsy.''

"I mean, I don't know whether it's perverted to tell you or perverted not to. I used to know . . .'' I sat up.

"It sounds lovely.''

"Then let's skip it—''

"Go ahead, Bits.'' He meant it.

I wished I could have said it was noble or fine or heroic, like holding an entire battalion at a standoff while I protected nine thousand barefoot orphans in the snow. It wasn't.

"If I tell you, will you not have a fit? I mean, it's all a really long time ago, but I just don't want you to—you know, have a fit or something.''

"It's a promise. I'm not given to fits.''

I'd never in the world planned to be a witness for the prosecution. I'd never rehearsed the speech, all I had were the damning facts. It was not going to be my shining hour.

"Well, you know those days I didn't feel so hot, when you got engaged? I didn't just not feel so hot, it was a little more than that—I never thought I'd be telling you this . . ."

"You've started, Bits."

"Yes, I have. Well, I decided you were such a stinkpot—"

"Stinkpot?" asked the State Department's answer to Blue-beard.

"Oh, Hayes, I'd run out of words. You made such a Thesaurus-eater out of me, but there wasn't one in it for you. So I settled for 'stinkpot.' Anyway, after I wrote you that tender letter wishing you all the luck in the world, I went upstairs to do a little Mary Martin. You know—some brain-laundry was in order. The bathroom always smelled like shampoo anyway. When I got there, there was this girl, sitting right smack on the john, taking notes on Nietzsche. I walked in on her by accident. Extremely funny. Except that I couldn't laugh. Nietzsche on the toilet. I opened my mouth and it was like falling down a crevasse and not being able to get a sound out.

"So, instead of reaching up for the shampoo, what ended up, very accidentally, in my hand was a Gillette Blue-Blade. You know, the ones that sponsored the ball games? I just turned around and got a shower curtain, I walked back to my room with it bunched up under my shirt and closed the door. We didn't have locks. I laid the shower curtain on the bed—and I put Brahms's First Symphony on the record player. I had one of those reject needles that repeats a record over and over so you could go nutty."

It would have been wiser to run naked down Nob Hill than to sit there and go on. Instead, the words kept coming out, accelerating like armed prisoners from a cell block. Shut away for years, mutiny propelled them beyond decency.

"I lay down on the shower curtain and found those two big veins the doctors in the D.O. always wanted us to fist up, and I took the Gillette Blue and I—"

"Bitsy, I don't think I want to hear any more—"

"Listen, you asked, you're gonna get the whole thing—I fin-gered the first violin part on my chest for awhile—Hayes, I've watched people going to *sleep* during the second movement—and I wondered why I wasn't. I remember getting almost through it. I played almost the whole A-flat ending—you know, where the bass voices have the E-natural?''

"Bitsy, be kind, for christ's sake—''

"I only *got* one and a half arteries and a tend—''

"I didn't *know*." He reached out and touched the jagged, ungorgeous welts on my inside elbows.

"Well, of course you didn't. But wait, you've gotta hear the rest. You'll like it."

"*Like* it?'' His hands moved a bit on my arms.

"Stop being squeamish for a minute. I'm sitting here, aren't I?''

"Go ahead then."

"Well, if you think about it, you'll remember that I never did quite pull off anything in its pure form. What I did was so dumb, they should've flunked me out for it—I lay too close to the edge of the bed. I guess I thought I was gonna writhe gracefully like some kind of Bernini twist—when I did get around to drifting out, instead of lying white and slender on the pillow like a Madame Bovary ballet, I fell plunk out of bed and woke the girl underneath me on the second floor. And I dripped on Camus.

"This girl, she must've had it with my noise by that time. She was some kind of descendent of an Articles-of-Confederation signer, her lineage sort of didn't take nimbly to being thumped on. She came busting in, yelled bloody Christ, and about six Muffy's, Puffy's, Katsy's and Toto's came tearing down the hall— somebody told me later the first movement was going full blast, there I was in all that spatter and ooze—I think it wasn't very patrician. It's a wonder I didn't wake up.

"The ambulance came, siren screaming, nobody'd remembered to turn the record off, it was around to the A-flat part again, the housemother was scooting around trying not to let anybody find out—with a siren going, blood all down the stairs and Brahms soaring away—''

This time they didn't bother with the Infirmary. "I don't know how much later, I woke up in Cooley Dickinson Hospital. A very quiet window display of hoses, bottles, clamps, bandages—I was strapped down.

"You know, three or four girls made it all the way while I was in college. For awhile I couldn't figure out why I had to be the one with the rotten luck.''

He was shaking his head back and forth, his eyes closed. Still with one hand on each of my arms. At least he wasn't having a fit.

"I did a lot of thinking, lying there. Very angry thinking. I don't think you want to hear. Then, just when the damned limbo I'd got myself into seemed the craziest of all, it sort of got clear. Through a glass lightly. The cosmic joke."

"The what?"

"You don't know?" I couldn't believe this *summa cum laude* didn't understand.

"Why don't you just try telling me?"

"Well, about the light for the children of darkness, the sculptor-father in heaven, the trip to the wilderness, the joking Jesus—you know."

"The what?" He was thinking fast.

"Oh, come on. What I couldn't figure out was why you didn't walk across the river. And how many guys you had supper with the night before they nailed your hand—were you anywhere near Oberammergau when that happened? And whether anybody in your family was named Mary. A mother or something."

He looked at me as if I were a fresh car accident. Then a smile spread the length of his face—a totally startled smile. He told me quite straightforwardly that I was crazy.

For a long time I'd thought I was the only person who'd gotten on the business end of that particular cosmic joke. The way you think when you're a little kid that you're the only one who dreams about showing up in the grocery store wearing pajamas.

"So. They'd let Mother and Fritz know, I had to call them and say it was a mistake, tell them it was someone with a name like mine—and not to hop a plane. Even lifting a phone, every time I moved, I pulled out some hose or other, strange fluids would squirt out, and they'd come in and plug me up again. I was laughing so hard by that time, I short-circuited every five minutes. You'd have fallen on the floor laughing."

"One comment, lady, then you can go on. You have the most macabre sense of humor I've ever seen."

"And one comment on your comment. It's not so macabre when it's a question of life or death. I guess you had to be there to appreciate its fine points."

While I'd been having stuff pumped into me, Hayes had been

appreciating the fine points of the nefarious and pungently nubile Nancy. How anthropometrical of him.

"So, I asked them to bill me directly—I couldn't let my family know about the circus of hoses and junk. You'd be hysterical over the crazy jobs I had to take to pay the bill.

"What they really wanted to do was send me to the funny farm up on the hill, as soon as they could disconnect me. I was very fuzzy upstairs, but you don't have to think too clearly to know you don't want to go there, do you? Do you?"

He leaned very mortally forward, put an elbow on one knee and said, "No, you don't have to think too clearly to know that."

"So, they sent a psychiatrist in to see me. A woman in a brown suit and a double chin. She sat herself in the chair where the nurses had been taking turns, and started asking me questions. I didn't even know what a psychiatrist looked like. And it's very hard to be incredibly sane when you're flat on your back plugged into a chemistry set, but I was *not* going to go up on that hill. I think I trilled a lot at her. Very soprano."

Beatrice, do you understand the significance of what you've done?

Yes, I surely do.

Why do you think you did it?

I lost my head momentarily.

Do you think you've learned anything from this experience?

Oh, I surely do. The steely jaws of death have taught me the most important lesson of my life.

And what is that?

How lovely the world is, how redeeming God's saving grace is, how valuable a sense of humor is in the face of certain trials . . .

And what do you think you want to do now?

Oh, Doctor, I want most of all to take my final exams.

Your final exams?

Oh, yes, absolutely.

"Now, what kind of nut wants to take a bunch of finals? Actually, it's a very nutty thing to want to do, but that's not the way they looked at it.

"So, they let me take them in Cooley Dickinson. I passed every one. And I got an A in Bach and Handel. They weren't even going to let me take the course. I took it instead of psychology."

Hayes was laughing, about a third of a laugh. And telling me that if I didn't mind his saying so, he thought it showed.

"I didn't get anything like a translucent sense of the eloquence of death, if that's what you're wondering, Hayes. None at all. In fact, it was terroriz—anyway, the exams were important. They kept me out of the crazy place."

I called Gayle in Princeton. Gayle, I said, I'm in big, big trouble, I did the dumbest thing you could think of. Hold on, she said, I've got hamburgers cooking, wait a minute. There now. What did you do—take another history course? Gayle, I said, I only had one reason for staying alive, and he's marrying someone else and I didn't know how funny it was when I sliced myself open with a razor blade— Sonofabitch, she said, where are you? I said, I'm in Cooley Dickinson. Sonofabitch, she said, hold everything, don't move. I can't, I said. She turned up a few hours later in her trenchcoat, and brought every exam to me, one at a time, and took them back when I was finished, even all the Bach and Handel apparatus, and what she did in the middle of it all was stick her arms around me, both of them, and let me cry all over them, and not tell me I was dumb and stupid right then and there.

I suppose it amounts to the old ski-tow loyalty, the reason why people show up for the pain of a gray-haired reunion. Gayle simply didn't drag her ass.

When I finished the last exam ("Discuss the use of irony in any three works read this semester...") Gayle made for the phone with Ann Arbor viciously on her mind. Gayle, I said, if you do that—if you ever do that—you're out of my life and I'm out of yours. The minute that phone connection gets made, there's no need between you and me, there's no love. Is it really worth that much to you to hear those *s*'s I've told you about? Gayle always was a very smart girl, and she decided she didn't have to hear the *s*'s. Bitsy, she said, you can't be stupid enough to think he was worth it, can you? You can't really be stupid enough to think he was worth committing suicide over. No, I said, I can't be that stupid. And I think this is a red-hot time for us both to stop calling me "Bitsy."

Gayle took her trenchcoat off the chair and turned it inside out. One arm dove into a sleeve. She asked me, Is that the way you do things out there in the Auragon woods? Grow the kind of mind that's gonna kill itself over some guy because he climbs mountains and convinces you he's got a Corinthian— No, Gayle, I said. That's not the way we do things out there in the woods. What we do out there in the woods is smell the pine needles and watch the squirrels. Corinthian didn't have anything to do with it; really, it didn't.

I lied about that part.

My right arm was terribly tired from writing exams, my hand was covered with ballpoint ink. It lay on the sheet like somebody perpetually ready to have her blood pressure taken. I'd been in the hospital for days, and was so very, very tired of the same four walls. It wasn't at all what I'd planned to be doing after exams. Gayle, I said, trying unsuccessfully for the seventy-ninth time to reach my left fourth finger with my left thumb, I think he was the only guy who ever took me seriously. Or I thought he did.

Gayle gave me her fiercely unhesitating look, smoothed down a loose, linty corner of adhesive tape on my arm, and said, Well, Beatrice, you're never gonna know, are you? I listened to the hallway full of shuffling nurses. No, I said, I guess not. She stirred the resident thermometer around in the resident glass of stale water. Gayle, I said, that's the only thing I can't stand not knowing. Whether he ever took me seriously. Well, she said, there's a phone right there— Gayle, I said, shut up.

She said, I bet you'll be playing scales by September. I hope so, I said. Gayle, I said, when they invented the red, calendared sisterhood I bet they had you in mind. Beatrice, she said, as a philosopher you're one hell of a violinist. She threw her trenchcoat down and sat on it.

"So, when I finally went back to the House—people just love to stare at freaks, don't they? Why is that?"

"I don't know, Bitsy. Yes they do. Were you so freakish?"

"Yes. I'd done that weird thing. But I just had two big band-aids on. You know what I wanted?"

"What?"

"I wanted you to be standing there, in a pair of jeans, holding a can of beer. We'd go on a picnic, I'd wear long sleeves. I thought, if he's so all-fired supernatural, why can't he be in two places at once?"

He wasn't.

"So, you weren't standing there, and we weren't going on any picnic. I went in and found all the letters I could. I threw them in the incinerator. And I got rid of the Salinger and Pogo.''

''That makes a certain cold sense, I guess.''

''Yes. Except, then I did the real figuring out. How long have you been sitting there waiting for that part?''

''For a while.'' If he was going to have a fit, at least he wasn't having it yet.

''I went and sat on the grass in the Quad, under a maple tree. I wondered how many girls had sat under that tree and decided to stay alive. It was late spring, lots of people had gone home. I couldn't go home. Anyway, it finally came to me. How it was the war. The peacetime war, the one that's always going on. As you said, take your pick. The horseshit that kids are thrown into when they're not ready. How we had that sunny, lovely, innocuous youth, and then the world sank its teeth in—more into you than me because—you know, the deadly inequality of it, how they send guys to carry guns and they send girls to college to write letters, only I hadn't done my share . . . ''

''You're getting platitudinous, Bits.''

''I don't care how damn platitudinous I'm getting. It's the truth. I was still mad as hell at you, in a half-assed way. The point is, I knew it was half-assed. So I ran in and dug the letters out again. Seared around the edges, some of them. But I did. Don't tell me how silly that is.''

I couldn't help wincing under the scrutiny of the two youngsters who stood in the shadows among the suitcases.

''No, I won't tell you just how silly it is.'' He looked at his hands. ''You weren't—this is a strange question to ask now—you weren't busy with some guy all those months?''

He couldn't know how hard I'd tried to go to the phone, and how I'd found out I'd forgotten how to talk in plain English. ''Sure, I was busy with some guys. I was busy with T. S. Eliot, and with Melville and Faulkner and Shakespeare and Nietzsche and Proust and the rest of them. You know how much they meant to my heart? About as much as blowing your nose. That's about how much.''

He looked at my hands. All ten fingers, four callused.

''Anyway, I had to wait until the next Christmas to go home. You know, deck the halls, cold weather, long sleeves . . . I spent the summer with Gayle and Eugene, in Princeton, in their apartment.''

Proofreading Eugene's dissertation on Three Dichotomies Inherent in Basic Christian Existentialism. Eugene's a hell of a nice
guy, who saw what I meant when I said that stuff had a way of
following me around.

Gayle reiterated that she wouldn't slice herself up over a green
smutted fag who'd send a newspaper clipping in the mail, and
besides, the one in the picture was probably a guy anyway. I said I
didn't think so, the picture was smirking, and I didn't think guys
smirked. She said guys smirked, all right, you just had to catch
them at it, which wasn't easy. I told her I wouldn't eat graham
crackers instead of taking a history final. We agreed that there were
different kinds of lunacy afoot in the world, we read parts of *Myth
of Sisyphus* to each other, and smoked our first joint. I don't
remember what they were called in those days. We ate peanut
butter sandwiches while Eugene typed his inherent dichotomies,
providing me with more proofreading by repeating "the blockades
to authentic living are all too often obscured in a nebulous" six
times. Their apartment was decorated in Early Orgasm—Gayle's
term. I had to take her word for it.

Gayle and Eugene have gone through a closed marriage, an open
marriage, and a contractual marriage. The day before I left for San
Francisco I had a card from her saying they'd renewed it again, all
four kids voting aye. She also said their new house was decorated
in Early Counterrevolution. I had a feeling she'd taken a belated
interest in history.

"I shot my music almost to hell. Especially the left side. That's
the artery I got, and the . . . they were a little reluctant to let me
switch to a music major, but they did. Can you imagine them
looking at somebody with slashed elbows wanting to be a violinist?"

"I'm trying to imagine that very thing."

"They were sort of inclined to be charitable to late bloomers. I
wondered for a while if I did it just to find out if Camus knew what
he was talking about. Do you suppose so?"

"I don't know. I don't know what to say about any of it."

HOW MANY BOYS, HAYES? HOW MANY GIRLS? DO
THEY HAVE LANKY POISE AND *MAD* COMICS AND
BIKES?

"That's okay. I didn't either, for a long time."

He changed position. I couldn't tell if he was bored. "Bits, let's get Room Service and have a picnic. You hungry?"

"Sure. After airplane stuff? Of course."

We had a picnic. Filet mignon and salad all over the sheets. I finally heard about Tokyo. And Madrid, Oslo, Helsinki . . .

As he hopscotched his way through the self-serving careers of the pricks and horses' asses in those scenic spots—he hadn't lost his propensity to run into horses' asses—he began to sound like a Victrola that needs winding. As if he didn't want to tell me about them at all.

"Bitsy," he said, in the middle of the bureaucratic tangle of Madrid, "are you saying your mother doesn't know? About your arms?"

DO THEY GO LAUGHING UP AND DOWN HILLSIDES IN THE SUNSHINE, HAYES? IN FIVE OR SIX LANGUAGES?

"Right. I go home at Christmas—"

"Bitsy, what I think we've got here is a—" He looked at me with cordial and immoderately spontaneous compassion. "It's a situation for which there isn't much of a precedent. I'm trying to make sense out of it—"

"Don't bother. I don't think it makes much—"

"You never told your—" With the measured concentration of a dedicated band-aid expert he put one index finger on one of my lavender welts. "Did it hurt badly, Bitsy?"

It hurt like leaping crazy hell. "Yes, it hurt badly, Hayes."

He pushed the flying lock of hair out of his eyes. "You can't spend the rest of your life in long sleeves, Bits. You can't do that."

"Hayes, I'm a grown-up. And my name's Beatrice. And I'll make my own choices."

"But it's not a logical choice. That's what I'm—"

"Logic interests me not one bit anymore. I've seen enough logic to give me an immunity for life. You know what logical people do, Hayes? They dry up. They go to sleep in the middle of concerts— do you go to sleep in concerts?"

"I've been known to."

"See what I mean?"

"You know what I'm noticing about you? You have all the enlightened reasoning of a koala, Bitsy, you really do."

"Not like you, I guess. You just ended up logical as hell,

enlightened reasoning and all. You probably knew the egg cartons wouldn't be enough. Music gets you farther away from the fascinating world of logic the longer you—''

"Not when you consider how it's related to the mathematics, the Pythagorean harmonies—''

"Oh, for heaven's sake, Hayes, don't tell me about music. And I won't tell you how to run an embassy, okay? You know, you've really got nice eyes—the whole world is crazy, anyway. It operates on a sideways ethic. Judy said that.''

"Bits, you can't blame the world for your own lack of logic. But Judy's right. That's as good a name as any. The world's run by phobic creeps. Always. And the part that really decimates you— logically and every other way—is that there's no system that's been invented yet that includes Freak. You know where he is? And thank you.''

"Yes. I saw him once. I wouldn't call him terrifically logical. If he'd employed any logic, he'd have—''

"That's not the point. You see what our phobic world did to him?''

"Yes, it is the point. I think he's a very happy man, Hayes.''

He looked as if he were trying not to ask me to define happiness.

DO THEY GO SKINNY-DIPPING WITH THEIR GIRL-FRIENDS YET?

"Could I ask you, Hayes, what are you doing about it? About the world? You, personally.''

He didn't miss a beat. "What do I do? I do my job. Trying to help the planet stay ahead of total economic disaster . . . I simply do my job. I'm good at it.''

"I'll just bet you are.''

"Bitsy, that sneer doesn't look good on you.''

I didn't realize I was sneering.

Saving the world. Being President. The prince of peace. Quadruple horseshit. A middle-aged, slightly wrinkled brilliant economist with an attaché case full of fiscal enlightenment. Lucky Nancy.

"You know what, Hayes? I'm disappointed in you.''

"What the hell did you expect?'' He smiled.

I heard my tongue clicking. "I expected you to be President, I think.''

He laughed without, as they say, visible amusement.

"Hayes, you're not the kind of person who sits at a desk and wields economic dilemmas around. That's *bland*. I've watched it happen to other people—but I can't believe it's happened to you. What do you do for excitement?"

He licked the back of my knee. I ignored it.

"What do you do—what do you do for nobility?"

"You mean with swords and coats of arms? I go to dinner at their castles sometimes—"

I moved my entire body out of his reach. "Hayes, I believe you've become a fatuous charade of a human being, I wish I'd never crossed paths with you, I—"

"Bits, did I make pronouncements about your character? Did I tell you you were a *disappointment*, for christ's sake?"

"But you didn't expect me to—"

"You know what I expected of you? I expected that you'd play in Carnegie hall—"

"I've done that."

"And I expected you to go dashing around the world with freshness and vision and—"

"I tried, Hayes. I did try."

"I know." The only part of me he could reach was my back. "I know you did. I try, too. But the odds are pretty good that I'll never be President."

The realist. "Why not?"

"Listen, Bits, you want to know what I do, and I don't really want to tell you. But I think I'm going to."

"You already have."

"Not all of it. When I was in Sweden—"

I turned around. "You didn't mention Sweden."

"Stop interrupting. Sweden's a very funny place, Bitsy. They've got a lot that's wrong, and a lot that's contradictory, but what they've got that's right is an enlightened neutrality, and along with that goes an open door for deserters, guys who don't find any particular romance in defoliating Indochina and setting fire to crippled children and—"

"Stop it, Hayes, I can't stand to hear—"

"Exactly. Now, it philosophically started with Freak, damn near twenty years ago. My empathy with various disaffected activities. Just an empathy, understand, nothing more than that. I didn't know what I was going to start once the poor bastards began hitting Sweden in hordes. Some American deserters crashed the embassy one Fourth of July, got hauled off to jail, and I thought, Wait a minute—that's Freak and that's me, and that's my kids, give or take a few years and a few ideological miles, there's the whole goddamn mess. The decision happened that fast. I wondered why it'd taken me so long. It was after My Lai. You know, these were guys with a very unsteady political commitment, if any—and intellectually, pathetically meek. They just happened to be draft age, they accidentally got their consciousness raised while they were in—do you know there are probably half a million guys— half a million—who've got no country and no rights because they refuse to take part in war crimes?"

I was a little shaky. "Don't justify it, Hayes, just tell me."

"So, I investigated some ways I might do something about it. Do you know what a man without a country is? Helpless. No money, no language, aliases—anyway, mine was an idea whose time had more than come, as the history books'll say someday. An underground railroad home. You'd be surprised how many people I found who were willing to help. Journalists, all kinds of people. Even two intelligence guys, my own personal *coup*—I met them skiing. People who were willing to go out of their way to insure safe passage to deserters, or 'self-retired veterans,' as we're calling them. Even when they get here they have to live under aliases, but—"

"How many people have you got involved in this, Hayes?"

"At State, or all together? State, scattered, forty-two. All together, into the hundreds. And someday the idea of universal amnesty is going to get through to the phobic—"

"I'm amazed. You've got so much to lose—"

"Everybody does, Bits. Forty-two guys, some of them women, you'll be happy to know. Careers down the toilet in two minutes if—"

"Is that why you're in Japan now?"

"Indirectly. Things got a little hot, eventually—"

"When did you learn Japanese?"

"A few years ago. It was economics-related. Just before Washington started the diplomatic war with Sweden. I had a feeling some people were going to start asking a lot of questions around Stockholm. I was right."

The thinker. "Jesus, Hayes. And there you were, being a splendid economist, studying Japanese."

"Yeah. And learning to eat with chopsticks. Had a little trouble with the left hand . . . " he laughed. "Now I handle the Tokyo connection, small as that is."

Another reversal. "Hayes, maybe you're not out of Terry and the Pirates."

"What?" He was pantomiming chopsticks.

"I mean—maybe this won't make any sense to you—just maybe you exist after all."

"Shit, what kind of thing is that to say about somebody?"

"Oh, damn it, you're a hero."

He scratched the terrific chest. "What do you mean, damn it I'm a hero?"

"You don't go thundering dangerously down secret passageways like that in the name of freedom if you're not a hero."

"Bitsy, there's absolutely zero thundering involved."

"How many men do you think you personally got—"

"I don't think, I know. Fifty-three. Whether or not any of them'll get a respectable amnesty, it's a shell game—"

"Fifty-three! I think it's noble. I wanted you to be a hero, and at the same time I wanted you to be tromped on and splattered all over the—I wanted to hate you and I couldn't stand the thought of hating you because I don't even understand the whole—the whole *dedication* that goes into the act of hatred—and besides, how can you hate somebody who—but there you are, a Goddamn hero. It mixes me up something fierce. And your *s*'s knock me out."

"Shall I tell you a trivial truth, Bits? You're the only person who's ever been knocked out by my *s*'s."

"Are you sure?"

(Dearest, why didn't your parents see to it that your bite got taken care of?

Does it bother you, Nance?

Not exactly. But it's a little annoying sometimes.)

"Bitsy, I'm very sure."

I was. Is. Am. Are. Knocked out. They must have stirred my first uncurlings of sensuality. Those and the pine pitch, horse sweat and T-shirt. I just didn't know it.

What most women and a few men know about sex is so sweetly
simple: it is an art form. What most women and *very* few men sense
is that because the planet has been strewn with a feast of beauty in
texture, line, rhythm, contour and light—one art form passionately
becomes another, the minute we are willing to participate in the
merger. Unexplainably, Hayes was one of those very few men. In
the next few minutes I heard the Bach B Minor *Sanctus*, the
six-winged seraphim dancing the oldest dance in the universe, the
vast dance of praise and joy.

As Bach ebbed away, and we eyed each other with that mortal,
silent, heavy-breathing how-did-*you*-become-such-a-magnificent-
lover gaze, he crossed one leg over the other, like Tom Sawyer
fishing. "Bits, how long did it take you to get rid of the prehensile
virginity of yours?"

"I don't want to tell you. You'd be disappointed. And do you
always talk that way? That prehensile virginity thing?"

He'd never in his life hear about the sneaky underwear. Men will
always joke about girls' virginity, but I'd be damned if I'd give him
another reason to joke personally about mine.

"No, I don't think it applies to too many people." He got up,
walked around the room, spent a few seconds bent over my luggage
tag. He came back to the bed and lay down. He asked me what my
name was. I reminded him.

"You mean you're not married?"

"No, Hayes. I'd have told you."

He looked at me and pushed the flying lock back. "You mean
you don't have a bunch of musical kids?"

The Rances? My belly swollen like a stolen watermelon, throbbing with the heartbeats and flailing legs of Swiss-Chinese truthful
unslapped canoeing newt-catchers with flying locks of hair? Morn-
ing-sick all day long while Hayes held my head and laughed and
said, Bits, will you stop throwing *up*, for christ's sake, so we can
go swimming?

"Sure, I've got musical kids, the ones I teach—"

"Jesus. What would you want to do that for?"

"Oh, for heaven's sake, Hayes. Not everybody gets—"

"You, Bits. Why you?"

"You really want to know? Yes, I guess you do. It's because
your first love loves you yourself. After that, anybody who comes

along gets somebody different. It's like the virginity of the mind, I think. You lose it to somebody, you're never the same. I just couldn't put all that together and marry somebody. Not yet, anyway."

"Bitsy, how can you be so wise and so excessively dumb?"

I never thought it was dumb before. Uncomfortable sometimes, lonely sometimes, but not dumb. "I don't know. There's probably a psychological name for it. One time I made a choice between analysis and a new bow. You're looking at the owner of a beautiful Tourte bow. Seventeen hundreds. That's years, Hayes. It's got resilience that makes your mouth water—"

He laughed. I got up and walked away. He lay on his back looking at the ceiling. Probably thinking in lots of languages at once.

WHAT IF SOMEBODY DOES THAT HATE-TO-PUSH-IRONY-TOO-FAR THING WITH ONE OF YOUR LITTLE GIRLS, HAYES? WHAT'S SHE GONNA DO THEN?

"Bitsy, what would you think of taking a little trip to Tokyo?"

"Silly, Japan's got enough scars. They don't need me. Besides, the Philharmonic has auditions next month. Again."

"I'm serious. Suzuki and things . . . "

"Not on your life. I speak about four words of Japanese." I was looking at the Mensa card that had drifted serenely out of his wallet.

"Bitsy, will you listen? This isn't Berlitz we're talking about. We're talking about a little trip, a short trip."

> and I hope you will feel free to drop in on us if you ever get over this way. We're not the kind that feels any undue embarrassment over this kind of

God holy damn! I turned very slowly to face the thunderer into the lives of the meek. Across the room I faced him squarely, my arms stretched straight out. I said in my best ruthless Anglo-Saxon, "You know what else it isn't? It isn't a comic book. You can't close it and go to sleep, you glib, laughing bastard. You know what you've got? You've got a case of hyperventilation of the soul, that's what. What are you trying to do? It's serious time? I'll get serious. Look, Hayes. Take a good faceful of these arms. And don't rock the fucking *raft*! Do you want to do something like that to the woman who's had your babies and held you when you threw up and watched you be a hero—and stuffed suitcases every time things got a little warm with the State Department? You want me to *meet* her or something? You want her to meet me? Go shopping for kimonos together? You Goddamn arrogant grim reaper, what *are* you?''

He sat up like ten million volcanoes. "Guess what, Beatrice. Screw you. Screw your phony, ass-kissing integrity. Screw your violin. You want to cut a few scars? You're way out of your league, Beatrice. Screw your cocksucking insured eighteenth-century bow. Screw your self-pitying purple elbows, screw your vengeful suicide story. Screw your protracted adolescent coquettishness— no wonder you haven't got stretch marks, you've never bothered to grow the fuck up. Screw your strident, baroque name-calling. Screw your smug, contrived, imitation ethics. Screw your chirpy little yellow suit, it's the costume of a goddamn transcontinental canary. Screw your perverted Oedipal craving. Screw your wise- ass demeanor that tries to pass itself off as intelligence. Screw your motherfucking cancerous piety, screw your shit-eating pretentious apologies. Godfuckingdamn it Beatrice, fuck you!''

When a Douglas pseudo fir falls it shakes the forest floor. Just once. Its final, definitive statement screams out its hurt, it settles and lies still while the sap drips out of the wound.

"Hayes, you know one thing we never did?"

"Holy jesus, Bits... " I was looking at a wounded human being.

"One thing. And this is Switzerland or maybe China notwith- standing. We never threw each other against a wall just to see what would spurt out. Whatever else we did, we never grabbed each other by the balls just to see what cruelty we could wreak. Now maybe that's not living, but... "

"Bitsy, you know what I'm gonna do?" He put his hand on my hip to make sure I was listening. I was.

"What?"

"I'm gonna forgive your hermaphroditic phrasing. And remind you of a couple of other things. You know what else we didn't do? We didn't keep score. That's for people who've taken out a membership in a—" He stopped and looked around the room. "—in a club devoted to ego-jousting and putting crampons in each other's faces. And much as you deserve it—or maybe you don't—I'll figure that out later—I wouldn't think of throwing you against a wall. But is that goddamn mutual?''

"Yes." I bit my lip. It tasted bloody. The squalid barbarity of two laughing berry thieves crowding into the parade of wall-throwers and truce-signers who creaked nervously, treacherously, in and out of that expensive room, stoking each other with filet mignon and sticking crowbars in each other's sensibilities until they bled—

The two youngsters, woodsmoke in their hair and Pogo books in their hands, looked at what they had become. They were appalled, horrified, most of all perplexed. They disliked us from head to toe, and it made them unbearably sad.

I wondered for a very brief moment whether I should have gotten both arteries. "Hayes, I've gotta get out of here, I really—"

I ran for the pile of clothes. A haberdasher's carnage, yellow skirt and belts contorted obscenely around pants and shoes, a garment-center *Guernica*. I began throwing things out of the way, no underwear to be found. I couldn't even remember what color it was. I'd have made a lousy soldier—I'd never find my uniform in time to come out fighting. My lip leaked a drop of blood on a cufflink. And I felt my skin coming off, like the seared, waxy knifings of a baked apple.

"No, Bits, you haven't gotta get out of here, you've gotta have dessert.''

I looked up. The thunderer into the lives of the meek was smiling like someone who told a fifteen-year-old kid what "ostensibly" meant. He was trying to pretend that both of us could escape blame.

"Just get up off the floor and go in the bathroom for a minute or so.''

I got up. SEE THAT FLYING SQUIRREL? The *Guernica* at my feet blurred. I started toward the bathroom. YOU AND I ARE GONNA GET TO KNOW EACH OTHER AND FIGURE IT ALL OUT. WHAT'S YOUR REAL NAME, ANYWAY? "Maybe I should—" I licked blood off my lip. GO ON ABOUT THIS GUERNSEY. "I could round up some of the other guests, we could have a game of soccer . . . ''

"No kidding, Bits, you play soccer?''

AND EVERY TIME I SEE A MOUNTAIN, OR EVEN A HILL "Once in a while.''

"Do me a favor, then." YOU'RE A LITTLE WEIRD YOUR-SELF, BITSY—THAT BEER IS SPILLING ALL OVER THE "Don't do it tonight."

BESIDES, I LIKE YOUR ARMS

I went into the bathroom and washed my face. The mirror could have borne one of Beth's notes:

> You are cordially invited to grow old with this person. How does that grab you?

Beth, Judy, Gayle, Fred, Pogo, those figures of my youth: why had every single one of them known more about life than I had? We have met the enemy and it is us.

"Put this on, Bits." His shirt. It reached to my knees, blood drying on one cufflink. "Now, jump in bed like a good girl and close your eyes when Room Service gets here."

I did.

"You crazy sonofabitch."

I don't often cry at dessert. But I wasn't expecting anything as consummately corny as a gigantic bowl of fresh strawberries.

"Bits, you may not believe me, but I didn't mean to hand you another cry." Tears rolled gracelessly all over the monogram.

"And I didn't mean to throw my arms at you like a bloody piece of revenge. Did you really think I'd do that? I *loved* you. With the most ferocious, unflinching, dumbest kind of—what do you have to do in this world to let people know you love them? Scream at them or something?"

He looked at the wet shirt front. "Yes. Yes, I think that's what you have to do."

I picked up a spoon. "Room Service must have thought something weird was going on," I said. Strawberries and cream. Old Waltzing Matilda.

"Not really. I said you were blind and it was your birthday. Then he wanted to get candles—take off my shirt."

Off went the wet monogram. We finished the strawberries and sat French-movie fashion. Judy would have gentle hysterics. Freak would say something about bits and pieces and shake his head. He was probably already bald.

The underwear I got for Ann Arbor had been yellow and blue. Blue for my initiation into delicious prurience, yellow for spring-time and scared.

"Hayes, could I ask you something?"

"Go, Bits."

"Couldn't you have picked up a phone? Couldn't you have said with your own voice 'I'm gonna get married and not to you . . . ' ?"

"Bitsy, I was afraid."

"Of what in the world were you afraid?"

"Of what in the world I was afraid was, you'd say, 'Hayes *who*?' "

"Dear God. While I was being afraid I wouldn't be enough for you, you were being afraid I wouldn't know who you were. Goddamn world."

"You'll have to watch that trenchant thinking, Bits."

"And do you want to know what I think of people who make sweeping, torrential love and then go around saying something dried-up like 'trenchant thinking'? Do you?"

"No," he laughed. "No, I do not."

I was coming to like Nancy more and more. If it weren't so perverted and twentieth century, the kimono-shopping would have been fun. I even began to regret wishing she wore a forty-eight stout.

(Now, Beatrice, I'll handle the language, let's just select two at a time to try on. I always like something versatile—oh, this one is delightful!

Yes, and the puce goes so nicely with your smile. You're so logical and trenchant, Nancy.)

"Bitsy, if you'd done a little trenchant thinking of your own, you wouldn't have tried to kill yourself. You know that, don't you?"

Hayes, bless his trenchant heart, wasn't standing near a razor blade with a newspaper clipping in the pocket of his jeans wondering why he couldn't laugh. Existentially it wasn't much of a moment, but it was all I had.

> *Dear Bitsy,*
>   *I've met this smile who*

No, not quite.

> *Dear Bitsy,*
>   *Just on my way out the door, but thought I'd drop you a line*
> *to say I won't be dropping you any more lines*

No.

Dear Bitsy,
> *I'm going to write as many pages as it takes to tell you truthfully how I feel because two human beings who've done as crashing a thing as love each other deserve that*

He couldn't write it. Because when he was hurt and angry and lonely and disillusioned, "one" had told him that Nietzsche and T. S. Eliot were vey sorry for him, that James Joyce and Herman Melville loved him dearly. And "one" had added later quite coyly in a burst of spring that Geoffrey Chaucer, Marcel Proust and Antonio Vivaldi wanted to jump into bed with him and consummate the divinest of loves.

God holy damn! I didn't like, not one single bit did I like, the volcanic truth that shot out of the top of my head on filet-mignon-stained sheets in San Francisco. The person who was willing to go as far as she could into loving—and that meant go the whole hiking, climbing, swimming, laughing, screaming way—that person had slouched slowly beneath the grim and threatening shroud of M3's desk and begun to disappear. Hayes couldn't write pages of flowing, scrawled honesty to someone who'd been gone a long time, could he?

"Bits," he had his hand on my knee, "what would you think of skipping your music thing tomorrow?"

"No. It's the first day. This isn't a hobby of mine, this is my life. Music isn't something I do in my spare time—"

"Well, if you could, I could take a later flight, I know where we could go canoeing, the weather's gonna be nice—"

"Hayes, when I was in college I had a pretty persistent fantasy about going canoeing with you and telling you all about Shakespeare's sexual metaphors. But it's not something I want to do or have time to do now. And you ought to get yourself home."

(Really, Nancy? That's what he meant by orchards and—

Sure, Hayes, and I've got more for you as the years go by. Go to port a little.)

I hunched up on my knees, the way you do when you're trying to clean out the remains of the old campfire. "Let me ask you—what did you get out of that whole thing? Besides the overstated hero worship?"

The third of a smile appeared. "You're not going to believe—"

"Sure I am. Go."

"You're not gonna believe it because it's so starkly innocuous. And not so terribly easy to say at this time in my life. It has to do with—you know, youth. . . . "

Sexiest *s*'s I'd ever heard in my whole bleeding life. "That's starkly innocuous, all right."

"Here it is. If you climb a mountain with somebody, and you steal strawberries with them—and if they play the violin way the hell off at the edge of the orchard while you're thinning little green apples and it's a wonder you don't break your goddamn neck—and when your friend is singing a dumb song about a mountain by a windy campfire . . . and you notice there's one person with her head leaned to the side, long hair hanging down over her knees, she's humming—and you see this silly, gutsy, hopeful—non-sensical—tear rolling down her chin—and she doesn't even know it—you don't forget it. Okay?"

I'm the first person to grant a grown man the right to cry if he wants to, I'll even lick the tears off his nose. Most men would have been embarrassed.

"Bits," he said, holding both my hands, "let's play a game. Let's play why-did-you-fly-exactly-today?"

"Oh, I was going to fly yesterday, but I had a kind of quarrel to settle . . . "

"A lovers' quarrel?"

"Sort of. I decided they needed me in a demonstration, a peace march thing, you know they always like body counts in peace marches—anyway, I changed the flight to today."

"Oh." He rubbed his chin with one hand, holding both my hands with the other, the way you do when you share the keel of a capsized canoe. "Would you like to hear the topper, Bits? I was going to fly tomorrow."

"Oh." I looked at my knees. "Why didn't you?"

"Well, I finished with a meeting early . . . "

"Was it a bold-thrust meeting, Hayes?"

"You'd call it that. It was a food crisis symposium, we came up with some proposals, none of them very workable—and I ended up flying today . . . "

I thought God had a finely tuned sense of humor, but I didn't mention it. One, we were laughing too hard to talk. And two, I was weary of theology.

"Hayes, shall I tell you what I like about you?"

"Then or now?"

"Both."

"Go."

"Your stride. You walk around like—in the airport, I wanted to tackle you there—"

"I've got a good sixty pounds on you, at least. I'd wipe you out."

"I know. Don't forget, you almost did. Anyway, it's like—have you ever seen a really hot skier who knows just—"

"I *am* a really hot skier." He looked almost apologetic.

"Then you know what I'm talking about."

"Tell me about my stride."

"Okay. When you see a mogul coming—or a gate or something—you deal with it before it's there. You weave a little, you go into the wind, it whips you about a little bit, you go sailing, breezing straight through, even if you've got a face full of blowing snow, you just keep right on. That's poise, Hayes."

"Thanks, Bits."

The light was off. A watch ticked near my hand.

"Bits, how embarrassing is it to know you didn't really want to commit suicide? If you'd wanted to do a good job—"

"Not at all. Not at all embarrassing. Very nasty for my music, there are some things my left hand just won't do, and never will. But not embarrassing. I don't talk about it much, because most people are squeamish, and Mother would have a fit. But you know, no matter what anybody says, people are going to go right ahead and do things like that. Every generation has a few. You know."

"I know. I still don't understand it."

"I don't think I do either. But it's a thing about sending signals to yourself. Kind of outrageous, masturbatory SOSes, ostentatious shrieks—just something to try to get back whatever it is you've lost. Me, it was a sense of humor. I don't know what it is with other people. They ought to read more Camus, that's for sure."

He thought awhile. I liked listening to him breathe. "You know, Bits, I still might be President someday."

"Good. Then you can go to sleep at concerts right in your own house."

"How would you like to be Desdemona with a pillow over your—"

"They'd never elect you President. Things like that have a way of getting—"

Now if Sibelius and Beethoven and Brahms and Schubert and Bach and Vivaldi and Handel and Stravinsky and Brubeck all got together—and if they combined their lyrical strains to echo the consummate grace of the flight of summer wind over water—I wonder if the State Department takes more than a casual interest in that sort of major breakthrough. I suppose not.

I knew my toe itched. I'd scratch it if I could remember where it was. "Hayes," I asked, trying to find it, "did being a *summa cum laude* have anything to do with being such a sexy bastard?"

"Bitsy, that's not a very patrician thing to say."

"I know. But I've got another thing to tell you."

"Go."

"There's not another person in my life that I never purposely lied to. I've lied to everybody else sometime or—"

"Really?"

"Really."

"Jesus. That's a hell of a tribute. You know that?"

"Sure. I know it. You mind if I turn on the light?"

"No. Why?"

Sometimes I play without clothes on. In San Francisco I gave Hayes the second movement of the Mendelssohn Concerto. The soccer players slept right through it.

I was rubbing rosin off the fingerboard when Hayes decided to tell me what he thought of it. The music lover.

"Bitsy, you're a wistful broad."

"I know. Do you know he was only thirty-eight when he died?"

"That's not what I meant. Not Mendelssohn. You."

Oh. "Hayes, I'm no more Goddamn wistful than you are."

"What do you mean by that?"

"Oh, you're so bloody impregnable—you're so darned strong. Please don't laugh. Right down there in the—in the very retina of your heart, you've got this little soft Ionic curl. It's the part where you stop laughing at everybody and everything for just a moment, it's the part where you actually admit joy and tears. It's the part where you shine. I think that's wistful."

He only laughed a little. "Sonofabitch, Bits. Nobody ever said that to me before."

"Well, now somebody has." I tucked the violin and bow away in their crimson silk.

I hadn't had such a good night's sleep in years.

The Mark Hopkins, with its crisp mind on busily bouncing matters like the day at hand, said cordially that it was time to get up.

I didn't. Quite reasonably.

Warm, drowsy, surprising sex in the early morning is one of my hobbies. Out of the accidental blue had appeared a fellow hobbyist—one of those Very Few Men—to ring in the morning with new splendors and to ring out the season of the old romance. The *Liebestod* from *Tristan und Isolde* tolled its unequivocal eulogy, riding double-reined with triumph and farewell.

I suppose we women have always tended to drift off to sleep afterward. I imagine it was during this smiling, spent doze that they sneaked out and slew the mastodons. Well, somebody had to, or we never would have reached the point of microencapsulations and pioneer breakthroughs. I suppose the State Department has taken careful note of all that.

"You've changed your mind about canoeing, then?"

I looked at my watch, still on New York time. No.

The shower was more than steamy. I wrote with one soapy finger on the immaculate shower wall:

Dear Nancy,
*   Thanks for getting me off the hook several springs ago. I still don't understand it completely, but thank you very much.*

Then I scoured the room, looking for the remains of me.

"What're you doing, Bits?" he asked around a yawn.

"I just want to make sure I haven't left anything."

He picked up an invisible microphone. "And now the little lady is gonna sing for us all she can remember of that torchy Tony Bennett hit—"

He threw the microphone to me. I caught it. "The word isn't 'little' anymore, Hayes." I threw it back.

"Bits, do you seriously want me to call you Beatrice?"

"Hayes, I seriously don't want you to call me."

"Oh." He looked at me without a trace of the old fractional smile. "I do come to New York fairly—" He breathed in and out. Twice. I was counting. "It'll take some self-control. Just dinner, maybe?"

The outline of his body under the sheet would have pleased Michelangelo.

"Just dinner. And a hop into bed. And a hop out of bed. And a trip to an airport. Leaving me to launder the sheets. How sophisticated of us both. Don't do it to me, Hayes."

"Goddamn it, Beatrice, you are exasperating. And you're also right."

I closed my suitcase, and took a few more seconds to look around. I noticed that the two youngsters were no longer there. Ghosts of summer past, they had floated through a wall, taken flight without baggage, drifted off to join the carbon cycle. I wished them well.

"Listen, Bits, I want you to leave laughing . . . "

"I'll vote for you. For President—"

"You take care of that laugh, now. You feed it just right—"

Part of me wanted to plunge my Tourte through his jugular vein. The rest of me decided it wasn't such a charitable thing to do to a lovely person like Nancy.

(Hayes, guess what.

What, Nance?

Another child is coming to live with us.

Another one?

Oh Hayes, he's an orphan, he's been thumped, Japan has so many scars—

Nance dear, don't say that just now. You're making me nervous.

All right. But wait 'til you see this sweet, frightened child. Oh—and we've got strawberries for dessert, and—

Oh my god, Nancy.

Why, I thought they'd be a nice surprise. Didn't you tell me you used to steal them a lot?

Jesus. Once.

You'll love this child; he needs us.

You're a wonderful woman, Nancy.)

He swung the long legs out of bed and headed for a toothbrushing operation.

I ran to the phone and made a brisk call. When he emerged I stood by the door. I still didn't know whether the wielder of all those languages knew how to say good-bye.

I got on the end of a nice and neighborly forehead kiss, and then I shoved my violin and suitcase through the doorway and got the hell out. I was almost at the elevator when I heard a roaring whisper.

"Hey, Bits—come back here, I've got concluding remarks!"

He would. I went. I felt like a peddlar of Roccas at the door.

"Bits," he pulled me softly inside by one arm, leaving the door open a few inches. "You know about the ducks? In the winter?" He was whispering, in mannerly deference to the sleeping soccer players.

"You called me back here to say that?"

"Listen. It's not where they go, it's how. They go together, they pair off, so the trip won't be so cold. Winter's cold, Bits, you can freeze your ass—"

"You don't have to tell me that."

"Bits, you find somebody and you pair off. Some musician or—"

"Maybe. Maybe I will."

He poked my belly with one finger. "Now, you get yourself to that—'

But I already was. I was almost inside the elevator when a baritone shout resounded the length of the hall. "AND GOD-DAMN IT, BITSY, MAKE SURE THE SONOFABITCH SHINES!"

Down to the wire, stark naked, he was giving me orders. Shouting with wistful bravura, he stood vindicated, recharged and graceful, profoundly boisterous, hauntingly profane.

I got into the elevator before the soccer players charged out in their pajamas.

When I soap-fingered the bathroom wall in the Mark Hopkins with my thank-you note to Nancy, I meant what I said. As I matched fingering, bowing, and methodology with a hundred-odd Suzuki experts in the next two days, what I hadn't understood in the shower began to rise to the top, like Guernsey cream in a milk bucket.

Item: Playing with your own irretrievable innocence, laying it out on a table and going at it with scalpel and forceps, is never a very good idea. It is dangerous terrain.

Item: Exorcising your devils, whoever they are, if the exorcism is nearly complete, is worth the pain you incur in the process.

Item: Hayes and I couldn't have made it together. When we had exhausted drollery and orgasm, when we had reached the limits of irreverence and joy, we would have, as if by mutual vow, gone for the kill. The crowning achievement of our unendurably precarious union would have been the savage destruction of a woman and a man.

What Bitsy had joyed in and longed for, the reason why Beatrice had never let herself think seriously about marching down an aisle with any ordinary man—the joy, the longing and the reason had confronted us both in San Francisco, and had been found wanting.

In three days I'd been privileged to find out what some people go around for their whole lives not knowing. God works in mysterious ways.

A Christmas or so later (after the western world had blown up in the face of the terrorizing realization that the Presidency of the United States of America was indeed a cruel joke), among the greetings that found their way to the log house through a snowstorm and got opened in front of the stone fireplace (while the venerable Fritz and quite a nice young man with something like burnished humor gave out some lusty Mozart for violin and cello, and while through the corny long hair hanging around my face I watched my mother smiling in the firelight while she decided which poor to invite), a card appeared, in the lanky scrawl I'd almost forgotten how to recognize. Inside was a wry, aging Santa trying to right an upended Christmas tree. And beneath him, like the footprints of small conniving elves:

> *In case you're still not reading the papers, I got the ambassadorship (note lower case) to wherever it is.*
>
> *And do you want to know what I think of people who never lie to you and then order you a triple breakfast of fried trout, when you're not even hungry? The state department takes careful note of such things.*
>
> *There's a concert tonight, right in my own house, a string quartet. I'm going to try to stay awake.*

> *Love,*
> *H*

The Sensuous President? By H? $7.95? I'd buy a copy. I suppose Freak is headed for law school right now. Funny, I always thought he was one man who couldn't be corrupted. Merry Christmas, Fred.